THE STRANGER
A LEGACY OF LOVE NOVEL

MELANIE DOBSON

EMBER ROTH BOOKS

Jon

*Thank you for showering
our family with your love*

INSPIRATION

Tucked into Iowa's beautiful rolling hills is a cluster of seven quaint villages called the Amana Colonies. The settlement was birthed in 1855 when thirty-three Inspirationists arrived from Ebenezer, New York, to build the main village of Amana. By the end of 1864, more than twelve hundred people lived in this new colony.

The Amana people share a profound spiritual heritage as their ancestors lived by the words of the Bible and inspired prophets called *Werkzeug* whose quotes are included in this novel. For eighty years, the Amana Society provided food, housing, medical care, and schooling for every member until they voted to dissolve the commune in 1932.

While the Amana Colonies are no longer a commune, many of the people living in Amana still worship and work together. Grapevines adorn the brick and stone homes today, and aromas from the bountiful gardens and bakeries waft through the streets. The Iowa River weaves through the villages along with a peaceful canal that once powered the textile, grain, and saw mills.

Charming inns and good German food abound in these

INSPIRATION

colonies, and visitors spend days touring craft shops, art galleries, museums, wineries, quilt stores, and an original communal kitchen. With the exception of the trains that whistle their way through these Colonies, the nights are calm, and when the clouds are gone, thousands of stars illuminate the dark sky.

Welcome to a quieter place, a retreat from the frenzied world outside.

Willkommen to the Amana Colonies.

THE AMANA COLONIES

- WEST AMANA
- HIGH AMANA
- MIDDLE AMANA
- AMANA
- EAST AMANA
- SOUTH AMANA
- HOMESTEAD
- Lily Lake
- Millrace
- Iowa River
- Railroad

N

*Whoever does not wander through the dark
wasteland of his heart cannot enter
into the new and peaceful land.*

Christian Metz, 1833

CHAPTER 1

JULY 1894, CHICAGO

The morning fog lingered in the alleyways and draped over the iron palings that fortified the row of saloons along Harrison Street. At the corner of Harrison and LaSalle, a gas lamp flickered in the mist, its yellow flame spreading light over the alley tents. Only a few more blocks until they were safe in the depot.

In the distance, the station's clock tower glowed like a beacon, beckoning him to hurry, and Jacob Hirsch patted the back of his daughter, asleep on his shoulder, before checking his breast pocket. The two train tickets were tucked safely inside.

Adjusting the strap on his satchel, he took a deep breath and hurried toward the train that would take him and his daughter far away from Chicago.

Cassie squirmed against his chest and lifted her head. "My throat hurts, Papa."

"I know, Pumpkin."

She tried to smile. "I'm not a pumpkin."

"You're my pumpkin," he replied softly. He put her down for a moment to shift his satchel to his other arm before he picked her up again. Laying her head back on his shoulder, her breathing deepened as she drifted back to sleep.

Shivering in the morning air, he pushed himself to walk even faster to get her into the warm station. Almost a week ago Cassie had started complaining of a sore throat, and he felt useless to help her. His money was almost gone, and they were just two among thousands who had no place to sleep tonight.

This city was the only place Cassie had ever known, but there was no future for them in Chicago. Tens of thousands were unemployed—strong men willing to work and educated men who could no longer provide for their families. These men walked the dirty streets during the day, searching for work, and a tent housed them and their families at night.

A tramp lay sprawled across the sidewalk in front of Jacob, inches from the door of a saloon. He stepped over the man, but a familiar queasiness clenched his gut. So many people were struggling to survive while others tried to drown the country's economic depression by drinking themselves to death.

He'd considered the latter himself, using the last of his money on liquor instead of train tickets, but the streets in Chicago were already crowded with children who'd lost both of their parents—he couldn't think about what would happen to Cassie if he weren't here to protect her from the scum who patrolled for orphans.

Jacob's stomach rumbled, but he ignored it. Cassie was the one who needed to eat. Cassie and the other young victims of the financial tsunami that had hit the East Coast last summer and swept across the plains and mountains, devastating families and businesses and farms in its wake.

Jacob checked his pocket again for the train tickets. They were still there. He'd pawned the last of their furniture along with Katharine's wedding ring to buy these tickets and garner two additional dollars to buy Cassie food during their journey west.

Three months had passed since he'd lost his job at the bank, and almost a year had passed since he'd lost...

He shook his head, focusing on the depot's bright clock tower instead of drowning himself in the past, for Cassie's sake.

They would take the early morning train to Minneapolis and then on to Washington State, where there were jobs waiting for men willing to work. He was more than willing.

Someone tugged on his trousers, and he looked down to see a young girl not much older than Cassie's four years. Her hair was matted against her head, and tattered rags hung over her shoulders.

"Can you spare a nickel?" she whispered.

Behind the child was a row of tents in the alley. "Where are your parents?"

Her scrawny finger pointed toward one of the tents. "Mama's in there."

"You hungry?"

She nodded, blinking back her tears. The New York Stock Exchange was eight hundred miles away, yet the impact from its crash trickled down to the least of these on the streets of Chicago. The pain wasn't in their wallets. It was in their bellies.

He couldn't spare a nickel but—

Cassie lifted her head in her sleep and snuggled into his other shoulder. What if it was his daughter begging for food?

The girl stepped back, her head hung with resignation, and he couldn't help himself. Digging into his pocket, he pulled out one of his precious nickels and handed it her. "Buy some bread when the bakery opens."

"Yes, sir," she replied, the strength returning to her voice as her fingers clenched the coin. "Thank you, sir."

During the colder nights, swarms of homeless slept in the hallways of city hall or in the basements of saloons. When those got overcrowded, the chief of police opened the doors to the station and crammed young and old alike into cells alongside the criminals for the night.

A jail cell was no place for a child.

He shifted the leather bag on his shoulder again and Cassie stirred, coughing against his suit jacket. He rested his hand on her back until she stopped coughing and then turned the corner toward the station and the passenger train that would take them west.

A half dozen people crowded together on the corner in front of him, and Jacob shuffled across the street to avoid them. He'd read plenty about rings of thieves that stalked the night hours on the Near West Side. He couldn't afford a confrontation this morning, nor could he afford to lose the last of his money or his train tickets.

A rough laugh passed through his lips at the irony of clinging to the two dollars in his waistcoat. A year ago, he'd been bringing home sixteen dollars and forty cents every week while employed as a clerk at Chicago's prestigious Second National Building and Loan, and he'd been on his way up the ladder with his sights on becoming president one day.

"A promising future," the president of the bank had told him in the spring of '93, and Jacob believed the man. Back then, his future was full of promise. More responsibilities were ahead. A reputable title. And, if he kept working hard, a lot more money.

For most of his life, he'd respected the power of a dollar. Even more than providing for his family, it was his livelihood, and he thought he'd understood its worth. But he didn't truly understand it until most of the bank's reserves were washed away in the Panic of '93 along with his salary. Never before had he known what it was like to have the future obliterated, to only have two dollars to his name. Nor had he understood real desperation— the need for money because of the love for his daughter and the hunger in his own belly.

And now here he was, on this chilly summer morning, afraid

that thieves might steal a measly two dollars from him. And even more afraid that he might be tempted to steal like them if he didn't find work soon and provide for his daughter.

Cassie moaned against his shoulder, and he kissed the lopsided part between her braids. The train station was only three more blocks away, straight down LaSalle. When she woke again, he'd feed her the crackers and apple his kind neighbor gave them last night.

The bell in the clock tower chimed five times. The train wasn't scheduled to depart for an hour, but even so, he hurried toward the depot. They would be ready to leave whenever the conductor called for them to board.

Nothing would stop him from getting on this train.

Dim rays of sunlight began to clear the gray fog, and the LaSalle Street Station rose through the mist like an ancient castle. The place spoke of a time past. A time of money and power and prestige, when more people wanted to visit their great city than run away from it.

Ahead, forty or so men crowded around the depot, and at the front of the mob, a man in a black overcoat shouted and raised a shovel in the air. Jacob's entire body tensed when the crowd raised their voices in response.

Why are they so angry?

Skirting around the group, Jacob pushed open a side door and shuffled into the marbled lobby of the train station. Golden ceiling tiles towered above them with a crystal chandelier that cascaded light onto the granite pillars below. Dozens of people slept on the stiff benches around the station, wrapped in blankets or covered with overcoats.

Cassie squirmed in his arms, lifting her head to take in the grandeur. "Where are we, Papa?"

His heart softened at her voice. "At the train station, sweetheart. You keep sleeping."

"I don't wanna sleep," she said, nestling her head back into his shoulder.

"Of course not." He laughed softly as her breathing slowed again.

Long glass windows overlooked the train platform on the far wall, and near the windows was the train counter. He rang the bell, and then rang it again when no one came to the counter.

A stout man slipped up beside him, a cigar hanging out the side of his mouth. His nose was swollen and red. "They're all outside."

Jacob turned toward him. "What's happening?"

"The railway strike."

"I thought the workers were striking down in Pullman."

"That was last week." The man blew smoke in Jacob's face. "The big whigs down there ain't budging an inch, and now the union is wailin' mad."

"The trains—"

"A few of them are still moving." The man slid the cigar out of his mouth and twirled it in his fingers. "Where you headed?"

"Minneapolis and then Spokane."

He pointed his cigar toward the glass windows. "You best get yourself onboard. They'll be leaving early today."

Early? Jacob slid back from the counter, the man's words propelling him through the station and back out into the morning air. On the other side of the platform, five trains were lined up on a maze of tracks, and the train closest to him was a passenger train. The train taking them to Minnesota.

He scanned the platform for a brakeman or conductor to open the closed doors, but he didn't see one. Turning, he watched the darkly cloaked man march onto the platform, thrust his shovel into the air, and shout about the Pullman dogs. The leader would be frightening enough by himself, but this morning, an entire crowd mimicked his tirade.

Dozens of men marched onto the platform brandishing

shovels and pitchforks, and they were all chanting. "*Strike. Strike. Strike.*"

"Papa?"

Jacob glanced into his daughter's frightened eyes. He had to get her out of here.

The whistle blew on the passenger train, and he hopped onto the steps and tugged at the locked door. Something whizzed by his head, and the window beside him shattered.

Floundering backward, he protected Cassie with his arms, and his chest muffled her cries.

More rocks followed the first one. More glass splintered onto the platform and the tracks. A rock clipped his ear, and he stumbled away from the firing line.

Shovels plunged into the windows of the depot, glass pouring to the ground—and then the train in front of him started to quake. Turning to the right, he sucked in his breath.

"Dear God," he whispered. The mob was rocking one of the Pullman sleeping cars, trying to tip it over. No one from the station was even trying to stop them from overturning the car.

His ear stinging from the rock, he tried to back away from the madness, but they were trapped on the platform. A gunshot blasted through the station, and the throng of men spun into a rage. People scattered in all directions, screaming, but whoever was rocking the train car didn't stop.

Steam puffed out of the engine on the far side of the tracks, and Jacob glanced around at the unruly mass. No one seemed to notice the steam. Covering Cassie's head, he ducked through a pelting of rocks as he cut between the train cars. He didn't care where the other train was headed. He'd get Cassie on it, and they'd escape this madness.

The freight train was thirty feet in front of him, the wheels already turning. He tripped over the tracks as he raced for an open boxcar, and Cassie cried out as they hit the ground.

Quickly, he pushed up from the gravel, but as he started

running again, someone shouted behind him. The mob had spotted the moving train.

The train's speed escalated as it fled the station, and Jacob ran harder than he'd ever run in his life, over the gravel and rails, toward the boxcar at the end. His hat flew off his head, but he didn't turn around. The crowd was swarming behind him now. He couldn't stop running, nor could he do anything to stop Cassie's tears. He would get her on that train, and then she'd be okay.

A crashing sound exploded through the station, shaking the ground. For an instant, the noise seemed to paralyze the crowd. They stopped running. Stopped shouting. And then they began to cheer. The mob had crippled the passenger train.

"Stop that freight!" another voice yelled over the roar.

The train in front of him increased its speed, and Jacob sprinted beside the boxcar, sweat pouring off his face. No matter what, he would protect his daughter.

Swinging the bag off his shoulder, he thrust it into the open door. Cassie clung to his neck, sobbing against his shoulders.

"C'mon, Cassie!" he shouted over the commotion.

"No..."

There was no time to hesitate. He pried Cassie's fingers and arms from his neck and swiftly pushed his daughter onto the train.

Let no one be dismayed, rather, resign yourselves to the Divine Will in the spirit of the Redeemer; then you shall cross this valley of tears safely and be comforted and sustained....

Johann Friedrich Rock, 1748

CHAPTER 2

JULY 1894, IOWA

The bell on the bakery wagon chimed outside the window, and Liesel Strauss rolled over, burying her head under a pillow. She should have been up twenty minutes ago, but she'd rather stay hidden under her covers than face this day.

Rain pattered on the window, stirring her to peek out from under her pillow at the gray clouds that blocked the sunlight from warming her room. Perhaps if she went back to sleep, she could pretend this morning never happened. Tomorrow she would spring out of bed and go about her daily duties as if nothing had changed.

She rolled over and closed her eyes as the bell rang again below her. Ludwig Kampf and his father rose before most people in Homestead to bake bread, and it was almost as if Ludwig enjoyed waking the town with his bell as he delivered his bread to Homestead's ten kitchen houses before breakfast.

In the large room below her bedroom was one of these kitchens, and the aroma of coffee brewing over the fire wafted upstairs. It was Thursday, so there would be coffee cake laced with streusel this morning along with oatmeal and crispy fried potatoes. Her stomach rumbled at the thought of the warm, sweet cake with her coffee.

Ludwig pulled his cart farther down the street, the clang of his bells fading away as another bell rang out below her window. The milkman was delivering his pails, fresh from the barn.

She inched upright on her bed and slowly opened her eyes to the same sight that greeted her every morning. Pale blue walls surrounded her, and four walnut posts braced the head and footboard. Almost twenty years ago her mother had quilted the yellow comforter that covered her, and six months ago Liesel's father gave her the treasured piece when she relocated from the neighboring village of Main Amana to Homestead.

In five more months, when their separation was over, she and Emil Hahn would marry and she would take the bedspread back with her to their new home in Amana along with the chest of her belongings.

She clenched her hands over the hem of the quilted comforter. She couldn't tell anyone, but the thought of marrying Emil filled her heart with almost as much dread as facing this day.

The clock by the door read 5:45, and she finally pushed herself out of bed. Placing her feet on the cold floor, she shivered. Today would be hard enough without mulling over her fears of marriage.

Lifting her coarse white stockings off the back of the chair, she inched them on and then buttoned the Dutch blue front of her calico dress.

"Clothe me with the garb of salvation." She prayed the familiar words as she looped the straps of the black apron over her arms and tied the strings behind her. "And clothe me with the purple garment of Christ."

She poured water from a ceramic pitcher into a basin and cleansed her hands and face. As she washed, she continued her morning prayers. "Give me true cleansing from sin today and sanctify me with the blood of the Lamb."

The routine of cleansing, praying, and braiding her hair mirrored her daily schedule in the Amana Colonies. Life in Homestead was steady and predictable, and while she appreciated the ease of their routines, some days she longed for a bit of change in the normalness of her routine. Nothing as extreme, though, as saying goodbye to her best friend.

She reached for the brush beside the basin and swept it through her long hair until it was smooth. Weaving the blonde strands into two braids, she twisted and pinned them to the back of her head. Beside the window, she laced her boots and watched other villagers stream down the narrow pathway that connected the houses, toward the kitchen below her.

Her father lived in Main Amana, the village north of Homestead, but these men and women were like family to her. She loved and respected them, and even though they all dressed similarly, she knew what made each of them unique.

Fixing her homemade hairnet over her braids, she tied the strings at the nape of her neck and slipped her pale orchid sunbonnet off its hook by the door to carry with her to breakfast.

I won't cry, she whispered, closing the door behind her. Cedar Rapids wasn't that far away—only a short train ride back to the Amana Colonies. And the mail came every day by train as well. She would write letters. Hundreds of them.

Still, the thought of writing letters didn't dry her tears.

Bells rang out in the village *Glockenhaus* as she rushed down the narrow stairs, under an arch, and into the kitchen. The *Küchebaas*—or kitchen boss—waved her past the wide, polished stove top brimming with kettles and into the dining room, where she sat down at one of three tables, the table designated for the women.

On top of the table were eight white plates, eight bowls, and neatly placed tin silverware alongside a coffee cup.

At the table across from her, most of the men were already seated, but no one looked her way. Their heads were bowed in quiet contemplation before the day's first meal. She bowed hers as well and waited for the food.

The bench creaked beside her, and she peeked over as Sophie slid into the seat. She closed her eyes again, but in the quietness, she reached out to her friend and squeezed her calloused hand. Tears were coming again; she could feel them brimming under her eyelids, but there was nothing she could do to stop them from tumbling down her cheeks.

With a bang the door to the kitchen opened, and she glanced up. Two kitchen workers breezed into the room with iron coffee boilers for each table. Releasing Sophie's hand Liesel filled her cup, and the steam warmed her face, clearing her tears for the moment. She took a sip of the hot drink.

Another kitchen girl placed two white bowls on their table beside the coffee boiler. The first bowl was filled with oatmeal soaked in molasses, and the second held potatoes that had been panfried in bacon grease. Another small bowl brought out next held chunks of soft hand cheese, and slices of coffee cake filled an oval-shaped platter. With her fork, Liesel snagged a piece of the yellow cake, placed it in her bowl, and then poured fresh cream over it.

The cake was rich and sweet, but she didn't relish it like she did most Thursday mornings. She could only think of what she was about to lose on this Thursday—the treasure of sharing all her meals with her best friend.

Sophie usually devoured the potatoes and oatmeal before another hard day of work in the gardens, but today her friend swirled the oatmeal in her bowl. Liesel longed to reach out and hug her, to talk once again about the trying days ahead for both of them and how she wouldn't let a day pass without writing to her.

Avoid useless words, for they deprive you of the strength of the soul.

The rules of conduct taught to them as children stated that dining tables were for eating, not talking, and none of them chattered and slurped like a worldly man or woman did. She'd seen firsthand how the outsiders could chatter when transients stopped by their village for a bite to eat. While filling their bellies, these men rattled on about their travels with no thought to the silence the rest of them maintained in the dining room.

Just this once, however, Liesel wished she and Sophie could whisper to each other over their meal. Her friend knew how much she would miss her, but it didn't seem like she could tell Sophie enough times. From the bottom of her heart, someplace so deep inside her that she didn't know from where it stemmed, there would be a vacancy. A hole. The pain hurt worse than the time she'd fallen out of a tree and broken a rib...worse than the time she'd burned her arm on the kitchen stove.

The doctor had tended her wounds after both the fall and the burn—and the *Küchebaas* asked the Elders to relocate her from the kitchen house to the gardens. But there was no salve available this morning to soothe the burning in her chest.

Glancing beside her, Liesel saw Sophie's cheeks damp with tears and her fingers rolling over her swollen belly. In two months, Sophie Keller would become a mother.

Liesel couldn't think about missing her dear friend's event or the opportunity to pour love and affection on her friend's little one. She'd dreamed of the day when she could be a *Tante* to Conrad and Sophie's children, and now Sophie's husband was stealing that away from her. From all of them.

When he was sixteen, Conrad Keller had been assigned to work on the dredge boat in the summer and the sheep barns in the winter. He was twenty-four now and tired of the work.

THE STRANGER

His father was an Elder in Homestead, and Niklas Keller—as well as the other seven Elders—listened to Conrad's complaints, but as Conrad was one of the few men in the Amanas who knew how to swim, they needed him to stay on the boat.

Ever since Liesel had known him, Conrad poured over the daily newspapers arriving in Homestead on the train. He was intrigued by the court cases reported in the papers along with the political maneuvering of the leaders in the land. Then, last spring, he met one of the tourists visiting their villages. A vacationing attorney from Cedar Rapids.

Conrad had spent hours talking to the man. Then he announced suddenly that he wanted to become an attorney. Unfortunately for Conrad, the Amana Colonies had no need of a man skilled in the law—they paid a solicitor in the county seat of Marengo when they needed legal papers written up for the state. There wasn't enough work in the Amanas for a full-time solicitor, but there was plenty of work in dredging the Mill Race Canal during the warmer months. In the winter months, they needed Conrad and the boat crew to care for the Colonies' sheep.

So Conrad had to make a choice, and after much deliberation, he decided to leave his work in the Amana Colonies and attend law school in Cedar Rapids. A career in law was more important to him than supporting the community that had cared for him his entire life.

Liesel spooned up another bite of the creamy cake before taking a long sip of coffee. Then a familiar thought slipped back into her mind. If she wanted, she could get on a train with her friend today and follow her to Cedar Rapids. Sophie had asked Liesel to accompany her and Conrad to the city and live with them in the apartment Conrad had secured. Where he'd gotten the money to pay for an apartment, no one seemed to know.

Liesel's stomach clenched at the thought of leaving the Colonies, and she set down her cup.

At the table across from her Conrad ate his food in silence like the rest of the men, yet there was a smile on his face. He'd been smiling ever since he decided to leave.

She couldn't imagine leaving the Colonies. Not for any reason. She'd heard stories about the outside—the sordid worldliness of those who pursued their own ambitions over the truths of God—and she had no desire to venture out of the seven villages that made up their community. Her family was here. Her church. Her work in the gardens. And her friends were in the Colonies—at least most of them.

Cedar Rapids isn't that far, she told herself yet again. It was only twenty-two miles away. Forever by buggy, but not so far by train. Not that she had money to buy a train ticket, but when Conrad was a successful attorney, getting paid to work, surely he could send Sophie back for a visit.

She stirred the cake in her bowl while Sophie pushed her potatoes back and forth across her plate. The clanking of forks and spoons echoed around them, but no one seemed to notice that she and Sophie had stopped eating.

Sometimes when she was in the gardens, pulling one more potato or carrot or stalk of rhubarb out of the ground, Liesel considered saying goodbye to those she loved and going to Cedar Rapids with her friend. Yet even if she decided to leave Homestead, her father, and her betrothed behind, she couldn't rely on Conrad to care for her, not while he was supporting a wife and child as well as paying his way through school. And she didn't know how to support herself.

One of the transients who'd visited their village had marveled at the opportunities for women in the Amana Colonies. There was no need for women to marry here since everything was provided for them, and married or not, the women all worked outside their homes, in the gardens or kitchen house, as a midwife, or even in the *Kinderschule*.

In the outside world, the transient man told her, the opportunities for single women to work were limited to housekeeping, fieldwork, factories, and the saloons. She told the man that she worked in the gardens in Homestead every day; she could certainly work the fields on the outside. The man had laughed at her—laughed hard—and she was mortified when he explained that working as a field hand didn't compare to working in the peaceful Amana gardens.

Yesterday Sophie said she would send for Liesel when Conrad completed school and had enough income to provide for all of them. The thought lingered in her mind, but even so, Liesel couldn't imagine ever leaving the Community of True Inspiration. By the time Conrad finished school, she would be the wife of Emil Hahn and perhaps expecting a child of her own.

Lifting her eyes, she glanced across the room again at Conrad Keller and watched him spoon oatmeal into his mouth like he hadn't eaten in days. He didn't seem to be having any trouble with his stomach this morning, nor did he seem to have any regrets about his decision to leave their community to chase his own ambitions.

Let everyone seek to be most humble. Flee ambition and exaltation of one over another.

The *Kinder-Stimme* doctrine often sprang up in her mind as answers and comfort in dark times. This morning, though, in the chilly dining room, anger flooded through her— Conrad had chosen selfish ambition over the good of his own soul and that of Sophie's and their child.

She prayed quietly as she took one more bite, prayed that God would take away her anger and fill her with peace and purpose.

The wall clock chimed behind her, and each person pushed back on their bench and stood in unison. Then, in perfect order, they all filed out of the dining hall, ready to work their professions in the barns, gardens, butcher shop, carpentry, and general store. Each person had his or her own duties, and they took pride in the work assigned to them.

Liesel set her sunbonnet onto the top of her head and tied it beneath her chin, the material draping over her shoulders and ears. Sophie reached for her hand, and they stepped out of the building together. Only one road ran through the village, and they walked down it, between the apple and cherry orchards that stretched for acres on each side.

Sophie squeezed her hand. "The train doesn't come for three more hours."

"Three hours...," Liesel repeated. The hours would go by too fast.

"I don't want to go," Sophie whispered.

"I know."

Ahead of them, Conrad clapped the back of another man. *Surely,* Liesel thought, *he must have some regrets over leaving his hometown.* Yet the smile spread across his face didn't communicate any regrets. In fact, he seemed to be filled with anticipation for their journey ahead.

At least one of them was happy about this change.

Liesel stopped walking. "Phyllis said I could come to the station."

Sophie managed a thin smile. "You're sure you can't come to Cedar Rapids with me?"

"It's not that I can't...."

"I know." Sophie hugged her. "I just keep hoping you'll change your mind."

Liesel glanced around her, relishing the view of apple trees and brick houses and budding pink blossoms on the grapevines. "This is my home."

Sophie followed her gaze. "Mine too."

"Cedar Rapids will feel like home soon enough."

"You'll write, *ja*?"

Liesel kissed her friend's cheek. "Every day, silly."

"I'll probably write you twice a day."

A raindrop splattered on Liesel's nose, and she brushed it away with her fingers. These Colonies would feel strangely vacant without the woman who'd been like a sister to her.

She hugged her friend and then stepped back. "You'd better finish packing."

"Three hours," Sophie reminded her.

"I'll be there."

*Persevere on your journey holding only to God,
whose protective shield has covered you
and will continue keeping you safe.*

Johann Friedrich Rock, 1720

CHAPTER 3

The train moved even faster now, out of the LaSalle Street Station and into the fog. Jacob sprinted beside the boxcar, trying to pull himself up into it, but he wasn't fast enough nor was he strong enough to climb inside.

"Come on, Papa!" Cassie shouted over the roar of the mob.

The train picked up speed, its wheels sparking against the debris on the tracks. Ahead of him were dozens of men hammering the sides of the metal cars with shovels, trying to stop the train, and in seconds he would be caught between the shovels and the train.

"Scoot back!" Jacob shouted, and Cassie retreated into the darkness.

Reaching up, one of his hands clenched the side of the door, and he clung to the car. Then, with a quick jump, he pulled his chest inside the car. Metal clanged ahead of him, and he sucked in his breath, hoping to cushion the blows of the shovels that would pound his legs dangling over the edge.

He sucked in his breath, and he prayed. Prayed that he wouldn't get dragged under the wheels of this monster. Prayed that God wouldn't take his life before he took Cassie home.

His daughter crawled toward him and reached for his arm, her eyes wide with fear and sorrow. He didn't try to stop her.

"You can do it, Papa," she said.

His body felt as if it was about to be ripped into two pieces, but he couldn't give up now. With a loud grunt, he heaved one leg into the car. And then the other.

Shovels rattled the metal walls around them, the entire boxcar vibrating with the madness of the angry mob as he gasped for breath. Somehow, by God's mercy, he'd gotten on the train.

His daughter crawled over, snuggling into his arms, and he kissed the top of her head as he pulled her close to him. He didn't know where they were going, but he and Cassie were on their way out of Chicago. Nothing else mattered at the moment except that they were together.

"Didn't think you was gonna make it."

Jacob jumped at the sound of the raspy voice in the corner of the boxcar and squinted toward the source. In the dim light, he saw the shadow of a woman.

"Me neither," he said.

"Good thing you did, mister. I ain't got no idea how to care for a kid."

Cassie's tears were soaking his only good suit jacket, but he didn't push her away.

Her entire body was trembling, and then he realized he was shaking as well. The truth hit him even harder than the shovels that hammered the sides of the train.

He'd almost lost his daughter.

What would he do if he lost Cassie? He wouldn't be able to live with himself if she had ridden away on the freight train alone.

He should have waited to get on another train. They could have gone west another day, once the strike was over.

Yet if he'd waited...who knew when the strike would be over

or if the passenger line would honor his train tickets next week or next month? Not that his train tickets did him any good. Here he was, riding the rails like a vagrant, and he'd brought his daughter along with him.

If they'd stayed in Chicago, they would have spent the night on the floor of City Hall or, heaven forbid, in a prison cell. He'd had to make a choice, and there were no good options. Kissing the top of Cassie's head, he thanked the Lord they'd both gotten on the train.

The woman shuffled in the hay that covered the floor of the boxcar. "First time ridin' the rails?"

"Yes, ma'am."

The woman laughed at his words. "My name's Etta."

"I'm Jacob Hirsch, and this is my daughter, Cassie."

Cassie's shaking started to subside, though her voice was strained. "Pleased to meet you."

Etta laughed again. "A pleasure indeed."

Jacob inched up the corrugated wall of the boxcar, Cassie on his lap. The shovels had stopped their pounding and the train now rattled across a trestle, racing above the city. The fog had started to clear, and he could see the tall buildings near Lake Michigan, the city where he'd spent most of the past eight years.

Etta inched closer to them. A worn bandanna covered her hair, and a long scar cut like a channel across her leathery forehead.

She wasn't focused on his face, though. Her eyes were on his leg. "You know you's injured?"

"Injured?" He looked away from her, down at his left leg. His trousers were soaked with blood.

Scooting Cassie down beside him, he carefully pried up the sticky material and rolled down his sock. Blood pooled over a gash on the side of his leg.

A shovel must have gotten him after all.

"Does it hurt?" Cassie asked, her voice trembling again.
A bolt of pain shot up his thigh. "Just a little."
"You want me to kiss it?"
"Maybe later, sweetheart."
Tugging a handkerchief out of his pocket, he wrapped it around the wound. Then he took off his jacket and tucked it around Cassie, hoping she would fall asleep again so she wouldn't see him in pain.

Strange that he hadn't even felt someone hit him with a shovel. He'd been so intent on getting on this train that he'd blocked out everything else, including the gash in his leg.

Etta dug into a satchel tied around her waist and held out a tin flask. "This'll help." She passed the flask under his nose, and the rancid smell made him choke.

He turned his face away from the bottle. "What is it?"
"Whiskey."
"It doesn't smell like whiskey."
She shrugged. "It'll knock out that pain of yours."

Another ache rippled up his leg, and he grabbed the flask and took a swig before he reconsidered. The drink burned down his throat, but seconds later, the pain began to subside.

Etta screwed the lid onto the flask and settled back onto her blanket. "What kind of hell broke loose back there?"

In the distance he could see the dome left behind after the Chicago World's Fair. "The bad kind."

"No kiddin'," she squawked. "Strikers?"

Cassie sighed beside him, but her shaking didn't stop.

"The workers down in Pullman started it, but it's rippling through the city."

"They got a decent reason for striking?"

He curled Cassie's braid in his fingers, grateful that her breathing had slowed again. "The company cut their wages but refused to lower the rent on their houses."

"Are these houses—" she began. "Do they have to live in them?"

He shrugged. "If they want to work for Pullman Palace Car."

"Then I can't blame them for striking."

His laugh was hollow. "At least they have a job."

"Too many spineless people in the world," she mumbled. "Someone twists their arm and they roll right over and play dead."

"Those would be the hungry people."

Cassie leaned forward, coughing, and then nuzzled back into his chest.

"Her cough don't sound good," Etta said.

"I can't seem to get her better."

"She don't have a sore throat too?"

"A slight one."

Etta's tone turned suspicious. "You got to get that girl to a doctor."

He wiped his hand across Cassie's warm forehead. "I can't afford a doctor."

Etta tsked at him under her breath, and he stiffened. How dare she judge him for how he cared for his daughter? He'd been stomping the pavement in Chicago for months, trying to find work. Trying to take care of his child. The moment he found a job, he would get her to a doctor.

Etta straightened the blanket under her. "Ridin' the rails ain't for kids."

"I don't have a choice."

It was like she didn't hear him. "I met a family once on the rails, mother and three kids. A boxcar done run over their daddy."

Cassie shivered under his jacket, and for a moment, he wanted to jump right back off the train. This was no life for Cassie…and it was no life for him either.

"Where you headed?" Etta asked.

"Minneapolis and then Spokane."

"This train's going to Iowa."

Iowa? Somehow he would have to find a train that was headed west and then north. A train they could ride without a ticket.

"Washington's a long way," she said, like he hadn't spent days preparing for this trip.

"Almost two thousand miles."

"Whatcha gonna do when you get there?"

"Get a job."

They passed a row of dirty tenements, and the dark buildings reminded him of blackened tombstones lined up in a graveyard.

"You got work waitin' for you?" she asked.

"Not yet."

She cleared her throat. "I hate to tell you, mister, but there ain't no work in Washington neither."

"But I read—"

She cut him off. "I've met whole camps of people traveling east from Washington, going to cities like Chicago to find work when there ain't a lick of work out East either."

His mind raced. He'd read about the opportunities for work in the newspaper—the need for miners and loggers and railway workers throughout the Great Northwest. He'd never worked in a mine or a logging camp, but he figured he could learn the work quickly. He'd do almost anything to provide for Cassie.

"The *Daily News* said there was work in Washington."

Etta laughed again, and the sound grated on his nerves. "You believed some newspaper?"

"Of course." Why wouldn't he believe the article?

"Can't tell you how many hobos I've met on the rails who were scrambling to catch the next train because of some silly article."

Her words tumbled around in his mind, and the horror of

them closed in. Would someone from the newspaper really write an article to rid the clogged streets of some of their homeless? Send them off to the West with a promise of work when the entire story was a fabrication? Propaganda.

Last summer people across Chicago had panicked when the stock exchange crashed, streaming through the doors of banks to withdraw their savings until some of those banks were forced to lock their doors. Some were temporary closures. Others were permanent.

Jacob banged his head on the metal wall behind him. He'd read in the papers that the panic closed out banks across the West as well, but he'd also read that there were still jobs in the forests and mines. Had he been so desperate for work that he'd blinded himself to the reality? Or had reality been so hard for him to face these past few months that he'd grasped any glimmer of hope?

Cassie lifted her head and coughed into her arm again. If only God would help him, for the sake of his beautiful daughter.

Dull light streamed into the car as they raced out of the city and into the countryside. He could barely make out the fields of corn and wheat as they flew by, the wind whipping through the open doorway. The handkerchief stopped the bleeding in his leg —and Etta's drink put a temporary end to the pain—but not even alcohol could stop the pain in his heart. It could dull it for a while, but it wouldn't go away.

Cassie scooted back up onto his lap and shivered. Then she opened her eyes and smiled at him—Katharine's smile.

He smiled back at her.

Just a year ago, Cassie, Katharine, and he were living safe and secure as a family in their rented home near Hyde Park. He adored his wife, and Cassie adored her as well. There was laughter in their home along with hope and faith and an indescribable joy.

His wife had been the warmth of their home. A ray of light in their dark city.

And he'd lost it all, shattered like the window on the train. His job, his house, his wife, his baby son—all gone.

All he had left was his daughter, and he wasn't going to let anything happen to her.

There is nothing in this time except misery and pain, work and struggle, day and night.

Johann Friedrich Rock, 1733

CHAPTER 4

Liesel lifted her hand to wave goodbye as the passenger train crept out of the depot in Homestead, traveling east. Even at this distance, she could see Sophie's nose pressed against the window and the forlorn look in her eyes. Liesel was afraid for her friend.

A small crowd gathered in the field beside the depot to wish Conrad and Sophie well on their journey and their new life in Cedar Rapids. Sophie had never been outside the seven villages in their Colonies. The Amanas were her home. Her security. Conrad would be in school all day and her dear friend would be alone in a world she didn't understand.

Someone cried out, and Liesel turned her head to see Conrad's mother, Hilga, sobbing in her hands. It seemed so wrong, so unnecessary to break the hearts of loved ones in their community to pursue one's own ambitions. Why couldn't Conrad be satisfied with the work the Elders assigned, like the rest of them were?

She choked back her tears, sadness clinging to her like dew on the grass. Who else would share her secrets? Who else would understand?

She had plenty of women friends in Homestead and Main Amana, but there was no one like Sophie. Her friend hadn't passed judgment in the days after Liesel's engagement, even when Sophie wasn't certain that Emil was the man for Liesel. Sophie didn't scold Liesel when she used her coupon book to buy peppermints and black licorice from the general store instead of saving it for something more practical like thread or new shoes. She didn't laugh about Liesel's fear of water…or her fear of marriage.

The tears fell fresh down Liesel's cheeks, and she pushed back the top of her bonnet so she could watch the train press toward the jungle of trees that sheltered their village.

Sophie's face was gone, but even still, Liesel stared at the last of the passenger cars, waving with both arms until the caboose vanished into the overgrowth.

Rain sprinkled down the sides of her sunbonnet and onto her cheeks, blending with her tears. If only it was all a bad dream. She could wake up, relieved that her friend hadn't left Homestead. That nothing had changed. She could meet Sophie for breakfast, walk out to the garden, and laugh at her silly dream.

Conrad's mother cried out again, and she watched Niklas Keller try to console his wife. It wasn't a dream. Sophie and Conrad were gone.

Liesel scanned the crowd, searching for Sophie's mother among the sunbonnets and dark dresses, but she didn't see her. Perhaps it was too hard for her to say goodbye to her only daughter with everyone watching. As the crowd dispersed, Niklas escorted his wife away from the tracks, his comments carrying in the breeze.

"So many young people leaving for the world," Niklas said to his wife.

"He'll come back." Hilga struggled to steady her voice. "He and Sophie will both come back."

Niklas placed his hand on Hilga's back. "*Ja*, of course they will."

Hilga's eyes were swollen, her cheeks blotched with red. As she and Niklas drew near, Hilga met her eyes and rushed over, reaching for her hands. "My dear Liesel. You hurt too."

Liesel tried to nod her head.

"So much pain," Hilga said, more to herself than to Liesel.

"I miss her already." Liesel sniffed as she released Hilga's hands. "Terribly."

"You will join us for dinner?"

"No...," she replied. "No, thank you."

Hilga nodded, patting her arm, and the Elder and his wife shuffled toward Moershel's Kitchen. It was almost noon—dinnertime—but Liesel's feet seemed to be frozen in the tall grass. She couldn't imagine sitting on a bench, eating her tomato soup and noodles, without her best friend....

In minutes, she was the only one left at the depot, and loneliness pierced her heart. Twenty-two years in the Amanas and she had never once felt lonely, but now...now she felt terribly alone.

Slowly she backed away from the tracks until she was leaning against the fence. Sheep bleated behind her, but she didn't turn. Instead, she stared at the tracks, hoping that one day these same tracks would bring Sophie back.

She closed her eyes. What was she going to do without her friend?

They were in Iowa now, or at least that was what Etta said as the train cruised over the grassy hills. The woman hadn't stopped talking since they'd left Chicago four hours ago, entertaining him with stories about her travels from coast to coast. She looked to be fifty years old, so he was shocked when she told him she was thirty-eight. Only ten years older than he was.

Cassie shivered against his shoulder, and he rubbed warmth into her arms. Etta kept talking, more to herself than to Jacob. She'd been married once, she said, when she was nineteen. Her husband died a year later in a mining accident and there weren't any reputable jobs for a woman near Sonoma, so she'd jumped on a train and headed east.

"I worked a bit here and there and slept most nights in the hobo camps or on the trains."

"No one caught you?"

"Course they did. Four times." She paused. "Three times a bull took me to the sheriff, who done locked me up for a night. Then the sheriff took me back to the train station the next morning and told me to git out of town."

"What about the fourth time?"

"That bull beat me senseless with his club. Never will forget his eyes—angry as a viper when he caught me."

"What's a bull?" Cassie whispered in his ear.

"It's a guard who makes sure the right people ride the trains," Jacob explained quietly before turning back to Etta. "The man hurt you, but you still ride the rails?"

"Ain't no other way for me to live." Etta laughed again, but the sound didn't bother Jacob as much this time. For all she'd endured, it was good she could still laugh.

They slowed down at a station, the engine hissing as it crawled to a halt.

"Welcome to Oxford," Etta whispered from the corner. "They'll be checking the train here."

He gathered Cassie even closer in his arms. What would a bull do if he caught them in this car? Probably not stop to find out why Jacob was riding the rails with his daughter instead of using his paid ticket on a passenger train.

He'd promised Katharine he would take good care of Cassie,

but he was doing a terrible job. She'd be heartsick if she knew what had happened to them.

The train stopped with a sudden bump and threw them back a foot or two. Cassie hit her head on the wall and cried out.

"Quiet," Etta hissed.

Jacob held Cassie close to him, trying to soothe her. "Shh, sweetheart. We're only stopping for a moment."

Her torso started shaking. "My head hurts."

He picked her up like a baby and rested her body against his chest. Her face burned against his cheek. "I'm so sorry, Cassie."

"It hurts…."

"Hush up," Etta whispered again.

A club banged the metal car in front of them, and Jacob whispered in his daughter's ear, angry at himself for making her stifle her cries. She shook in his arms, but she didn't make another sound.

Their car rattled against the slam of a club, and Jacob held his breath, waiting for the bull to catch them and drag them off to a jail cell. Seconds passed slowly, but the man didn't even glance into the doorway. Jacob's shoulders slumped in relief.

Cassie jerked away from him, and he saw the tears smeared across her cheeks. This time she didn't scream, but her voice was desperate. "Papa…"

"You did good, sweetheart."

"My head hurts…and my throat."

Etta spoke, moving a little farther from them. "Your throat hurts, Cassie?"

His daughter's voice was strained. "Yes, ma'am."

"And she has a fever?"

Her forehead burned against his palm, but he didn't tell Etta.

"It hurts," Cassie moaned again as she closed her eyes.

The train jolted forward again, slowly gaining speed along the tracks as he held his daughter. As the minutes passed, Cassie's breath waned, and fear gripped him again.

Alarmed, he whispered her name to wake her, and when she didn't respond, he began to gently shake her. Her eyes fluttered open, glassy and confused, almost as if she didn't recognize him.

"Hang in there, sweetheart." He held her close and rested his face on the top of her head. "I'm going to find someone to help you."

Even as he said the words, he didn't know where he was supposed to get help. If they got off the train in a farming town, no one would want to help a transient with an injured leg, nor would they want to come near his very sick girl. They would tell him to keep on riding, away from their town, and he couldn't blame anyone for putting him back on a train. His daughter might be contagious, and he couldn't afford a doctor's bill to get her better.

He needed to press on to Des Moines. Perhaps they could find help in a public hospital.

Smoothing his hand over Cassie's auburn braids, tears sprang up from a reservoir he thought was dry. If something happened to her…the end of her life would be the end of his too.

Cassie opened her eyes, her voice clear. "Do you see her, Papa?"

He followed her gaze to the dark corner of the car. "See who?"

"She has the prettiest blond hair."

His heart lurched. "Who has blond hair?"

She pointed at the corner. "The angel."

Cassie rested her head on his shoulder and closed her eyes once more, but her words shook him. Why was she dreaming about angels?

Etta gulped down a swig of her whiskey and glanced at him. "You'd best get off at the next stop."

"I need to find work," he stated like Etta didn't already know how desperate he was.

"Next town is Homestead, Iowa. One of them Amana Colonies."

"Amana Colonies?"

"You ain't heard of the Amanas?"

He shook his head. He hadn't heard of them, nor did he particularly want to hear about them right now. A plan was what he needed. Help for Cassie.

"They're a strange folk," Etta rambled. "They live in a world of their own, but they're always good for a meal."

He swallowed. *Always good?* Perhaps they would be good to Cassie and him. "You've been to Homestead?"

"Oh no." She chugged the whiskey again. "I ain't needin' no pity or piety."

"Piety…" The word tumbled off his lips.

"Those Amana folks got all sorts of rules and prayers and traditions. They might give me a meal fast-like, but I'd muddy up their religion if I stayed too long. Probably boot me right out of their pretty little town before suppertime."

What if he got off the train here and they booted him out of town? Then where would he go?

No, he couldn't get stuck in the middle of Iowa's farms and fields. He needed a city doctor who knew what to do. It wouldn't be that much longer until they reached Des Moines.

The train started to slow again, but Jacob didn't move toward the door. "What are you doing?" Etta asked.

Cassie moaned against his chest. "I'm going to get off in Des Moines."

As the train stopped, Etta moved closer to him, her finger waggling in his face. "You gotta git that girl of yours off this train before it's too late."

Without battle there is no victory;
without night, day cannot follow.

Christian Metz, 1833

CHAPTER 5

The whistle of the Rock Island train snapped Liesel back to reality. How long had she been standing in the drizzle, staring at the railroad tracks? Three mill workers and two covered wagons waited by the depot, ready for the transfer of crates filled with woolen blankets from Amana onto a boxcar, but no one else lingered on the streets. Most of the villagers rested after the midday meal.

She brushed her hands over her wet sleeves. She should be in her room now as well, out of this dreary weather...but the thought of going back to her room seemed even lonelier than standing in the rain.

The whistle grew louder and the ground vibrated underneath her. The engine was still hidden behind the curtain of tree limbs, but its brakes squealed in the distance. Steam puffed over the crowns of the trees, and it looked like a dragon was about to surge into the sky.

Seconds later, a black engine pushed out of the forest, its wheels screeching against the tracks. For the briefest of moments, Liesel wondered if Sophie and Conrad had changed their minds. Perhaps they had turned around in Cedar Rapids and took another train back home.

But this was the Rock Island line—coming from Chicago instead of Cedar Rapids— and it was a freight. The only passengers on those trains were hobos. Most of them wanted food, but very few wanted to do the work the Elders offered in exchange. Every once in a while someone opted to work in the fields or the mill, though these men rarely stayed longer than a month or two. The temptation of worldly pleasures lured them away from the Amanas.

The train stopped in front of the depot, and the mill workers unloaded their wooden crates into an open boxcar. The brakeman slid the heavy door shut, locking it behind him, and one of the workers lifted his cap at the engineer as the train edged forward. In two hours, Amana's woolen blankets would be at their distributor in Des Moines, ready to ship across the country.

Guard against mental and physical idleness as a state in which the Enemy is able and likely to overpower you most easily.

She glanced down at her arms, the wet sleeves covered with soot. She didn't want to move, but any minute the bells in the *Glockenhaus* would ring and the colonists would emerge from their homes to return to work. Even in the rain, she would join the other women in the garden, and the work would be good for her. A guard against the enemy's power and threat in her life.

As she stepped toward the lone dirt road that traveled through their village, a groaning sound rumbled across the grass, followed by a cry. A sheep stuck his head over the fence, and Liesel reached out and rubbed her fingers over his matted head as she scanned the heads of the flock in the pen for an injured animal. None of the flock looked wounded or cast down.

The cry came again, and she strained her ears. The sound…it

wasn't an animal bellowing. Instead it sounded like a human cry.

Swiveling, she faced the tracks again, and on the other side, she saw the head of a man peering out over the tall grass.

Was this man crying? No, that didn't seem right. He looked confused, but he wasn't crying. He was calling something out. *Cassie.*

Standing still, she stared at the man. Why was he crouched down in the grass like that, shouting this word?

She glanced quickly around her. The mill workers were already riding away from the station. She raised her hands, trying to signal the men, but they didn't see her waving, nor did they seem to notice the transient man as they headed north, toward the village of Main Amana.

Liesel took another small step toward the tracks, and then another, watching the man on the other side. The prophet Isaiah commanded God's people to defend the oppressed, and their Society cared for the transient men whenever they could. She'd talked to these men and ministered to them, but she'd never approached a transient by herself. She didn't want to scare him.

She stopped walking.

What if she didn't scare him? What if he threatened her instead? She'd read stories about dangerous men and heard of them as well from people passing through their town. She glanced at the doctor's residence behind her, across the street from the depot, and her confidence surged. If she screamed, at least Dr. Trachsel and his wife would hear and come running to help her.

The man was trying to stand up now. His brown hair was neatly trimmed, and he wore a brown sack coat over his matching waistcoat. Almost like he was a traveling businessman.

But why would a businessman be riding on a freight?

The man reached into the grass and then hoisted a lumpy bag over his shoulder. When he lifted his head, his eyes locked with hers. He wasn't that much older than her and might even be a comely man if it weren't for the sorrow etched in his gaze.

She stepped closer, staring at the load on his shoulder. At first she thought it was a bag of flour or clothes, but now it looked like he was holding…

Lord, have mercy.

It looked like he was holding a child.

Jacob's leg buckled under him, so he crawled forward, searching until he found Cassie in the wiry grass. Her face was ashen as she struggled to breathe. Smoothing his hand over her hair, he pulled her close to him. If only she did have a guardian angel to help them both.

"Can't breathe…," she rasped when he lifted her in her arms.

He couldn't carry her far, not with his injured leg, but he perhaps he could signal for someone to help them. He hoisted Cassie farther over his shoulder, and then scanned the village across the tracks, searching for some place to take his daughter.

On the other side of the tracks he saw a woman staring at him. Her hair was hidden under a long bonnet that enveloped her head and shoulders, and she looked frightened. When her gaze wandered from his face to the shoulders of his daughter, she picked up her skirt and raced toward him.

Cassie whimpered on his shoulder, and the woman gently placed her hand on Cassie's back. "*Ist das Kind krank?*

Pain pierced the back of his leg as he tried to take another step. "What?"

"*Ist das…*" She hesitated. "Is your *Kind* sick?"

Kind? The word slowly sparked a memory. *Kind.* Child. The woman spoke German— the language his grandparents had spoken when he was a child.

"*Ja*," he said, limping toward the tracks. "She's very...*sehr krank*."

Her eyes traveled down to his knee and then to the blood-soaked hem of his trousers. "You are ill too?"

"*Nein*," he started, but there was no use lying. It was obvious he'd injured his leg. "It's a small wound."

"Not so small," the woman said, before holding out her arms. "Let me carry her."

He shook his head, clutching Cassie to him. It didn't matter how much his leg hurt.

No stranger was carrying his daughter.

The woman glanced around their feet, and when she spotted his satchel, she flung it over her shoulders like the bag was filled with cotton instead of clothes and books.

Then she turned back to him, her arms outstretched again. "Let me have her."

He lifted his leg over the track, trying to ignore the pain. Cassie's breath was shallow as she lay against his chest. "I need to carry her."

The woman studied him, as if she might wrestle Cassie out of his arms, but she relented. Looping her arm under his left arm, she helped him maneuver across the tracks.

"The doctor lives over there." She pointed at a stately brick home across the street. "He can help you."

Relief washed over Jacob and he moved faster, leaning on her for support. They strode toward a weathered barn surrounded by a slew of fencing and sheep. The animals gathered to the side of the fence to watch them, but Jacob's eyes were on the home in front of them. If he had to, he'd get down on his knees and beg the good doctor to help them.

"If Dr. Trachsel is away, his wife can help."

A lump formed in his throat. The doctor had to be home today. He had to help them.

The woman released his shoulder to knock on the door, and within seconds an older woman answered, wearing a dark calico dress identical to the woman at his side. Her hair was pulled back sternly away from her face, but her eyes were kind.

"Liesel?" She glanced back and forth between him and Liesel and then she focused on Cassie's braids. *"Was ist das?"*

"It's her throat," he said. "She's having trouble breathing… and she has a fever."

The woman reached for his shoulder and pulled him into the door. "Quickly, now."

She led them to the second room in the house, and he laid Cassie on a narrow bed. His daughter opened her now-swollen eyes, peeking out at him, and he kissed her hot forehead. "It's going to be okay."

She tried to smile back. "I know, Papa."

Liesel handed him a wet cloth and he looked up, surprised that she had joined him in the room. Her bonnet was on the countertop and strands of her pale blond hair stole out of her hairnet, but her eyes were wrought with worry as she examined Cassie's face. For a moment, it felt good to have someone worry with him.

He wiped the cold cloth across Cassie's forehead, and his daughter reached for his hand and squeezed it. He squeezed back.

The doctor rushed into the room, his unkempt hair pressed to his scalp. Slipping a pair of spectacles over his nose, he glanced down at Jacob's bloody pant leg. *"Sprechen sie Deutch?"*

Jacob handed the wet cloth back to Liesel. *"Ein bisschen."*

"So we speak English, *ja?*"

He didn't care what language they spoke as long as the doctor could make his daughter well again.

"You have injured your leg, yes?"

The doctor crouched down to look at his calf, but Jacob waved him toward the bed. "My daughter is sick."

The doctor stood, his gaze pivoting from Jacob's leg to Cassie's face. Stepping rapidly away from Jacob, the man retrieved a tongue depressor off the counter. In rapid sequence, he listened to Cassie's heart, felt her forehead, and probed the sides of her neck.

His daughter gasped, struggling against the man's strong hands.

"Rosa!" the doctor shouted over his shoulder, and seconds later, his wife entered the room with a basin of water in her hands and clean cloths draped over her arm.

As he rattled off instructions in German, Rosa set the basin on the counter and riffled through a cabinet until she removed several bottles and a hard rubber tube. She handed the tube to the doctor, and without even glancing at Jacob for permission, the man slid it down Cassie's throat.

Jacob jumped, reaching for the tube, but the doctor blocked Jacob with his arm. "*Halt, mein Freund.*"

Cassie gagged at first, choking, and for a moment Jacob was back in that drab hospital room in Chicago, dying inside himself as he tried to help Katharine breathe her last breath.

The doctor was hurting Cassie. Suffocating her. He'd brought her to a doctor for healing, not to make her worse. He struggled against the doctor's arm. Losing his wife was too much. He couldn't lose Cassie too.

He pushed harder, intent on overpowering the man, but in the midst of his struggle, Cassie's breath filtered through the tube and into the air. It was a small breath at first, but then she breathed again, deeper this time. Her body fell back against the bed, and Jacob slumped into a chair.

The doctor barked out another order, and his wife handed him a syringe. Jacob stared at the needle. He should be doing something—consulting with the doctor and asking questions before they treated his daughter—but the doctor didn't even glance his way.

Something was terribly wrong, and Jacob decided not to fight the man.

The doctor held the syringe in the air, checking the measurements in the light before he poked the needle into Cassie's upper arm. Cassie bolted upright in the bed, screaming, and the doctor yelled for help. Liesel rushed to his side, bracing Cassie's arms as the doctor emptied the medicine into her skin.

Helpless. The feeling returned with a vengeance, the same feeling that haunted him for a year. All he could do was sit on the sidelines and hold Cassie's hand, not even able to give her much comfort or help make her body better. He was a useless father to this precious child.

"Let her go," the doctor said in English, and Liesel released her hold on Cassie's shoulders. Cassie's eyes flickered shut, and Jacob stared at his daughter.

This was how it happened before. He was with the doctor trying to save Katharine, when she slipped away from them. He'd lost his wife in those healing hands and now...

He buried his head in his hands. He couldn't bear to lose his daughter too. The doctor clasped his shoulder. "She is resting, my friend."

Jacob lifted his head and looked into the man's kind face. The doctor turned toward Liesel and his wife. "You both need to leave this room."

His wife nodded and shuffled out, but Liesel didn't move. "What is it?"

The doctor glanced between Liesel and Jacob. "She has diphtheria."

Jacob's heart plunged. *Diphtheria...* Diphtheria lingered on the threshold of death's door.

"Where are you from?" Dr. Trachsel asked.

Jacob's gaze lingered on Cassie's still face. "Chicago."

"You have had diphtheria there, *ja*?"

"A few cases, but not in my neighborhood."

"It spreads like fire."

Jacob opened his mouth, wanting to ask something, but he didn't know what to say. Liesel stepped forward, addressing the doctor. "Will the antitoxin cure her?"

"We must pray that God will cure her."

Jacob was good at praying, but God wasn't very good at answering his prayers.

"You need to go home, Liesel." Dr. Trachsel washed his hands in a basin. "This girl must be quarantined. *Sofort*—immediately."

Liesel's chin rose a notch. "Someone must care for her."

The doctor glanced over at him, like he was doubtful Jacob would be much help. "Her *Vater* will assist me."

Liesel pointed at his leg. "Her *Vater* is injured."

Harsh fragments surged out of the doctor's mouth like rocks plunked into a riverbed.

Sick. Danger. Death. Jacob almost wished he couldn't understand German.

The doctor quieted for a moment, giving Liesel the opportunity to leave, but she refused to walk out the door. Her hands on her hips and her face resolute, she spoke firmly back to him.

The doctor waved his finger in her face, his tone stern, but she interrupted his verbal assault to argue with him. It was almost as if Jacob had been transported back twenty years ago to that tiny kitchen in New York where his grandparents had lived. His grandfather used to make those same grunting noises when Jacob's grandmother had argued with him. He didn't remember one time his grandmother backed down.

Finally the doctor turned back to him and spoke in English. "I cannot allow you or your daughter out of my home."

Jacob brushed his hand over the blanket that covered Cassie's legs. "Yes, sir."

Dr. Trachsel pointed to the ceiling. "There are three rooms upstairs you can use."

Jacob nodded again.

"You must stay in those rooms."

"We will," he replied. The doctor had no idea how grateful he was simply to have a dry place in which to spend the night.

"I only have two dollars—" Reaching into his waistcoat, Jacob dug out the coins secured inside his pocket and held out the measly pile to the doctor. "Actually, it's a little less than two dollars, but as soon as I find work, I will pay you back for your care."

The doctor motioned for him to put the money away. "We will discuss payment later."

Jacob held out the pile of coins further. "I want to pay you now."

"Later," the doctor repeated as he reached for another bottle in the cabinet. "We must get you and your daughter well first."

Liesel dipped the washcloth into the basin of cool water to apply to Cassie's forehead, and the doctor pointed at his leg. "Pull up your trousers, *bitte*."

Jacob leaned over and slowly peeled back his trouser leg to reveal the stained handkerchief he'd wrapped around his shin. Blood caked under the white cloth, concealing the wound.

The doctor fixed a towel on the floor under Jacob's leg and examined his calf before lifting a glass bottle above his skin. "This may sting a bit."

Jacob braced himself as the doctor poured the antiseptic. The clear liquid bubbled over the wound, and he clenched his teeth and fists, trying not to cry out.

Through the blur of his pain, he watched Liesel move toward him with something in her hand. She plastered a coarse, cool washcloth over his forehead, and cold water trickled down his cheeks and nose, chasing away the heat that was spreading through his body.

However, even with the cloth, the searing in his leg didn't subside.

Liesel stepped away, and he reached out, grasping for her. She held out her hand, and he squeezed and then released it suddenly, afraid he'd hurt her.

She reached down and took his hand again. "*Ist* okay."

And so he squeezed her fingers until he slipped away.

*Help one another. Encourage, understand,
and nurture one another for the betterment of all.*

Christian Metz, 1825

CHAPTER 6

Second National Building and Loan was a small yet reputable bank for Chicago's wealthier citizens, and as the bank president, Frank Powell liked to tell himself that it was one of the most respected banks in the country. His father passed on the building and loan to Frank in 1846, and he'd worked tirelessly to keep its doors open throughout the Civil War.

Over the years he'd reluctantly accepted deposits from the lower classes, but he didn't like the risk involved with such accounts. He preferred the clientele who entrusted him to invest their money securely for the future instead of the middle classers who were forever depositing and withdrawing funds. Still, he couldn't seem to help himself when an engineer or teacher asked to open an account.

His customers trusted him to guard their money, and he'd done well for them by investing their savings back into Chicago businesses and making them loans to buy houses in the city. And with a small percentage of it, he'd invested overseas in countries like England and Argentina. Then England and

Argentina went bust like the rest of the world and that portion of his capital was forever gone.

Wall Street and the U.S. government messed with the finances of their great nation, and they'd mucked it up. Then people across the nation followed suit, rushing on banks for all their cash even though it was spread in investments around the world.

When a customer decided he wanted his money returned, Frank didn't blink or beg. He returned the entire sum without question. Even when half of Chicago marched into his bank last summer and demanded every dollar and cent in their savings, he'd coughed up fifty thousand from the bank's reserves. Unfortunately, he couldn't march right back to the doors of their homes and businesses and demand every dollar and cent he'd loaned them.

A hundred other banks went under last year, but Second National kept their doors open. They'd survived the worst crash he'd seen in his lifetime, but they were still stumbling to get their feet back on firm ground.

He'd had to let two of his three clerks go—not because he wanted to, but because he'd had no choice. At the time, he'd hoped that he could rehire them within months, but even now, three months later, he couldn't afford to hire another soul. Orwin Tucker wasn't the brightest clerk who'd ever worked for him, but as long as he kept trying to learn the business, Frank couldn't let him go.

The president's office was separated from the main lobby by a wall, a long window of frosted glass, and a door that allowed him to see his customers entering and leaving the bank while sitting behind his mahogany desk. This afternoon, when Stanley Roberts entered the bank, he knew the man wasn't here to deposit cash. At this time of day, he should be out laying bricks at one of the few construction sites left in the city.

Frank waited for Orwin to handle the man's transaction

from the teller cage before he went out to greet the man. Turning the page of the *Daily News*, he hoped for something positive in the midst of all the articles raging over the Pullman Strike, but there was not a stitch of good news.

Minutes later Orwin appeared at Frank's door with Stanley close behind him. His bank clerk was a wiry fellow with thick hair and even thicker spectacles. Stanley was a few inches shorter than Orwin, and his bushy beard matched his stout frame. At the moment, neither man looked pleased.

"What is it?" Frank asked.

Orwin scooted into his office and placed the ledger of the bank's accounts on his desk. "Mr. Roberts is here to withdraw from his savings."

Frank pulled the red-and-gold-colored volume close to him and scanned Stanley's record of deposits and withdrawals. At the beginning of January, the man had a little over a hundred dollars in his account, but he'd withdrawn twenty-five dollars a month during the first part of the year.

Frank pushed the book aside. "You have fifteen dollars in your account, Mr. Roberts. Would you like to close it?"

Stanley stepped up to his desk, an enflamed red climbing up his neck. His voice shook when he spoke. "Not fifteen dollars, Mr. Powell. I need my hundred and fifteen."

Frank reread the numbers on the ledger. "But you already took out your money."

"No, sir. I've been saving my money so I could move my family to a bigger flat, but now I lost my job and I need my money to make rent."

"The fifteen dollars should pay for your rent."

The man's lips trembled. "I've got other bills to pay too, Mr. Powell, and it's my money I've been saving. I don't need to tell you where I'm spending it."

Frank turned the ledger around. "See these lines."

"I see a bunch of numbers, but it don't mean nothing to me."

"This says that on January fifth, you took twenty-five dollars out of your account. My clerk initialed the transaction." Frank pointed to Jacob Hirsch's initials on the line.

"But I didn't take out the money."

"Then on February tenth, you withdrew another twenty-five dollars."

"No, sir."

"Orwin here approved that transaction."

"Do you remember that?" Stanley asked, looking over at Orwin, but the younger man shrugged.

"That was six months ago."

Stanley turned back to Frank, and there were tears in the man's eyes. "I trusted you with my money."

"And I took good care of it."

"But I didn't take it out!"

"I'm sorry, Mr. Roberts." If it had been one transaction, he may have thought it a clerical error, but Stanley had taken out the money four different times with three clerks signing for it. Frank felt sorry for the man, but he couldn't give him someone else's money either.

Orwin held out the cash in his hand. Fifteen dollars.

Stanley pounded his fist into his hand, and Frank eyed the telephone at the edge of his desk. Perhaps he should ring the police station.

"How is my family supposed to live on fifteen dollars?"

"I don't know, Mr. Roberts."

The man swiped the cash from Orwin's palm. Cursing both Frank and Orwin, Stanley turned and stomped out the door. Orwin apologized for the interruption as he backed out of the doorway and moved toward his teller cage.

Frank sat back in his chair, rubbing his temples. Stanley didn't seem like the kind of man who would try to trick the bank into giving him cash. Even so, you could never tell about people. Over the years he'd learned that some of the seemingly nicest people could bite you in the backside.

In days past, he might have given Stanley a bit more money than fifteen dollars since the man had been a faithful bank customer, but times were different now. In the past twelve months, Frank had liquidated the bank's overseas and domestic investments at a frightening rate to keep up with the requests of people who were taking their money out of the bank and hiding it under a floorboard in their home instead—like no one would find it there. Even though a year had passed, many of his former customers hadn't returned their savings to the bank, and now they were faulting on their bank loans as well. House loans. Business loans. Even farm loans.

Second National didn't have much cash these days, but they sure did own a heck of a lot of barns and office buildings that no one wanted to buy. Some days he felt like a chicken perched on a nest full of eggs that would never hatch.

Liesel knew the instant her father stormed into the good doctor's home. It was barely first light, and Cassie was sleeping in fits on the bed in front of her. Jacob was awake, sitting in vigilance on the other side of the bed as Albert Strauss stomped his feet below them and demanded the release of his daughter.

Dr. Trachsel told her father that she'd refused to leave when she had the chance, but her father was insisting it wasn't too late. Liesel could go home with him now. Silence followed, and she imagined the doctor down below, shaking his head while he explained to her father what he'd explained to her. The suffocation from diphtheria. Paralysis. If Albert exposed himself to diphtheria and carried the disease back to Amana, they could have an epidemic on their hands.

Her father continued to argue. He was an Elder in Amana, a

respected member of their Society, but she prayed quietly that the doctor wouldn't back down under her father's pressure. The moment she saw Cassie and Jacob across the tracks, she knew she was supposed to help them. It was almost as if God had placed her there at the depot and allowed her to linger until Jacob and Cassie arrived.

Outside Cassie's room was a sitting room, and on the other side of the family room was a bedroom for her to use. She hadn't slept in the bedroom last night. In fact, she hadn't slept much at all. She'd stayed up most of the night, keeping the girl's face moist and putting blankets back on her small frame after she kicked them off. Every three hours, she administered the whiskey-and-milk mixture that Dr. Trachsel had prescribed to soothe Cassie's throat and help her rest, but the whiskey didn't seem to be working.

She strained her ears, trying to listen to the conversation on the bottom floor as the doctor explained that Jacob did indeed need help caring for his daughter.

Jacob's fingers picked at the wool on Cassie's blanket, his eyes on his daughter's face. He didn't ask, but even so, she wanted to explain that her father had a compassionate heart. He just wasn't the least bit generous about allowing his only daughter to be quarantined with a worldly stranger, no matter what the condition of the man or the man's child.

The arguing continued downstairs for at least twenty minutes, and after it quieted, someone slipped a folded piece of paper under the door. She opened the note and scanned her father's admonitions and reminders from the Scriptures. If Jacob threatened her, he wrote, she was to notify the doctor immediately so she could serve out her quarantine in a locked room.

When she read those words, she glanced across the bed at Jacob's bone-tired face.

She'd been with him and Cassie all night and never once did

she feel threatened. Most of the time he didn't even seem to notice that she was in the same room.

Jesus himself had reached out to those who were dirty. Unclean. He'd touched the lepers when no one else would go near them. She was only doing a very small part to follow His example.

As she folded the letter, Jacob looked at her. "I've caused a lot of trouble, haven't I?"

"It's not trouble." She slid the letter into her apron pocket. "My father's only worried about me."

"He's right, you know." He took a deep breath, and for an instant, she was afraid he would send her away. "You should have left when the doctor told you to go."

"I wanted to help you…." She looked down at Cassie. "And help her."

He cleared his throat, and his voice cracked when he spoke again. "I'd never hurt you."

Her eyes flickered up, ever so briefly, and met his intense gaze. She saw the power and kindness in his eyes. "I know."

His gaze softened again. "Cassie thinks she has a guardian angel."

"Her faith is strong, Jacob. This is *gut*."

He paused before he spoke again. "She thinks her angel has blond hair."

Heat climbed up her neck, and she hoped he couldn't see her blush in the morning light.

*So now cast aside all fear and, with a childlike heart,
immerse yourself in fulfilling mercy, love,
and faith of your Immanuel.*

Ursula Mayer, 1717

CHAPTER 7

Hail hammered the shingles on the doctor's house, plunking bits of ice against the bedroom window. Lightning illuminated the tangled branches outside the dark glass, and a violent crash followed the flash of light, shaking the walls around Liesel and her patient. Even with the lightning and thunder her patient didn't open her eyes, but the light and sound were welcome company for Liesel.

God's in His heaven; all's right with the world.

God was in heaven, of that she was certain, but she wasn't sure she could agree with Mr. Browning's words about all being right in the world. God was here tonight, in this room, but nothing seemed right in her world.

Cassie groaned on the sweat-soaked bed, tossing her head back and forth on the pillow. Liesel dipped a washcloth in a bowl of tepid water, wrung it out, and wiped the puddles of sweat from the child's face. Instead of getting better, Cassie's health continued to spiral downward. They'd forced the last of the whiskey through her lips hours ago, so Jacob had gone downstairs in search of more to ease Cassie's pain and help her rest.

THE STRANGER

The water didn't seem to be doing much good on Cassie's skin, but the work gave Liesel something to do and some way to at least pretend she was helping to keep Cassie from slipping through death's door.

The doctor ventured up the stairs at least once a day to give them medicine and advice, but he never crossed the threshold to check on Cassie. Of all the people in Homestead, he had to be the most careful to not expose himself to the disease any more than he already had. No one else was qualified to care for the people in their community.

Rosa Trachsel had left liver sausage, potato salad, and tins with tea and milk outside the door for supper. The woman had knocked to alert them to the hot food, but by the time Liesel rushed to the door to ask for whiskey, the woman had disappeared back down the steps.

Jacob had wanted to go downstairs right then, but she'd asked him to wait until the doctor came and checked on them for the night so they wouldn't break their quarantine.

Hours passed and the doctor never came...so around nine, Jacob had walked out the door.

The kerosene lamp flickered, and shadows danced around the twin beds and the two chairs alongside Cassie's bed. Beside the bed there was also a large dresser and a clock in the corner that kept time but never chimed.

With a loud moan, Cassie thrashed and kicked at the heavy blanket on top of her, sending it off the bed. Liesel picked the wool blanket off the floor and tucked it around the girl's hot skin once more to help her sweat out the fever.

Three nights had passed since Jacob and Cassie arrived in Homestead, and Liesel had only left this room to use the chamber pot in her bedroom. She'd slept very little since volunteering to help Jacob Hirsch, only briefly napping in the chair while he attended to his daughter. Every once in a while, he would doze off as well, but then he would force himself to wake again, pacing the floor and sipping the coffee that Rosa brought them. Jacob ignored the doctor's instructions to rest so his body could fight off the infection in his leg. It was almost as if he didn't care about healing his leg or even if he survived...like he was ready to go to the grave with his daughter.

Liesel soaked the washcloth again and wrung it out. She'd never had the privilege of birthing a child so she couldn't imagine the grief over losing one, but even so, it was for God—not man—to decide the time for each of His children to come home. Until God called this precious soul to him, she'd work as hard as she could to keep both father and daughter alive.

The swelling around Cassie's throat had started to subside, but the fever kept burning her skin. They'd never had a case of diphtheria in the Amanas before, but she was grateful that Dr. Trachsel and their Elders had had the foresight to purchase the antitoxin serum long before their village needed it. The doctor had specifically requested the antitoxin, thinking it was critical to fortify themselves against this rapidly spreading disease. Not only had he administered the serum to Cassie, but he had given it to Jacob, Liesel, and Rosa as well, to help protect them from the disease. Still, even with the antitoxin, Dr. Trachsel didn't know how long it would take for Cassie to recover...or if she would recover. But he told them that the colonists in all seven villages were praying for Cassie's healing and that Liesel and Jacob would be protected from the disease.

Liesel heard the door open, and when she turned her head, Jacob limped into the room, carrying a small jug in one hand and a bucket of clean water in the other.

"How is she?"

Liesel walked over to the window and dumped out the basin of stale water she'd been using. "She stopped moaning."

When she returned to the bed, he refilled the basin with clean water from the bucket. "Is that a good sign?"

The cold stung her fingers as she soaked the washcloth for

another sponging of Cassie's skin. She couldn't answer his question. Cassie's face looked peaceful, but she didn't know if that was good or bad.

"Where's Dr. Trachsel?" she asked instead.

"Apparently someone is having a baby tonight."

She looked back at him. "Who?"

He mixed the whiskey and milk together in a tin. "I didn't ask."

"Marga? Greta?"

"I said, I didn't ask."

She glanced out the window's dark glass. The lightning was further away now, flashing in the distance. The news may not be important to him, but she was hungry for information. A new baby! They were welcoming a new life into their community, and she didn't know who was having the child.

Jacob was hovering over the bed now, pushing hair out of his daughter's eyes. He lifted Cassie's head, trying to force her to take a sip of the mixture, but his hands shook and he spilled milk down her neck and hair instead.

"Sit down," she said, her voice barely a whisper.

"No…"

She pointed at the full plate of food on the stand beside his chair. "Did you eat the sausage?"

He set the tin on the bedside table. "A little."

"You can't help your daughter if you don't take care of yourself."

"You don't know what I need." He turned his eyes from his daughter, glaring over the bed at her. "You don't know…."

"You're right," she said quietly. "I don't know."

He grabbed the washcloth from her hands and swabbed Cassie's neck and arms. Then he tossed the cloth onto the bedspread and collapsed into his chair, his head sinking into his hands. His shoulders trembled like they were carrying a burden so heavy that his entire body was about to break under the load.

Liesel reached for the cloth and wrung it over the basin. She didn't know what any of them needed right now.

The fading lightning flickered through the room again, and the walls rattled with another rumble of thunder. The hail had stopped beating against the glass, but the skies were now pouring rain.

Liesel slid back in her hard chair after glancing at the clock ticking behind her. It was almost eleven o'clock now, and everyone else in the village would be asleep except perhaps Dr. Trachsel, the midwife, and the woman giving birth.

Part of her wished she could be outside this room, ready to help the new mother, but she knew that God wanted her here, caring for this child...and for her father. So she was content to stay right here, in the stillness of this room, until Cassie was whole again. In the darkness, Liesel prayed for the health of the new Amana baby. And the health of his mama.

Jacob shifted in his chair, and Liesel looked over at him. His firm chin was speckled with stubble, and dark shadows clung to the skin under his eyes. Even so, he was a handsome man. Handsome and haggard.

Liesel's father had loved and protected her for her entire life, the fierceness of his protection compounding in the years after her mother went away. She'd heard that worldly fathers often left their families when they hit troubled times, but not Jacob Hirsch. He was staying with his daughter through the worst of times, guarding and caring for her needs, doing work that women usually did.

Where were the women in Jacob's life? She'd wondered it over the past few days but didn't dare ask. Did he have a wife? If not, who was Cassie's mother—and more important, where was she when her daughter needed her so badly?

In one of their brief conversations, Jacob had told her he'd grown up with his German grandparents in New York, though he lived in Chicago for almost a decade. He certainly remembered enough German to communicate with her, but she preferred to speak English with him. Seven years ago, she'd finished her lessons at their English-speaking school, and she had only been able to practice English when tourists or transients visited…or when she and Sophie worked in the gardens. It was her secret language with Sophie—a language many of the older people in the Amana Colonies didn't understand.

Jacob Hirsch was nothing like most of the transients she'd met over the years. He wasn't crass, nor had he asked for ale or whiskey like so many of the hobos who passed through their town. She'd never even seen him steal a swig of the whiskey the doctor prescribed for Cassie.

He'd been terse when she questioned him, but his rudeness was laced with confusion. His love for his daughter was palpable in his pain and frustration at not being able to rescue her from this cruel disease.

Jacob lifted his eyes to meet hers again, and she blushed when he caught her staring at him. His voice was softer this time. Broken. "I'm sorry, Liesel."

She looked down at the basin of water instead of meeting his strong gaze. "It's okay."

"No, it's not."

She picked up the wet cloth and wiped it across Cassie's forehead. This time the girl didn't thrash her head across the pillow. "You don't have to pretend that everything is okay, Jacob. Not with me."

She dared herself a quick glance over her arm and saw a spark of appreciation in his light green eyes. "Thank you."

She nodded slightly, folding her arms across her chest and squeezing her elbows.

When she shivered, he turned around and snatched the comforter off the bed next to Cassie, the bed where he was supposed to sleep. When he handed it to her, she placed it over her shoulders and thanked him.

He reached down and propped up his injured leg on a stool. "You need someone to take care of you."

A soft laugh escaped her lips. How ironic that Jacob would talk about her lack of care when he refused to care for himself. She almost protested, saying that she could take care of herself, but that would be a lie. "Our community cares for each other."

Quietness settled over the room as they both watched Cassie. For the first time in three days, she was sleeping peacefully. Minutes passed before he spoke again. "Your father cares for you."

"*Ja*. A little too much sometimes."

He watched Liesel in the dim light. "I suppose you have a suitor who cares about you as well."

She squirmed in her chair. She craved the companionship of a friend, conversation. Still, she didn't want to talk about her family or her future with this man who refused to tell her about himself.

Jacob waved his hand in front of his face. "It's none of my business."

She brushed her hands over her dress. "I'm supposed to be married this winter."

"Is your fiancé in Homestead?"

"He's in Main Amana." She knew her voice sounded weak, but she couldn't let this man know the turmoil the word *fiancé* caused within her.

"He is counting his blessings, I'm sure." He paused. "Why didn't he come to visit with your father?"

She shrugged, pretending like it didn't matter even though she'd asked herself the same question already. "He has an important job in Amana."

"It must be very important work."

"He's the…" She couldn't tell him that Emil's important job was baking bread for the village. An outsider wouldn't understand. "We're not supposed to see each other anyway."

"Not supposed to see each other…" He repeated her words like he was trying to understand. "That's odd."

She bristled, waiting for him to tease her like so many of the tourists did who didn't understand their ways. "Not in Amana."

"But why can't you see each other?"

"All the engaged couples live apart for a year to make sure they really want to marry."

"So it's like a test."

"I suppose."

"How long have you been separated from—"

"Emil." She twisted the hem of her apron in her hands. "Emil Hahn."

"How long has it been since you've seen Emil?"

"We've been separated for six months now, but I saw him in May."

"I bet he's counting down the days until he can see you again."

"Right," she mumbled as she stretched out the edge of her apron and twisted it again. Six months ago, she had accepted his proposal. After all, she and Emil had grown up together, and they were the best of friends when they were children. He'd teased her through *Lehrschule* and lingered at her kitchen house when he delivered his bread.

Since their engagement, they'd had three visits, but her last visit with Emil had been so miserable that she doubted he would want to see her again, perhaps not even until their wedding. They'd picnicked along the banks of the Iowa River, but Emil—charming, dashing Emil—had barely acknowledged her presence. She'd chattered on like a woodpecker intent on penetrating a tree, but Emil never cracked. No matter how hard she tried, he didn't want to answer her many questions.

Fortunately, the Elders had assigned two of their childhood friends to be informal chaperones. As he fished, Emil laughed with Margrit Poetsch and her brother Franz , but Liesel felt like a foreigner in a different land. Franz teased her. Margrit tried to include her. But Emil…Emil ignored her, and the thought of being married to a man who no longer enjoyed her company terrified her.

"So do you still want to be married?"

She blinked. "What?"

Jacob repositioned his leg and then looked back at her. "After six months, do you still want to marry this man?"

"I…" She smoothed the edge of her apron back on her lap. "I don't want to talk about him anymore."

Out of the corner of her eye, she watched the edge of Jacob's lip arch, like he wanted to smile. Was he mocking her? Or empathizing?

It was none of Jacob Hirsch's business if she still wanted to marry Emil Hahn.

She pulled the blanket over her legs and rested her head beside Cassie's feet. She was done thinking about Emil tonight. She was here with Jacob and Cassie, and she was content.

"I'm going to sleep," she whispered as she closed her eyes. If Jacob wished her a good night, she didn't hear him.

Quietly and yet so very powerfully, Love flows forth, miraculous, still, and blessed. The soft pure breath of Love is awakened within the profound.

Johann Friedrich Rock, 1720

CHAPTER 8

Someone wove her fingers through Jacob's hair, and he smiled in his sleep. Katharine was there, twirling around and smiling with him. They were so very happy. So in love. He knew it was a dream, but even so, he didn't want to wake up. He wanted to stay here beside his wife. He wanted to laugh with her and remember their good years together.

"Papa," someone whispered, pulling him away from Katharine. He pushed the voice back, fighting to keep his eyes closed, fighting to keep his wife beside him.

"Katharine!" he called, as she disappeared into the darkness. He didn't want to open his eyes. He wanted to stay beside her.

"Papa," the voice said again, and he jolted upright. He'd tried to stay awake, but his body wouldn't cooperate with him. Sometime during the night, he'd fallen asleep on the edge of Cassie's bed. Glancing around the room he started to panic...until his eyes rested on the face of his daughter.

Somehow, Cassandra Kate Hirsch had scooted herself upright on her pillows, and the morning light warmed the smile on her face.

His daughter was smiling.

He couldn't breathe as he examined her face. A healthy pink pallor had replaced the gray in her skin, and the sweat that had saturated her forehead and cheeks was gone.

Was he still dreaming, or had God blessed him with a miracle?

Cassie wagged her finger to scold him. "You scared me, Papa."

"I scared you?" Laughter poured out of Jacob. "You scared me!"

She grinned. "I'm hungry."

He glanced down and saw the leftover sausage and potato salad by his feet, but that wouldn't do at all for his little girl. His hungry girl.

Looking to his right, he saw Liesel asleep on the end of Cassie's bed. He nudged her arm. "Wake up."

She didn't open her eyes. "*Alles gut.*"

He prodded her again. "Wake up, Liesel."

Slowly she lifted her head, until she realized that Cassie was awake and watching her.

Then she leaped to her feet.

"Cassie Hirsch," she gasped. "You about gave me a heart attack."

Cassie blinked, her eyes wide as she stared at Liesel's hair. "Who are you?"

Liesel laughed with delight and reached out to shake Cassie's hand. "Liesel Strauss, and I'm very, very pleased to meet you."

"Are—are you an angel?"

Liesel giggled. "Oh no, my dear, sweet, wonderful child. I'm just a plain Iowa girl."

Instead of curtseying, Cassie nodded her head. "I'm pleased to meet you as well."

Liesel didn't release Cassie's hand. "I think we are going to be the best of friends."

Cassie reached out with her other hand and grasped Jacob's

arm. He gently squeezed her fragile fingers. He didn't know what was next in their journey, but his daughter was alive and awake. He was a blessed man.

Someone knocked on the door, and he scrambled around the bed so he could open it before Rosa Trachsel snuck away again. However, it wasn't the doctor's wife bringing up breakfast this morning. It was Dr. Trachsel.

He lifted his hat to them. "I'm sorry I couldn't come last night. I—"

"Who had a baby?" Liesel blurted out beside them.

Dr. Trachsel chuckled. "Greta had a boy."

"Are they okay?"

"They're both healthy."

Liesel clapped her hands. "God is good."

Grief seared him, but Jacob refused to let the memories overtake him. He was happy for this woman and her healthy baby too. No family should have to suffer the loss of a mother or a child.

"How is our patient this morning?" Dr. Trachsel's gaze traveled over their heads and landed on Cassie's bed. "Well, well."

The doctor scooted around both Jacob and Liesel and reached for Cassie's arm to feel her pulse. Then, opening his black bag, he worked swiftly, listening to her chest, pressing down her tongue, examining her throat.

When he finished his exam, he turned back to Jacob. "I believe we're on the other side."

Jacob sighed with relief. "Thank God."

"She still may be contagious." Dr. Trachsel untangled the stethoscope from around his neck and closed it back in his bag. "We will have to wait for the results of her throat culture to see."

With Cassie feeling better, he could take care of her now. Liesel had helped them both, taking care of his daughter and him when they needed her. She was an angel, but it was time to release her from her obligation so she could go home to her father and the man who was to marry her.

Jacob leaned forward, his eyes on the doctor. "Can Liesel go home now?"

Liesel jumped beside him. "What?"

"I can take care of Cassie."

She crossed her arms. "I'm not leaving."

"But your father—"

"You've done a terrible job of resting the past few days, Jacob Hirsch," Liesel said. "You sleep, and I'll help Cassie."

"Actually—" the doctor began, but Jacob wasn't done talking yet. Liesel had served her time, and he'd appreciated every minute of her help, but she needed to go back to her home. Before Cassie started caring for her.

"Your fiancé wouldn't want you here, Liesel."

"Emil doesn't care—"

The doctor interrupted again, this time with a chuckle. "Neither of you are leaving right now."

Jacob turned toward him. "What?"

"I'm sending a culture from you and Liesel off to the laboratory in Iowa City. Once those are clear, you can leave the house."

"How long until we get the results?"

The doctor shrugged. "I'm not sure exactly. Two or three days." *Two or three days?* He didn't want Liesel to be here that long. "How long until Cassie is released?"

"We will test her again in a week to see if her culture is negative." The doctor picked up his black bag. "Do you need anything else?"

He glanced over at Liesel, her face set like stone. She didn't look back at him. "I think we're fine."

Cassie tugged on the doctor's jacket. "Excuse me."

The doctor leaned over, and Cassie whispered in his ear. The doctor laughed at her words, and the sound reassured Jacob.

None of them had laughed for days, and with the doctor's laugh came the comfort that Cassie was indeed going to be okay.

The doctor turned to him with a wink. "Apparently, Cassie thinks you need a bath."

"I don't need a—" He looked down and saw his daughter's face, her eyebrows raised. "I just had a bath."

"When?" she asked.

He blinked several times. Surely he'd taken a bath in the past few weeks—but he couldn't remember exactly when. It hadn't seemed important to him before.

Jacob looked at the doctor. "My daughter is a smart girl."

"*Ja*, that she is."

He brushed off his sleeves as sunlight streaked across the room. "And if she says I need a bath—"

"Can you swim?"

"Yes, sir."

The doctor folded his fingers together and lowered his voice. "Tonight, after everyone has turned in for the night, you can walk down to the river and wash up."

Cassie tapped the doctor's shoulder. "I need a bath too!"

Jacob reached over and ruffled her hair, so glad to see her alert again. "You can't come this time, sweetheart."

Her smile tumbled. "Next time?"

He nudged her chin. "I sure hope so."

"You'll need clean clothes too," Liesel said.

"I have a change of clothes in my satchel."

Liesel tilted her head. "Are they clean?"

He sighed. The women were ganging up on him. "Of course they're clean."

Liesel flicked his sleeve. "Then I'll stitch your initials in these, and we'll send them off to the laundry after we're in the clear."

He wouldn't tell the women, but it would feel good to clean up and shave and put on some clean clothes. Perhaps a good bath would clean out some of the fog that blurred his brain. Almost like a new start for Cassie and him. With new clarity, he could chart out a course for their future.

The doctor left the room with a tip of his black hat. Outside the bedroom door was a tray filled with a pot of coffee, a slab of butter, buckwheat cakes, toast, and strawberry jam. Jacob's stomach rumbled.

Lifting the tray from the floor, he handed it to Liesel, and she carried it to the little table beside Cassie's bed. She made a small plate for Cassie, and his daughter slipped her feet over the edge of the bed and reached for a piece of toast with jam.

It was a new start indeed.

Frank Powell didn't have two thousand dollars on hand to close the Honorable Charlie Caldwell's account, nor did he know where Caldwell's money went, but he couldn't admit that to the man pacing in front of his desk. Caldwell was a bigwig judge in Chicago, and if he discovered that Second National had lost his money, there would be lawsuits and bad publicity and yet another run on the bank's dwindling resources. Frank couldn't afford any of it.

He glanced back down at the ledger in front of him as if the numbers might have evolved since the last time he'd looked, but Caldwell's record clearly showed that the man had taken out more than a thousand of the two thousand he'd entrusted to the bank—most of it in the winter and spring in the amounts of fifty and one hundred dollars.

Caldwell leaned across his desk, and Frank flinched.

"I never took out that money, Frank. Not even during the panic last summer. I sat tight, trusting you to care for it."

"I did care for it."

"Then where did my money go?"

Frank shook his head. Stanley had questioned him, and now Caldwell was asking questions as well. He was an honest banker, had always been an honest banker, and he watched over his customers' savings with more vigilance than a warden watched his prisoners. Never once had he doubted he could keep the money safe...until now.

"It's not gone, Caldwell. One of the clerks must have recorded the transactions under the wrong name. Someone else must have taken out their money."

"How many Charlie Caldwells do you have at this bank?"

"Only you, my friend, but there are plenty of other Charlies in the books. One of the clerks mixed it up." He delivered the words with much more confidence than he felt. It was odd that his clerks would have erred on the record over and over again, but he wasn't prepared to accuse Caldwell of lying either.

His friend crossed his arms and leaned toward the desk again. He wasn't a tall man, but there wasn't a more powerful man among his clientele. Right then, Frank wanted to strangle whoever made the errors, if it had been an error.

Everyone knew Caldwell dabbled in a bit of gambling—horseracing and that sort of nonsense—but neither Caldwell's gambling nor Frank's investing had paid off in the past year.

Caldwell rapped on the desk. "Times are hard, Frank."

He nodded. "I know it."

"I need that money."

"I'll find out what happened to it."

Caldwell stepped back toward the door, but he kept his eyes on Frank. "I'll be back on Friday."

Frank made a notation on the paper in front of him, like the problem could be easily resolved. "It may take me a few more days, Charlie."

"Monday, then."

He swallowed. "Monday."

The door slammed shut, and Frank sunk back into his chair.

He'd spent his life working in his father's bank, and if he weren't careful, his life's work would dissolve overnight.

He closed the ledger with Caldwell's name and opened up another book, skimming the surnames from F–K. Each transaction was scribbled in the lines. The date, amount, initials of the teller, and sometimes even the reason the customer was depositing or withdrawing their money. Frank was strict about the details and expected his clerks to be strict in their recordings as well. Even in the midst of the panic last summer, he expected their records to be impeccable, and they knew it.

He raked his stubby fingers through what remained of his graying hair and then twisted the diamond ring on his right hand before he turned back to Caldwell's record and ran his fingers along the scribbled notes and numbers in the ledger. It would be much simpler if only one clerk had recorded the withdrawals, but there were initials from all three employees—Orwin and the two clerks he'd had to let go.

He could quiz Orwin to see if he remembered Caldwell taking out the cash, but it wasn't like he could contact the clerks he'd released from his employ and ask about the missing money. They had no motivation to explain anything to him. There had to be another way.

He pushed the ledgers to the side of his desk, clearing a space in front of him. Then he leaned over, slipped a lined piece of paper out of a drawer, and scribbled the names and last-known addresses of Bradford Pendleton and Jacob Hirsch.

"Orwin!" he hollered. His clerk scrambled into his office with a pencil and paper in his hand. He seated himself in one of the polished chairs on the other side of the desk and crossed his legs. Very few understood the rush of the financial world, but Orwin was supposed to understand it. Banking was in his blood.

Orwin leaned toward the open ledgers spread across Frank's desk. "Is something wrong?"

Frank shook his head. He'd wait to ask Orwin about Caldwell's missing money. If they had another run on the bank, he'd never be able to appease the crowds this time. He would hold onto as much money as he could until he discovered the missing funds, and even then, he wouldn't have to let anyone know what had happened to the money.

He slid the piece of paper across the desk. "I have an assignment for you."

Orwin glanced down at the paper, but he didn't pick it up. "Anything you need."

"It's a small task, really."

Orwin's face fell slightly.

Frank tapped the list, and Orwin picked it up and glanced at it.

"I need you to find out where Bradford Pendleton and Jacob Hirsch are now."

Orwin's eyes narrowed behind his spectacles. "Where they are now?" he queried.

"I'm…," Frank started. "I've been concerned about them and want to know how they are faring after the loss of their jobs."

Orwin shrugged. "So I will send them each a letter."

"I was thinking more of a visit."

Orwin glanced down at the list again. "You want me to knock on their doors?"

He shook his head. "I don't want them to know I'm checking up on them."

"So you'd rather I knock on their neighbors' doors…?"

"Precisely."

"I'd be glad to check up on them but"—Orwin placed both feet on the floor—"are there any specific questions I should be asking?"

"Oh, no." Frank tried to make his tone sound casual. "I'd just like to know if they're doing well or if they're struggling to find work."

"Are you…" Orwin stuttered. "Are you going to offer them new positions?"

"No…I just want to know if I can help."

"You can't feel guilty about this. You had to let them go."

"I know, Orwin, but I still have a few regrets."

Orwin folded the list twice and dropped it into his pocket. "I'll find them for you."

Frank nodded. "Orwin…"

"Yes?"

"Please remember to do this discretely."

The man nudged his glasses back up his nose. "Of course."

*So now enter into the chamber of grace!
Here there is rest for all who are weary
and joy for all who suffer.*

Johann Friedrich Rock, 1725

CHAPTER 9

*L*iesel lit the kerosene lantern on the nightstand and quietly closed the door that connected her bedroom to the sitting room. Her fingers grazed the lock above the doorknob, but she didn't turn it. Her father would tell her to lock it, but she'd never once locked the door in her room above the kitchen house or in her bedroom in Main Amana. In spite of what her father said, she knew she could trust Jacob Hirsch.

Reaching behind her neck, she peeled the hairnet off her hair, then took off her apron, hung it on a hook over the door, and began to unbutton her long dress.

While Jacob rested today, she and Cassie played for hours in the sitting room. When the doctor returned this afternoon, he carried a beautiful bisque doll with him, a gift from Greta's oldest daughter. The doll had a delicate porcelain face with rosy cheeks and curly black hair and looked very much like the doll that Liesel played with as a child. Cassie snuggled the toy to her chest like it was a real baby, and Liesel understood. She'd spent many a night cradling her own baby.

Beside her dresser, Liesel washed her arms and face with the water waiting in a basin. Even though she'd teased Jacob about taking a bath, she needed one just as badly as he did. She couldn't go down to the river for her bath, though. The middle of the river was over her head and, like most of the colonists, she'd never learned how to swim. There was little time for recreation in the Amanas, and no swim apparel was appropriate for the women anyway. But even if she were permitted to swim, she would be too scared to go into the water.

At least once a week, the Amana women turned the community laundry into a washroom so they could take turns bathing in the hot water. When the doctor released them from quarantine, both she and Cassie would take a hot bath.

Fortunately, Mrs. Keller had delivered a clean dress for Liesel along with undergarments and her nightshirt so she would have fresh clothes to wear.

Climbing under the covers, Liesel stretched out her toes as far as they would go. The breeze whisked the branch of a tree through her open window, and when she blew out her lantern, the glow of moonlight cast a silvery sheen over the walls. She pulled the covers up to her shoulders and breathed deeply, the sweet air refreshing her lungs.

Thank God, Cassie was well again. Thank God, He brought them through the darkness and despair. Thank God, she could finally rest again.

It was the first night in a week she'd slept in a bed, and it was a relief to stretch out on a mattress. She and Jacob were blessed —so very blessed—that they didn't have to stay up all night again tending to Cassie, yet Liesel couldn't help missing the companionship. Families across Homestead were resting together tonight, but she was alone.

She closed her eyes, but sleep didn't come.

Today was one of the best days of her life. Not only was Cassie recovering, but Liesel couldn't remember enjoying a day so much—at least not since she was a child herself, playing with her own friends and toys.

Cassie was a delight, and she'd made Liesel giggle like she was a child again. And Liesel hadn't cared a bit if Jacob or anyone in the house heard her laughter. That was the beauty of being around a child. No one cared if one acted childish.

The *Gartebaas*—garden boss—often scolded her and Sophie for acting like children when they were planting and harvesting the gardens. They would manage to suppress their giggling for a while, but they'd get reprimanded again before long.

The truth was, Liesel loved to play and laugh. Happiness was elusive, to be sure, but the gift of God's joy strengthened her. And there was nothing more joyful to her than playing with a child.

They had a *Kinderschule* in their community to care for the young children while their parents worked. After her fire incident in the kitchen, she had hoped the Elders would reassign her to the *Kinderschule* to care for these children, but two older women already worked there. There was no need for her in the school, but there was a great need in the gardens behind the kitchen house...so she was placed outside.

She'd learned to enjoy working the dirt, growing things—and it was a delight to spend her days with Sophie—yet part of her still longed to spend her days in the *Kinderschule*.

Liesel rolled over on the mattress, trying to clear her mind, but her thoughts wouldn't rest. She couldn't stop thinking about her day...her many days spent with Jacob and his daughter.

Jacob was a blessed man to have a girl like Cassie, and Cassie was blessed to have a father who cared so much about her. His entire being had been focused on getting her well again, and Liesel couldn't help but admire a man who was so dedicated to his child. He loved Cassie, and she had been swept away in his love for his daughter.

Still, it made her wonder again if there was a woman in Jacob's life. Had his wife left him? Passed away? Or perhaps he never had a wife. She hoped there wasn't a woman looking for him.

Her eyes popped open, scolding herself for the thought. She should be hoping there *was* a woman in Jacob's life. A woman who loved both him and his daughter. Anything else was vile. Wrong.

She rolled over, trying to stop herself from wondering about Cassie's mother, but she couldn't seem to conquer the thoughts.

It didn't matter if Jacob was married or not anyway. She was an engaged woman herself, and the only reason she was here was to help Jacob until his daughter was well again. She had to focus her thoughts on helping Cassie, not on the private life of the girl's father.

Yet in spite of the circumstances, she was pleased to be able to assist Jacob these past few days. Their time together had been terribly hard, not anything like the lighthearted picnic she and Emil were supposed to have last May, yet she preferred her long hours working alongside Jacob to spending another leisurely afternoon with the man she was supposed to marry.

She rolled over onto her left side and shut her eyes again.

It didn't matter that she enjoyed her time with Jacob. Her focus was on Cassie, and she would care for this dear child until she was well again. Then she would have to say goodbye.

The train's shrill whistle awakened Jacob. He bolted up in bed and squinted in the moonlight to read the time on the clock. Eight minutes past three. If he hurried, he could sneak down to the river and be back in the house before sunrise so no one in the village saw him.

Creeping out of the bed, he placed his ear onto Cassie's chest and listened, relieved once again to hear her calm breath. She was resting peacefully now, her fever gone along with the sore throat. Dr. Trachsel believed that the danger had passed, yet he couldn't stop himself from checking on her.

Stepping around Cassie's bed, he propped open the door to the sitting room so Liesel could hear Cassie while he was away. He didn't want to leave Cassie, not even for an hour, but Cassie had said he needed a bath and the doctor had encouraged him to wash his leg. If Cassie called out, he had no doubt that Liesel would race to her side.

He almost crossed the room to knock on Liesel's door and remind her that he was leaving, but he didn't want to frighten her. He'd let the women sleep, and when they woke up, he would be refreshed and clean.

His gaze rested on Liesel's door for a few seconds before he backed toward the hallway door. She was clearly an angel of God, sent to help Cassie when she needed it most, but it wasn't fair of him to monopolize her time when she should be preparing for her marriage with Emil Hahn.

Yet today, when he'd tried to give her the out she needed to go home, she'd insisted on staying with them. It was almost like she was running away from something as well.

This afternoon, when Liesel and Cassie thought he was asleep, he'd listened to them laughing together through the walls. He wanted to open the door and go play with them, but he didn't want to interrupt their fun. Cassie was getting better, and she'd found a devoted— and charming—playmate in Liesel Strauss.

Still, even though Cassie was having fun, she was getting too attached to Liesel and it frightened him. And if he was gut honest with himself, he was getting a little too attached as well. It was time for Liesel to go home and definitely time for Cassie and him to move on.

When the quarantine was lifted, he would insist that Liesel leave right away—and he would need to leave as well, to find work to pay the doctor's bill and provide a living.

Draping his clean shirt and pants over one arm, he struck a match and lit the kerosene lantern hanging by the door. Then he bundled his razor and a bar of lye soap into a towel and snuck down the back stairs of the doctor's house so he wouldn't startle either Mrs. Trachsel or their two children.

The step under his foot creaked, and he held his breath. The house was silent, so he tested the next step and continued down the stairs, slipping out the back door.

The street was as quiet as the house. A few animals rustled in the barnyard, but none of them seemed to be startled by his presence. He hiked past the barn and over the train tracks as Liesel had instructed. Yellow light from the lantern washed over his feet and illuminated the tall grass in front of him. His leg still ached a bit, but the tight bandage circling his shin and calf reduced the pain.

A frog croaked in the darkness beside him, and something slithered in the grass.

He stopped for a moment, his heart pounding. What was crawling beside him? He took a deep breath and told himself it was probably a garter snake, but still, he had no idea what was living in the grass around him or the forest ahead.

He had no issue with walking the streets of Chicago at night—he knew what streets and what people to avoid. Most people were predictable, but he knew nothing about the backcountry of Iowa or the creatures who lived here, nor had he bothered to ask Liesel about wild animals or snakes. All he'd wanted to do was get outside and take a swim.

He ducked under a branch and skirted the narrow path through the trees. The air was cool in the early morning hours, a balm before the start of another hot July day.

He'd been so intent on traveling to Spokane that he never thought about taking an alternate trip—like a train ride to Iowa. Yet he was grateful that Etta had forced him out of the train at Homestead, grateful that Liesel had escorted him right into the doctor's office. Without Dr. Trachsel and his miraculous serum...

He didn't want to think about what would have happened if Dr. Trachsel hadn't given Cassie the antitoxin.

A breeze rustled the leaves beside him as he pressed forward along the path.

Not only had Cassie found a friend in Liesel, but the doctor had spent the day delivering new toys to their doorstep like he was Saint Nicolas. A doll, blocks, picture books, a baby buggy, colored pencils with paper...

Even now, Jacob was amazed at all the gifts, given to a child the Amana people didn't know, with no expectation that Cassie would be able to repay or even thank them. The strangers in Homestead were kinder to them than their friends had been in Chicago.

He ducked under another tree, and his head brushed a branch.

Squawk!

A wing clipped Jacob's head, and he almost dropped the lantern as he swatted the air with his free hand. Shouting in the darkness, he jogged ahead, hoping to deter the creature from swooping again. Did bats chase someone who'd angered them? He'd heard that a bird would chase you if it was mad, but he didn't know. He'd never been chased by a bird or a bat.

Steps ahead of the creature, he stopped and held up his light to illuminate the path behind him, but nothing seemed to be stalking him.

His feet moved faster now as he hiked further into the woods. The foliage was thick and imposing, and he tried not to think about what else could hide inside the shelter of the trees.

Less than a mile outside Homestead, he stopped at the top of a riverbank. In the moonlight, the wide river loped under the trees and wound toward a wooden bridge. The water was tame today, but it also seemed high, cresting three or four feet below the edge of the muddy bank.

Unbuttoning his shirt, the cool air swept across Jacob's chest and chilled his skin. He started to toss his shirt on the ground but stopped when he saw something hidden in the grass. Reaching for the lantern, he lifted his light off the ground and shined it on the grass by his foot. At first he thought it was an ordinary stick beside him, but it wasn't just a piece of wood. It was an oar.

Alongside the oar there was a pile of leaves, and as he brushed away the leaves and branches, he discovered an overturned rowboat underneath...almost identical to the boat he used to keep hidden along the marshy banks of the Chicago River.

His hand brushed over the flat bottom of the boat.

Before Cassie was born, he and Katharine often took their rowboat to the river on Sunday afternoons, exploring the wetlands near Lake Michigan. Sometimes they'd row all the way out to the Great Lake, and he'd splash and swim in the afternoon sun while Katharine, her parasol propped above her auburn hair, laughed with him from her seat on the boat.

When Cassie was a baby, they would take her out on the boat with them for an hour or two. Sometimes he would swim, while other days they would simply row along, pointing out butterflies and carp and rock bass to their daughter who was too young to appreciate the wildlife. Still, there was nothing more enjoyable to him than rowing the river with his family.

Then Katharine had gotten pregnant again. During most of her pregnancy, she was so sick that she became a prisoner of her bed. Their Sunday afternoon boat rides turned into a memory. They laughed about their times on the water. Remembered. But they never went back on the boat again. It would have been too much strain on Katharine and their baby.

How he missed his wife—desperately at times. Even so, he

was here now, in the Amanas, and Katharine had moved on to a much better place with the Savior she loved. He'd mourned for almost a year now. Perhaps it was time to start living again, for the sake of Katharine and his daughter.

When Cassie was released from quarantine, he'd try to bring her down here and borrow this old boat. Maybe she would enjoy boating as much as her mother had.

Unbuttoning his shirt, he laid it across the boat along with his shoes and tossed his trousers on top. Carefully he unwound the bandage from his leg and placed the white cloth beside the rest of his things. A scab had formed over the cut and a black bruise encircled it, but the pain was gone.

With the bar of soap in his hands, he waded into the cold water and then dove into the river. Soap and water washed off the weeks of dirt that had caked on his skin, and in some peculiar way, the river water almost felt like it washed away some of the fear that had been accumulating for weeks as well. Confidence was replacing his worry. And hope. He couldn't give up now.

If Katharine were still here, she would tell him to keep moving. Keep pressing until he found a position. She believed in him and in his ability to find a job. He was healthy, and he was determined. There had to be work someplace for him, and he would find it. Not that he wanted his daughter riding the rails, but perhaps they wouldn't have to go very far.

He dove under the water again and rinsed his hair.

Iowa seemed like a good place to raise a child, and he certainly liked the people here. Perhaps there was work to be found in Des Moines or Cedar Rapids or even over in Iowa City.

If only they didn't have to leave Homestead. The people here had been so kind to him and Cassie. It felt almost like the years he'd spent living near his grandparents—the one place that held the security of home.

The Amana people were gracious, but they were also part of a commune. A closed commune. Liesel told him they allowed tourists to stay in their midst, but few people were permitted to join the Amana Society.

From a purely financial perspective, he understood why the Elders wouldn't allow anyone new to join. It must take a significant amount of money and labor to support the seventeen hundred people who lived in the seven villages. The Society's operations seemed to run smoothly because everyone was dedicated to their faith and community. If someone joined from the outside world without the same work ethic and faith in God, they might stop contributing, and then the convert would become a burden on the society.

The Amana Colonies were a locked door to Cassie and him, but perhaps they could settle someplace nearby.

Reluctantly, he climbed up the riverbank to dry off and dress. The sun would rise soon, and out of respect for the villagers, he would hide himself back in the doctor's house before the bell tolled for breakfast.

*Your life is to be a pilgrimage and your
spiritual growth shall be accomplished in the Lord,
through whom you are moved.*

Johann Friedrich Rock, 1725

CHAPTER 10

Doll clothes, painted blocks, and pieces from a wooden puzzle were scattered across the sitting room floor along with a tiny crib the town carpenter had built for Princess Cocoa, Cassie's new doll. Liesel maneuvered a baby buggy around the toys, squealing as she raced through the maze. Princess Cocoa was supposed to be sleeping in the buggy, but no doll—or child—could sleep through this madness.

With a lurch, Liesel parked the buggy in front of the ottoman, inches from Cassie, and she gasped. "We must rescue the princess."

"Oh yes," Cassie giggled from her perch on the sofa. "We must."

"But…" Liesel leaned toward the buggy, checking the princess. "Oh, no."

Cassie pressed her hands to her heart. "What is it, Queen Liesel?"

"He's coming…."

Cassie turned toward the window, toward the rays that emerged from the glass panes. "Not the evil magician?"

She leaned down, whispering. "Even worse."

Cassie's eyes grew wide. "The dragon?"

"Yes, my friend." She reached down and pulled Princess Cocoa from the carriage. "That horrible, terrible dragon."

Cassie lifted her candlestick scepter. "You must save her!"

Liesel clutched the doll to her chest. "I will try."

Cassie looked back at the window. "It's too late."

"Oh..." She spun around slowly, the doll in her arms. "Oh, no."

Cassie giggled as Liesel spun one more time, and laughter tumbled from Liesel's lips as she collapsed on the floor. The door to the sitting room creaked open, and Liesel tried to jump to her feet, but she couldn't do it. Nor could she stop laughing.

Cassie stared at the doorway, and for an instant, Liesel didn't recognize the clean-shaven man who walked into the room. Jacob wore navy trousers and a white-cuffed shirt, and his hair was combed neatly behind his ears. There was no trace of hobo left on Jacob Hirsch.

Swallowing her laughter, Liesel gathered the hem of her skirt in her hands and hopped to her feet. What must he think of her, sprawled out on the floor like a child? He probably thought she was twelve instead of twenty-two.

"You took a bath, Papa."

Jacob sat beside his princess of a daughter, and Cassie placed her hands over his clean cheeks and turned his head slightly to examine his ears. Nudging his face upward, she checked his neck and then lifted her sleeve to rub a smudge off his chin. "Good job, Papa."

Jacob tugged her close to him. "I'm glad you approve."

He turned and looked at Liesel with a smile. "You're both up early."

"I...," she started—but her words jumbled. "Cassie..."

"I was the first one up," Cassie said.

At least one of them didn't have a problem finding their words. "I went to Liesel's room."

"You should have let her sleep."

"Oh, no." Liesel waved her hands. "It's not often I get to be queen for a day."

Jacob flashed her a smile of appreciation, like she had done something heroic by playing with his daughter, but she was having just as much fun as Cassie. Perhaps even more.

"Are you hungry?" Jacob asked his daughter, and she nodded.

Liesel brushed her hands over her hairnet. "We're having fried potatoes and bread and butter for breakfast."

"How do you know that?"

She shrugged. "It's Wednesday."

Seconds later someone knocked on the door, and Liesel swept across the floor to open it. The doctor stood in the doorway with the breakfast tray in his hands and a newspaper tucked under his arm. She took the tray of fried potatoes and bread and coffee from him.

The doctor tossed the newspaper to Jacob while Liesel began arranging the food on the small table. "It's three days old, but the Elders still thought you might want to read it."

Jacob caught the rolled-up paper. "Thank you."

"We should get the results back from the laboratory any day," the doctor said. "And then you can both leave the house."

Liesel's stomach flipped with his words. Of course she wanted the cultures to come back negative, but when they did, neither Jacob nor Cassie would need her anymore. Jacob's leg was healing, and without the fear of diphtheria hovering over them, Jacob and Mrs. Trachsel could care for Cassie without her. Jacob and Cassie would go back to being a family, and she would return to the gardens—back to the predictable, steady life in the Colonies.

She loved the Amana villages, loved the community that rallied around its residents and strangers alike. Still, an ember of discontent burned inside her. She didn't want to move away like Sophie, though. She'd stay here in Homestead with her remaining friends, but some days she craved purpose outside herself and her daily chores of weeding and harvesting food.

Staying here, caring for Cassie, sparked that sense of purpose inside her. It was almost as if God had planted this desire in her heart, so strong that it was impossible for her to ignore.

How could she convince the Elders that she wasn't losing herself to selfish pursuits because she desired to work with children instead of in the gardens?

Ignoring the breakfast tray, Jacob unfolded the newspaper and spread it out on a side table, as if news from the outside world would give him more sustenance than potatoes and bread. Like Conrad Keller used to do when the paper came to him.

She scooped up a serving of potatoes and handed it to Cassie along with a tin of coffee mixed with milk. Why was news from the outside world so important to men like Conrad and Jacob? She couldn't care less what was going on in the world outside the Colonies. Everything important to her was right here, including the people in front of her and right outside the window.

And the woman who'd left for Cedar Rapids.

Now that her friend was gone, Liesel did wonder, just a bit, what was happening in the city north of them. Sophie's new world.

Cassie scooped a spoonful of potatoes into her mouth. With bulging cheeks, she tried to speak. "Queen Liesel?"

"Ja."

"Will you play with me again after breakfast?"

Liesel bowed her head slightly, like she imagined a real queen would do. "I would be delighted to play with you...and Princess Cocoa, of course."

Cassie's smile warmed her heart, and of one thing Liesel was certain. She didn't want the quarantine to end.

The bank had closed hours ago, but Frank didn't leave the building. His wife was throwing a dinner party tonight, and he was supposed to be there alongside her, smiling and shaking the hands of some of his finest customers. His friends. He couldn't face the people who'd deposited most of their savings with him. They'd trusted him, and he was failing them...miserably.

For almost a week he'd poured over the ledgers on his desk, days and nights alike, and he'd discovered a peculiar trend. Some of his best customers' accounts had been depleted over the winter and spring in withdrawals of fifty to a hundred dollars—some of the men and women who were at his house at this very moment.

As he'd reviewed the accounts over the past year, he'd seen the transactions, but he'd never suspected that one of his clerks would record false withdrawals on the records. Though he trusted those in his employ implicitly, he still checked the accounts almost every day.

Nothing had seemed amiss.

Over the weekend, he had inventoried the basement vault, hoping that somehow the missing money would appear—Caldwell's thousand along with the thousands of other dollars he now speculated were missing. Without asking his individual customers, he had no idea how much was gone, and there was no way he could ask. They would want their money returned immediately, and if he had another rush on his bank, they wouldn't survive.

He opened up another ledger, searching the records for some sort of clue. If he searched long enough, he would discover where the money had gone, but it would pain him to discover that Bradford or Jacob—men he had trusted—had stolen from him.

Until he hired Orwin, Frank thought that Jacob Hirsch

would succeed him as president of the bank. He hadn't wanted to fire Jacob—he was talented and devoted to his career—but when it came time to let either Jacob or Orwin go, he'd had no choice but to terminate Jacob's position.

Someone coughed outside Frank's door.

Frank closed his book and looked up as Orwin walked through the door. "You're working late."

Orwin shuffled to the edge of the desk, but he didn't sit. Instead he handed Frank the names and addresses of his former clerks. "I just got back from visiting Bradford Pendleton's family over in Maywood."

Frank leaned forward, hoping Orwin had answers for him. "And?"

"Bradford is working as a city assessor."

"And how is he faring?"

Orwin coughed into his arm. "He seems to be getting by just fine. Not prospering, mind you, but he's living in the same home with his family."

Frank picked up a pencil and drew a line over Bradford's name. The man wouldn't have stolen money and then gone on to assess taxes.

He drummed his fingers on his desk. "What about Jacob Hirsch?"

Orwin reached into his satchel and took out a package wrapped in brown paper and twine. He set it on his lap. "I couldn't find him."

Frank slid forward on his chair. "Where did he go?"

"It's a bit of a mystery," Orwin said with a shrug. "His neighbor said he disappeared."

"Disappeared?"

The man nodded. "He and his daughter walked out of their house last week and never came back."

Frank slumped back in his chair. Jacob was plenty smart enough to embezzle money, but he had also seemed to be dedicated to his job, dedicated to the success of the bank. He'd always been an honest employee…or so Frank thought. Jacob had been overwhelmed with medical bills over the past year and taking care of his daughter when his neighbor couldn't watch her. There was no telling what people were capable of when they were desperate.

He circled Jacob's name on the paper. "The neighbor doesn't know where he went?"

"No idea."

Frank mulled over the words. *Where has Jacob Hirsch run?*

"Did his neighbor say how they were faring before they left?"

"Apparently they've been living quite well the past few months." Orwin folded his hands together and leaned closer to his desk. "She said she's been wondering how he's been able to afford so many new clothes and furniture pieces after he lost his position at the bank."

He stared at the man across from him like Orwin might tell him this was a joke, but Orwin didn't blink. How could Jacob have done this to him? To the men and women who had trusted him?

He needed to find out what happened to the bank's money, for the sake of both his business and his customers, but he didn't want to hear that the man he'd trusted had been stealing from him all along. If he couldn't trust someone like Jacob, who could he trust?

"Is that it?"

Orwin placed the package on the desk. "Not exactly."

Frank eyed the package. "What is this?"

"I went into Jacob's house."

Fear weaved up his spine. "How did you get inside?"

Orwin's thin lips eased into a smile. "You don't want to know that, sir."

He reached for the package, but Orwin pulled it back toward his lap. "What did you find?"

Orwin peeled back the brown paper to reveal a red-and-gold ledger covered with a thin layer of dust. He slid it across the desk.

Frank reached for it, his eyes wide. It was identical to their ledger for customers with surnames from A–E. "Where did you—?"

Orwin cut him off. "Under Jacob's bed."

Slowly, Frank turned the crisp pages until he reached Charlie Caldwell's record.

Scanning the record, anger and sadness twisted in his belly. He was too numb to react except to stare at the numbers before him.

The lines in Caldwell's record were filled with bank deposits over the past five years along with two withdrawals. His friend had been telling the truth. More than a thousand dollars was missing from his account.

Frank closed the book, trailing his fingers through the dust on the cover. Jacob had carried pocketfuls of money out of the bank and then kept a second set of books so no one would guess his game. He had to know that Caldwell and the other men and women would eventually ask for their money, but he'd been fired before the reckoning day.

Now the money was gone and so was Jacob.

Frank's head felt heavy, as if he could no longer support the weight on his shoulders.

His hands were almost too heavy to lift, but he picked them up and pushed the foul book away from him. For the first time in his life, he felt his seventy-two years.

Orwin's eyes were on him, waiting for him to speak, but Frank wouldn't tell Orwin the money was gone. Instead he would search for Jacob Hirsch until he found the man. And he'd get the money back for Stanley, Caldwell, and his other friends.

In such a free, unselfish and cooperative society, My light can evermore be imparted through Inspiration, thereby bringing fulfillment through the power of My grace....

Christian Metz, 1843

CHAPTER 11

*L*iesel was resting on the ottoman, her legs tucked under her dress and her head huddled over the Scriptures, when Jacob entered the sitting room. Her face transformed into a smile as he stepped toward her, and he almost smiled back at her...but he didn't feel quite as comfortable being alone with her as he had while Cassie was sick.

"Is she asleep?" Liesel whispered.

He nodded, sitting in the chair beside her. "Finally."

"God took care of her, Jacob."

He nodded. "That He did."

"And you took good care of her too."

He shook his head. He could have done so much more if he hadn't been distracted and tired, but even so, Liesel's simple words were a much-needed balm. Perhaps he'd done all right.

She closed the worn cover of the Bible and placed it on the table, beside the oil lamp that flickered between them. She watched him but didn't speak again, and he squirmed on the hard seat. Silence had been a welcome friend over the past week as he anguished over Cassie's health. There had been no reason to talk with this lovely young woman who'd labored over his daughter beside him. But now that the danger had passed, he didn't know what to say.

"Cassie seems happy, *ja*?" she asked.

He nodded, glad she wanted to talk about Cassie. "Your friends are spoiling her with toys."

"It's our way."

"What way?"

"It's how we demonstrate God's love."

"Aah…" They'd certainly demonstrated His love with every step, providing for Cassie and nursing her back to health. In fact, God had poured out His blessings ever since they'd arrived in Homestead in a way he'd never experienced in his life. "They've shared so much with her."

Liesel flicked a strand of hair off her forehead. "We share everything in the Amanas."

He paused. "You share everything?"

She tilted her head, brushing her hands over her apron. "Not *everything*, I suppose. We have our clothes and shoes and any items we craft in our homes."

"But who owns your homes?"

"The Society owns the houses," she said. "And our animals and wagons and all our land. We work together for the good of the community instead of collecting goods for ourselves."

He swallowed, marveling that they were able to own everything collectively. People were supposed to work together in the outside world, but it seemed as if everyone was really working for themselves. In fact, he'd never seen anyone work together like the Amana people supposedly did. It seemed too perfect. Utopian.

Once he was released from quarantine and could meet the other people, he was certain he'd find plenty of people working for their own good instead of for the good of the community.

"What about the food?"

She grinned. "The food is very good."

"I know it's good," he said with a wave of his hand. "But who buys it?"

"Our coffee is shipped to us along with some flour, but we grow or raise the rest of our food."

"Doesn't that concern you?"

Her smile fell. "Why should it concern me?"

Why should it concern her? There were more reasons than he could name. What if a storm destroyed their gardens or crops? What if disease swept through and killed their sheep or chickens? What if the Society couldn't afford to buy them enough food?

He glanced out the window at the quiet street. With less than two dollars to his name, he was very concerned about food. "How does the Society get money to buy your coffee and seeds and land?"

"Our Society sells woolen blankets and extra food, and the Elders use that money for supplies...but no individual makes money here, and we don't spend it. We work hard to contribute, and all our needs are provided for."

"But what if…" It sounded strange to ask, but he couldn't help but wonder. "What if you want more?"

She nodded like she'd been asked the question many times before. "Every year we get a ration of coupons for personal items from the general store."

"And if the store doesn't have what you want?"

"What more could I possibly want?" She paused. "Our Society is more concerned about supporting each other and serving and worshipping God together than accumulating new dresses or other things."

He crossed one leg over the other. Perhaps he had found utopia after all.

She leaned toward him. "What do you worry about?"

He felt a barrier go up between them, a guard to keep his heart and his mind in check.

It wasn't any of her business what worried him. He didn't need a community to support himself, nor did he need anyone questioning his motives.

She scooted closer, examining his face. Cool air poured through the window, and he wanted to push her away, to tell her it wasn't any of her business—but it was almost as if he was supposed to be here tonight with Liesel. Like he belonged. "I've had plenty to worry me lately."

She tucked a loose strand of hair back into her hairnet. "Like what?"

He fidgeted on his chair. It was more than not wanting to share. Liesel unsettled him, and he was scared to share his load with her...as if sharing his fears would give her a bit of power over his weakness. Yet he still wanted to tell her.

"I've been worried about Cassie."

"Of course you have."

"And I've been worried about finding work."

She repositioned her legs and tucked her skirt tightly under her. "What was your position in Chicago?"

"I was a clerk...at a bank. Second National," he said. Then he felt silly. She wouldn't know the name of the bank nor would she care. "We began to lose money last year, and the president could only keep one clerk."

Liesel straightened her back. "He should have kept you."

"The other clerk is his nephew."

"Oh...," she whispered. "I guess he had to keep his nephew."

"So now I'm looking for a new position."

"In a bank?"

"I'll take just about anything."

They sat still again, and he listened for Cassie. She was tired after her day of play. Tired and happy. Perhaps they would both sleep well this night.

"So what else worries you, Jacob Hirsch?"

The clear blue of her eyes unnerved him, and he looked

away. He wanted to tell her that nothing else worried him. All he needed was a job and everything would be fine.

"I'm worried about Cassie growing up without a mother."

The words hovered between him and Liesel like a thunderhead. He hadn't meant to say it, hadn't really been thinking about finding Cassie another mother. A mother for her would mean a wife for him, and he couldn't imagine marrying again.

The lamp flickered again. "I didn't mean to say that."

Her voice was quiet. "It's okay."

"No, it's not."

"What happened to Cassie's mother?"

"She..." His gaze trailed toward the window.

Liesel shook her head. "Never mind."

His mind wandered back a year ago. Outside the hospital walls, crowds swarmed the city for the World's Fair even as the financial world collapsed around them, but he didn't care about any of it. For one minute, he held his son—Jacob Thomas Hirsch II—in his arms. Sixty precious seconds with his child before the nurse whisked him away.

Then his world began to crumble from the inside. His baby son had been born dead, and the chloroform the doctor had administered stole his wife away from him. Weeks passed, but she never woke after her labor, never knew the fate of their son. For that, he supposed he was grateful.

A blast of wind gusted through the window, and he heard the rain begin. He didn't want to talk about Katharine tonight.

"Liesel...," he began. "What are you afraid of?"

Her eyes widened, like the very question of her fears frightened her most. Instead of answering, her black stockinged feet slid out from under her dress and touched the floor. "It's time for me to sleep."

"Surely something frightens you."

"Another time," she said as she fled into her chamber.

Liesel couldn't stop her fingers from trembling as she untied her hairnet and placed it on her dresser. She wasn't supposed to be afraid of anything, but she was. She was afraid of marrying Emil. She was afraid of the outside world. She was afraid of moving water. And she was a little bit afraid of Jacob Hirsch.

She couldn't tell him this, of course. She shouldn't be asking him such personal questions anyway. She was an engaged woman, and Emil would be furious if he knew she was staying up late in the darkness and communing with Jacob while his daughter was asleep.

Or at least, she thought Emil would be upset. She'd been quarantined for an entire week now but she hadn't heard a word from him. During their engagement, they weren't supposed to write and were permitted only the occasional chaperoned visit—like their dreadful picnic along the river—but surely the Elders would make an exception here because of the circumstances. What man wouldn't demand to know if his betrothed was well after being exposed to diphtheria?

A man who didn't want to marry her.

Perhaps Emil had changed his mind and no longer wanted to marry her. She hoped he'd changed it.

Absence makes the heart grow fonder. Or so Thomas Haynes Bayly had written in his famous poem.

She believed his words. Absence did make the heart grow fonder, but for her, the absence was making her heart grow fonder of someone else.

*Would a father give his child something
which that child could not put to use?
Have I given intelligence, will, understanding,
and wisdom in vain?... Determine what your best
talents are and put these talents to full use.*

Johann Friedrich Rock, 1717

CHAPTER 12

*J*acob unfolded the *Chicago Daily News* and spread it across the small desk in the bedroom...but instead of reading the headlines, he glanced toward the window. Blue sky had replaced the clouds, and for the first time in a year he felt God's presence, almost as if He was pouring His grace over Cassie and him along with the sunshine.

The door between his room and the sitting room was open, and he leaned back on his chair to peek into the room. Liesel and Cassie snuggled together on the couch reading a book, content in each other's arms. For an instant, he wanted to step away from the paper and join them, but what Liesel think of a grown man listening to her read a fairy tale?

The two were happy being together, and he would let them be for the moment.

He rocked the front legs of the chair back onto the floor, but his gaze wandered out the window again instead of on the paper. Life was so different here in Homestead from the rest of the world, certainly from his grandparents' home where he spent his childhood. His grandfather may have spoken the same language as the people in the Amanas, but his outlook on work was opposite from communal living.

As Jacob grew up, his grandfather instilled in him the importance of individualism and the drive for success. That he would have to be the best in his trade to get ahead. Life was a race—a competition—and his competitors were every person working around him. In order to succeed, he had to work harder and run faster than the rest of the pack.

He'd educated himself on accounting and banking and became the best bank clerk at Second National. Or at least he thought he had been the best. All of his hard work and drive crumbled the day Frank Powell walked into his office and told him, regrettably, that it was his last day. It wasn't because he was a poor manager of the bank's money or because he'd somehow failed at his job. He'd lost his hopes for promotion when Frank opted to hire his nephew and groom him for the role of president before Frank retired.

Jacob had run as hard and as far as he could, but Frank Powell had taken him out of the race before the finish line was in sight.

He leaned back in his chair, basking in the sunshine.

Perhaps Liesel and her friends were right to walk through this life arm in arm instead of pushing and shoving each other to win the race. He'd never met anyone quite like Liesel, so free from the cares of this world, and if he were really honest with himself, he was a bit envious of the peace that enfolded her.

Being quarantined in Homestead had been good for both Cassie and him. In the past week, they'd eaten better food than he'd ever had in his life, and they'd eaten in abundance. Cassie had regained her health quickly, and his leg had healed even faster than the doctor anticipated.

He was rested now and ready to get out of this room and start working again—as soon as the laboratory results came back from Iowa City.

His eyes focused back on Monday's headlines, three days past. The top story was about the Pullman Strike, the same story that ruled the front page since they'd left the city.

There were six thousand Army troops in Chicago now, and more than three thousand police and five thousand deputy marshals trying to stop the obstruction of the U.S. Mail and the destruction caused by the rioters.

If he and Cassie hadn't hopped on that train, they would still be in the city, and God only knows what would have happened to his daughter.

He listened for Liesel's soft voice as she read to Cassie, but all was quiet in the sitting room. He was so very grateful that Cassie was here in Homestead, safe from the disease and corruption and violence that plagued Chicago's streets. He didn't know where they were going from here, but he was certain they wouldn't be returning east.

Someone knocked on the bedroom door, and Jacob, expecting the doctor, called for him to come into the room. The door opened slowly, but instead of Dr. Trachsel, two middle-aged men stepped into his bedroom. The men wore denim pants and work shirts, and they both held hats in their hands.

Hurrying across the room, Jacob stretched out a hand to greet them but then checked himself and quickly retracted the gesture. These men shouldn't be here in his room, not until he was out of quarantine and they had confirmed Cassie's recovery.

Just before he asked them to leave, one of the men held out a piece of paper toward him. He scanned the short letter from the University of Iowa laboratory in Iowa City, the words registering slowly.

A sigh of relief escaped his lips, and he waved the paper in his hands. Neither Liesel nor he had diphtheria.

The men introduced themselves as two of the eight Elders in Homestead. Niklas Keller was a tall man with reddish hair cut close to his head. Adam Voepel was a few inches shorter and rounder. His green eyes twinkled when he smiled.

Jacob held out his hand again, and both men shook it in turn this time. "Thank you for providing me with the newspapers."

Niklas twisted his hat in his hands. "We have wanted to welcome you to Homestead."

Adam nodded. "The whole community has been praying for your daughter."

"Dr. Trachsel tells us that you are well now," Niklas said.

Jacob nodded.

"We are grateful to God that He healed you and your daughter."

Jacob thanked them both for their prayers and for their visit, but as he was talking, it occurred to him the real reason Niklas and Adam had come to see him. They'd been sent to collect for his doctor's bill.

They'd been kind to Cassie and him, but what would they do when they found out he only had a measly $1.95 to his name? It could be months before he had enough money to pay them back. Or even years if he couldn't find a job.

Instead of asking him about the money, Niklas surprised him with his next words. "Dr. Trachsel told us you know how to swim."

"I...," Jacob started, wondering at the odd question. "I learned when I was a child."

"Very few of our people are able to swim," Adam said.

"Not many people in Chicago swim either."

"Near the main village of Amana, we have a seven-mile canal called the Mill Race that provides power for our lumber, grain, and textile mills," Niklas explained. "Every summer we have to dredge it to remove the silt and debris from the canal."

Niklas blinked, and Jacob wondered what he read in the man's eyes. Desperation, perhaps. "One of our fine young men worked on the *grosse* boat, but he left for schooling in Cedar

Rapids. Now we need someone to take his place. Someone who can speak some German and, more importantly, someone who can swim."

Jacob's heart raced. "You want me to work on your boat?"

Niklas followed his words with a flurry, as if Jacob might think the work was below him. "We can pay you seven dollars a week plus your food," he explained. "The crew lives on the boat for the season, so your lodging would be provided as well."

The twinkle was gone from Adam's eyes. "We know it's hard work, but Dr. Trachsel said you are a good man. We thought that perhaps you could assist us for a few months. If you don't have any other obligations…"

"Obligations?" Jacob couldn't help his laugh.

"It would just be until October," Adam said. "You could continue on when the work is finished."

"What would I be doing on the boat?"

Niklas began twisting his hat again. "Sometimes the captain will need you to retrieve or fix things in the water. Sometimes he will need you to help remove the bridges so the boat can pass. When you're not needed in the water, the captain will rotate you with the other crew members."

For seven dollars a week, he would do whatever the captain needed. "Can Cassie stay with me on the boat?"

"Oh, no," Niklas said. "The dredge boat is too dangerous for children."

Jacob's shoulders slumped. He couldn't take the position if they refused a place for Cassie to stay.

Niklas patted the top of his hat. "She can't stay on the boat, but one of the *Tantes* in Homestead can care for her while you are working."

Jacob's mind raced at the man's words. Could he leave Cassie with a woman he didn't know, in a community he didn't understand? His daughter had endured so much change in the past year, losing her mother and her home and everything that seemed to be secure. Now he would have to leave her as well.

"You will only be a few miles away," Adam urged. "And we could arrange for you to visit her."

He brushed his hands together. The Homestead community had already been so good to Cassie and him, and now they were offering him work with decent pay and a place for both he and Cassie to stay. He could save every penny that he didn't spend on Cassie's care, and when the work was finished, he'd start building their life again.

"Could I speak with my daughter first?"

"Of course." Niklas nodded, taking a step backward out the door. "We will return in the morning."

*Detach yourselves from other purposes
and permit your hearts to be prepared,
so that I, speaks Eternal Love,
may communicate with each one of you.*

Christian Metz, 1819

CHAPTER 13

Sophie didn't like Cedar Rapids. She didn't like the granite buildings or the crowds of people swarming the streets. She didn't like the horrible smells that saturated her flat, making her nauseous, and she didn't like cooking three meals a day every day. *Monotonous* was how she described life on the outside. Monotonous and lonely.

Liesel turned the page of Sophie's long letter, her heart breaking for her dear friend. Cassie was tucked in close beside her on the ottoman, sound asleep, and Liesel couldn't be happier. Sophie, on the other hand, sounded miserable.

In the following pages, Sophie described the pitfalls of city life and most of all about her utter failings in the kitchen. She'd burned the potatoes on her first attempt at frying them with bacon grease. Then Conrad had brought home a slab of beef and she'd tried to boil it like the women did in the communal kitchen, but it was stringy and dry.

To make up for the disaster, she'd attempted to bake a blueberry pie, but the berries in the city weren't nearly as sweet as the berries in the Amanas, so she'd settled for a rhubarb pie with plenty of sugar. The pie had fallen apart when she and Conrad tried to eat it, and it was so sweet it tasted like syrup. She'd dropped her fork and cried over her dessert.

There was no one for her to ask about making rhubarb pie. No one to talk to about her disappointment with her new life or what she missed about her home. There were thousands of people in Cedar Rapids, but not a single person had befriended her.

Conrad told her it would be okay, that she'd make friends eventually, but she wasn't certain. She clung to her faith in God, but she dearly missed her mother, and she missed her hours spent with Liesel and her other friends in the garden.

Liesel folded the letter and set it in her lap. The outside world sounded as frightening as she imagined it would be. Why would anyone want to move away from the security of the Amanas? Here there was safety and community and people who cared for you when you needed help.

She couldn't console her friend, but she could pray for her. She bowed her head and prayed, the way she'd done almost every night since Sophie and Conrad had left. She asked God to comfort her dear friend, and she asked Him to change Conrad's heart and bring them back to Homestead.

Brushing her hand across Cassie's head, she continued praying until she heard a knock in the next room. Voices followed, but she couldn't hear what the men were saying. She fixed an afghan over Cassie's shoulders before she slipped off the couch and crept to the other side of the room.

Niklas Keller and Adam Voepel were with Jacob, and she listened as they offered him Conrad's job on the dredge boat.

Jacob, in the Amanas?

Her heart lurched at the thought.

She'd told herself over and over that one day Jacob and Cassie would climb on the train just as Sophie and Conrad had done. One day soon they would be gone. She hadn't allowed herself to entertain the thought that they might stay—well, at least she hadn't allowed herself to entertain the thought for long.

But what if Jacob and Cassie could stay in the Amanas for the summer—or perhaps even longer?

Reaching into her apron pocket, she ran her fingers across the edge of Sophie's letter.

She would be delighted if Cassie could stay. Overjoyed. But she wasn't sure she wanted Jacob Hirsch to stay in the Amanas. He was a kind man, but even so, he unnerved her. She couldn't imagine living out the next few years of her life with him here, knowing that she might see him at their prayer services or in the dining room or on the dark pathway between the houses.

Worse yet, she would see him and not be able to acknowledge him as a friend. She would be married to Emil, and it would be inappropriate for them to converse privately. They'd never be able to talk about their week shared together in the doctor's home.

Months would pass; the community would forget about her time here with Jacob. But even if they didn't forget, surely no one would suspect that she'd been immoral with this stranger. She guarded her chastity as closely as she guarded her heart.

The community may forget...but she would always remember the summer of '94. Even as Mrs. Emil Hahn, she wouldn't be able to stop the memories of her time spent with Jacob and his beautiful daughter.

Cassie could stay in Homestead, but as far as she was concerned, Jacob needed to move on. The dredge boat would be a good start since it was three miles from Homestead, but come winter...

Come winter Jacob would probably tire of the plain lifestyle anyway. He would be more than ready to move back to Chicago or travel to another big city where he could live the news he loved to read.

The door shut in Jacob's room, and footsteps crossed the

floor. Rushing back to the sofa, she tucked her legs under her and pulled Sophie's letter from her pocket, pretending to read the words again. When Jacob walked into the room, his gaze rested on his daughter, spread out with her doll on the sofa, and then he looked at Liesel.

"She's asleep," Liesel whispered.

Jacob waved her into the bedroom, and she followed him through the doorway.

Leaning against the wall, she watched him pace the floor.

When he arrived in Homestead, worry shadowed his face, but the shadows had slowly subsided during the past few days. A new strength had emerged, and this strength made her wonder what Jacob Hirsch had been like before the weight of the world crushed him.

He stopped pacing and turned toward her. "Two of your Elders came to visit me."

"I heard."

"Did you hear what they said?"

She rolled her fingertips over the blue paint on the wall. "Some of it."

"We're released from quarantine."

She mustered a smile. "That's good news."

"So you're free to leave whenever you'd like."

She nodded, but she didn't move. It wasn't time for her to walk out of this room. "Niklas Keller offered you a job."

He wandered over to the window and leaned against the sill. "On the dredge boat."

"Dredging is hard work."

He crossed his arms. "What do you know about dredging?"

"My best friend...," she began. "Her husband used to work on the boat."

"Ah," he replied slowly. "The friend who moved to Cedar Rapids."

He remembered.

"Conrad hated the boat. He said he'd rather get a tooth pulled than spend another summer on it."

"You don't think I'd like the work?"

"I think you'd hate it."

"Liesel..." Her pulse quickened as his eyes bore into hers. "Have you ever been hungry?"

His gaze was intense, but she refused to look away. "Not really."

"Have you ever wondered where you were going to sleep the next night?"

"Of course not."

"Have you ever been terrified because you couldn't pay a doctor's bill or the rent on your house?"

She blinked. "What's a rent?"

A smile flickered across his lips, and she felt silly for asking the question. Still, she'd never heard the word before.

He nodded toward the window. "You have to pay for everything on the outside world."

Pay for everything? She laced her fingers together, watching him. No wonder the worry had shadowed his face. There were so many burdens out there, and he had no one to help him carry his heavy load.

Pity weighed his gaze as he watched her, but he didn't have to pity her. She understood plenty, and the way she saw it, the only people that needed pity were those who didn't have anyone to prop them up when they fell.

Jacob brushed his hands over his trousers. "I've been out of work for three months, and now your Elders are offering me a job."

She glanced at her feet. Her feelings didn't matter. Jacob needed work, and it wasn't her position to convince him to move on to another city to find it. In her selfishness she wanted him to go, yet she needed to think of them before herself.

She met his eye again. "Then you must take it."

"Niklas offered to let one of the older women in the community care for Cassie while I'm working." He stepped closer, his eyes pleading with her. "Will they take good care of her?"

"The *Tantes* in Homestead have been part of raising almost every child in this community. They will care for her like she is blood." She squeezed her hands together. "But there's one problem—"

His eyes narrowed. "What is it?"

"Cassie is still in quarantine."

"Quarantine," he repeated like he'd forgotten. He started pacing again.

"You will need someone to watch Cassie until Dr. Trachsel releases her." A slow smile wove across her lips. "Someone who has been exposed to the disease."

He stopped walking and shoved his hands into his pockets as he fixed a stare on her. "Why don't you want to go home, Liesel?"

Her gaze wandered toward the window, toward the hot sun beating down on the men and women working the fields today. She couldn't tell him that she was scared for her life to move forward without Sophie, scared about her marriage to Emil. Nor could she tell him that she'd never been happier than she'd been the past nine days.

When she didn't reply, he stepped closer to her. "Cassie's not contagious anymore."

She shook her head. "We don't know that, Jacob, and Dr. Trachsel won't risk exposing anyone else to the disease."

His eyes wandered from her eyes to her hair and then back to her eyes. The intensity of his gaze scared her. She tried to scoot back, just one step away from him, but the wall was already behind her. The words from her father's letter raced through her mind. Was this the time to scream?

Jacob kept both hands in his pockets, but he didn't need his strength to make her quake. His words alone reached out and shook her. "What are you running from, Liesel?"

She rolled her shoulders back. "I don't know what you mean."

His tone was gentle but direct. "Is it your work in the gardens?"

When she didn't reply, he continued. "Because you seem like the type of person who would work hard no matter how difficult the job."

Her knees shook, but she tried to remain confident. Strong. "You don't know me, Jacob."

He didn't stop. "If it's not your work, perhaps you are trying to get out of something else."

She shook her head. "I'm not trying to escape," she insisted—but he didn't seem to hear her.

"Or perhaps…" He stepped closer to her, and she could feel the warmth from his skin. "Perhaps you are running from Emil Hahn."

Her hands sprung out, shoving him away from her. She didn't care if she hurt him. All she wanted was for him to go away.

He stepped back, his hands protecting his chest, but his face filled with compassion.

Unbidden tears filled her eyes. How dare he accuse her of running away from her betrothed? It didn't matter that he was right. It was none of his business, and she didn't owe him an explanation.

She swallowed hard. "This isn't Chicago, Jacob. We work together here, and our community needs to have the Mill Race dredged. I am offering to stay here and care for Cassie while you work, but if you continue to harass me, I will walk out that door."

She hid her trembling fists behind her back, praying even as she spoke that Jacob wouldn't make her go away. "I hope, for your sake, that the Elders will find another woman willing to come under quarantine."

Jacob stepped back slowly, like he wasn't sure exactly what would come out of her lips next or if she might shove him again. She wasn't sure either.

"That's a relief, Liesel." He reached for the hooks by the door and pulled off his cap. "I was worried you might be running away."

A new creation shall emerge when the Spirit of God lives and works within humankind.

Christian Metz, 1832

CHAPTER 14

On Friday afternoon, Frank picked up the earpiece on his desk telephone and asked the operator to connect him with the local precinct. Once she did so, he could hear people shouting in the background, and the man who answered had to ask Frank's name twice. He spelled his name and explained that he was the president of Second National Building and Loan—a title most people respected.

The police chief picked up the line, but he wasn't the least bit impressed by Frank's title or even particularly interested in it. Even so, Frank explained that one of his former clerks had embezzled money from his bank and disappeared.

The chief barked an order out to someone before resuming the call. "What did you say your name was again?"

He cleared his throat. "Frank Powell."

"Have you been out on the streets lately, Mr. Powell?"

He glanced out the window at his side; the sky was colored orange and yellow from the setting sun. "I have."

"Then you're aware of the crime infiltrating them."

He wasn't going to let the chief slight his duty by concentrating on petty crimes. "This man took at least twenty thousand dollars from me."

"I don't care if it was a hundred and twenty thousand, Mr. Powell." The chief shouted another order at someone else. "I don't have the men to chase down your money."

Frank squeezed the bridge of his nose. He actually paid taxes, unlike most of Chicago's business owners, who usually bribed their way out of a tax bill. He paid taxes to employ men to police their city, and now this man wouldn't even delegate a single officer to search for Jacob.

"If I were you," the chief said, "I'd hire a private detective."

"I don't have any money left to hire an investigator."

"You find your embezzler, Mr. Powell, and then we'll talk justice."

"You're supposed to help me find him!"

"Here." The man rustled some papers on the other end. "I'm opening a file for you. In our spare time, I'll send someone over to start on the investigation."

Frank hung up the phone. There was no justice these days in Chicago, even for a criminal like Jacob Hirsch.

Cassie's feet dangled over the edge of the bed as she watched Liesel don her black prayer cap in front of the oval glass. "It's so pretty."

Liesel took the cap off her hair, holding it out to the child, and Cassie gently brushed her fingers across the sheer material and the tatted loops around the edge before she put it over her braids. Liesel giggled and tied the lace strings under Cassie's chin.

"You look just like an Amana *Kind*."

Cassie hopped off the bed and admired her appearance in the glass.

With a deep breath, Liesel wrapped her prayer shawl over her shoulders. She'd taken a long, hot bath today in the washroom, and she felt ready to enter the village life again. Part of her was excited to see her friends, but she was nervous as well. Some of the older Amana women were perceptive, irritatingly so. What if they saw something in her eyes—something she was trying to hide?

Cassie handed Liesel her cap and she retied it, tighter this time so that it covered the tips of her cheeks. If only she could wear her sunbonnet to *Nachtgebet*, the nightly prayer meeting, so she could hide her eyes...

Cassie reached over from the edge of the bed and squeezed her hand. "I'll miss you, Liesel."

Liesel bent down and kissed the part in Cassie's braids. "I will miss you too."

Cassie didn't let go of her hand. "Do you have to leave?"

"It wouldn't be proper for me to stay, now that I'm no longer under quarantine."

"But when will you come back?" Cassie asked.

"Tomorrow morning. Just after the sun comes up."

Cassie smiled. "And then we will play."

Liesel grinned back at the girl, patting her on the head. "Play and play and play."

Someone cleared his throat behind her, and Liesel whirled around.

Jacob stood at the door, a smile on his face. "You look nice."

Without thinking, she smoothed her hands over her cap again and then forced her hands back to her side, silently reprimanding herself for caring even a little about how Jacob thought she looked. She muttered something that sounded like *"Danke schon"* to thank him and shuffled around his tall frame.

He looked down at her, still smiling. "You'll be back tomorrow?"

"*Ja.*"

He laughed. "*Ve vill* miss you."

She shook her head at his teasing, but she couldn't stop her smile. It was good to hear him laugh.

She rushed down the stairs and out the back door. Even though the evening air was weighted with humidity, she was glad to walk the narrow path. She had missed the fresh air...the soothing sound of sheep braying in the fields...the daily fellowship with the women in her village. The Amana tradition was engrained in her heart along with the familiar routines and friendships. Without these, she wasn't sure exactly who she was.

Except for the occasional illness, she never missed *Nachtgebet*, but now she had been gone for over a week, caring for a worldly man and his daughter. The Colonies didn't need a newspaper or even a telegraph to spread news like this. No doubt the women would ask question after question about the worldly visitors, but the questioning was no reason for her to stay away from the meeting. More than anyone, she needed prayer.

The evening's service was held in a brick house on the bottom floor, a block down the pathway. Her head bowed, she entered the home in reverence. A dozen other women sat on pale pine benches on the left side of the large room, and the men sat on benches on the right.

After the last person walked into the room, one of the men led out in song, and the others followed with familiar words.

Sit and pause a while,
my spirit this great miracle behold;
See the king of highest merit,
on the cross, so bare and cold!
Out of heaven God has given
His own Son in love untold!

The song faded and the words washed over her. She was grateful, so grateful, at the great miracle of what God's Son did for her on the cross.

As the lyrics lingered in her mind, invigorating her heart, Eduard Krupp stood up and read from Psalm 51. *"Create in me a clean heart, O God; and renew a right spirit within me."*

That was exactly what she needed. A new spirit and a right one before God. She could hold onto her bitterness at Conrad and her anger at him taking Sophie away from her, or she could give it up to the One who desired to fill her mind with joy and gladness.

The others spoke out in prayer around her, and she sat in silence...in gladness for God's gifts.

Jacob and the Elders had agreed that she could care for Cassie while she remained in quarantine. God had blessed her life with this little girl and she wanted to care for her. She would help Cassie, and with God's Spirit alive in her, she would face the days ahead without fear—even the day she would have to say goodbye.

The meeting ended, and the women shuffled out the left door in silence. The silence didn't last long, however. One of the younger women nudged her toward the lawn beside the pathway, and a half dozen other unmarried women huddled around them. The words of the hymn and Scripture lingered in Liesel's mind even as she braced herself for the questions.

Amalie spoke first, her big blue eyes sparkling in the setting sun. Her frame was larger than most of the young woman in their community, and she bubbled like a glass of sparkling wine whenever she spoke.

"We've missed you," her friend said as she gave her a hug. "The gardens are too quiet without you and Sophie."

Liesel reached out and squeezed her hand. "I've missed you too."

"We kept asking Niklas Keller when you would leave the doctor's house, but he wouldn't tell us a thing."

"He didn't know."

Amalie leaned closer to her ear. "So…"

Liesel smiled at her friend. "So, what?"

Two of the Elders strolled toward them, talking quietly to themselves. A hush spread over the group until the men had disappeared behind the greenhouse.

"Tell us about him," Amalie pressed.

Liesel glanced around at the group of women, who waited in expectation for her description of the man from Chicago. She shrugged. "About who?"

"About the worldly man." Karoline nudged her in her ribs. "We heard he was dashing."

She stiffened. "Who told you he was dashing?"

"Rosa Trachsel did," Karoline said with a giggle. "So…is he as handsome as she says?"

"I can't say that I've noticed."

"You've spent a week with him," Karoline said. "Surely you've noticed."

The women around her laughed, but Liesel didn't think it was funny. It seemed disloyal to be critiquing Jacob's appearance like he was a stranger in their village. He wasn't a stranger to her, and it didn't matter in the least if he were handsome or not. Jacob Hirsch had a kind heart and an ingrained strength that she couldn't help but admire.

His vivid eyes were a pale green—and his warm smile melted her—but she wouldn't trivialize his strength and kindness by talking about his appearance. Especially when she'd spent the past week trying to save Cassie's life.

Amalie tugged on her hand. "Black hair or brown?"

"It doesn't matter."

"Of course it matters."

Irritation sparked in her. "This man's daughter has been on the brink of death, and you ask me about the color of his hair?"

The laughter stopped, but the questions didn't.

"Is he married?" Karoline asked.

She sighed. "I don't think so."

Amalie stared at her for a moment, like she was the crazy one. "You didn't ask if he was married?"

"I told you..."

Amalie waved her off. "You would think the question of his wife would slip somewhere into the conversation."

A small voice piped up from the back of the women. "How is his daughter now?"

Liesel pushed herself up on her toes and saw Elise Bach peeking around one of the taller women. She looked like an angel of mercy.

"Bless you, Elise." She smiled. "Cassie is doing much better."

"We've all been worried about his daughter," Amalie said. "We've prayed for her every night."

Karoline's head bobbed up and down, agreeing with vigor. "But now that the daughter is well..."

"Now you are interested in her father."

"We're only curious," Karoline said. "It's not often that a handsome stranger gets thrown into our midst."

Amalie grinned again. "And one of our friends gets to spend an entire week with him."

"I didn't say he was handsome!"

Even if he was, he was leaving Sunday morning to live on the dredge boat. It wasn't likely she or any of these women would see much of him again. She and Jacob would go back to being strangers, and once Cassie went to stay with one of the *Tantes*, she would go back to working in the gardens. Life as usual.

For once, though, "life as usual" didn't seem as appealing as it normally did. Jacob and his daughter had arrived in her world uninvited, yet she didn't want either of them to leave.

Amalie tugged her arm. "Liesel?"

She glanced over at the kitchen house beside them. Her bedroom was upstairs in the corner, the window dark. She hugged Amalie's neck and then hugged the other women. "I must be getting up to my room."

Karoline sighed. "You won't tell us a thing, will you?"

"There's nothing to tell."

Whosoever sincerely seeks the treasure within their heart must seek with diligence, abandoning all else. You must search deeply until you reach the unfathomable. wherein you shall be absorbed.

Johann Friedrich Rock, 1717

CHAPTER 15

Smoke billowed out of the stack on the *grosse* boat as the giant shovel lifted another layer of silt out of the Mill Race and deposited it on the bank. The cumbersome boat snorted like a wild horse and its chains clinked as the crew moved the pulleys up and down.

Schoolchildren gathered on the levee, watching the final hour of dredging for the day, and Michael—the boat's captain—blew the whistle for their audience. The children laughed and called back to the boat, "Ship ahoy!"

About thirty feet from the bow of the boat, Jacob helped an elderly carpenter dismantle a bridge. They'd worked for four hours now, removing each plank and piling them on the bank so that the boat could move down the canal in the morning.

The sun emerged from the cloudy sky, toasting Jacob's neck and arms. Michael had given him Conrad's bathing costume—a sleeveless wool jersey and knee-length trousers—so he could work in the canal, but until today they hadn't needed him in the water. Instead he'd sweltered in the boat's dungeon, feeding wood into the boiler to power the dipper.

All the guys on the boat were much younger than him except

for the captain. Michael was at least forty and had a wife and son in Main Amana. A teenaged boy named David usually operated the boiler, but with Jacob's arrival, the captain had started teaching David how to drive beams into the banks of the canal to anchor the boat.

Jacob unscrewed a plank from its joist and pocketed the screw, grateful to be outside in the sunshine, although he wasn't enjoying the company. The carpenter worked the other end of the bridge in silence, speaking only when he needed something —and he rarely needed anything from Jacob.

Without looking over, the carpenter barked at him. *"Kann ich bitte meinen Schraubenzieher haben."*

The words tumbled in Jacob's mind. *Kann ich bitte... Can I please...*

The man wanted something, but Jacob didn't know what.

"Ich verstehen nicht," he replied with a shake of his head. *"I don't understand."*

The man repeated the words, much slower this time, and Jacob realized he was asking for the screwdriver. He handed the man the tool and then sat back on the edge of the plank, stretching his toes down to the water.

A cloud momentarily erased the glare of the sun and cast a dull light over the slow-moving water and the fields that framed the Mill Race. Downstream from their boat was a bell tower and a cluster of stone and brick homes—the village of Main Amana.

They were only a quarter mile west of Amana but a good three miles from Homestead. Leaving Cassie on Sunday was one of the most difficult things he'd ever done. Liesel was right —working the dredge was hard work, but it was good, manual labor. He enjoyed working with his hands and he was grateful for the opportunity to provide for Cassie, but he missed his daughter, plain and simple.

Liesel would care well for her while he was gone, but a child needed her parents, and Cassie only had one of those left. And the truth was, he needed her, perhaps even more than she needed him.

Splash! The water rippled to his left, and Jacob glanced over at the panicked face of the carpenter. The man was pointing toward the water. *"Schraubenzieher!"*

Jacob drew in a deep breath and dove into the murky water. The Mill Race was only eight feet deep, but the silt would swallow the tool in seconds. His arms outstretched, he sifted the water around him, hoping the water had slowed the screwdriver's descent.

His hands touched the slimy bottom, and he began to dig, sifting through the mud and leaves under his fingers. Thirty seconds passed, and his lungs started to burn. In fifteen seconds, he needed to ascend. Twenty, tops.

But he wouldn't give up. Not yet. Anyone could run the boiler room in the boat's belly, but this was his chance to prove they needed him as a swimmer...and that he was worth paying seven dollars a week.

Seconds ticked by as he scrounged through the muck. His head throbbed, and his lungs cried out for air.

It's only a screwdriver. The tinsmith can make another one.

Yet it was about much more than the screwdriver. It was about convincing the carpenter and Michael and the Elders... and Liesel...that he could do this job.

His fingers brushed over the long handle of the tool, and he grasped it. With a strong scissor kick, he shot toward the surface. Light filtered through the dirty water, and he burst through the surface gasping for air.

He heaved in long breaths, and in the midst of his breathing he heard cheers. The schoolchildren were shouting, celebrating his return. It was a small feat, but he held the screwdriver above his head, and they rejoiced with him.

The whistle on the boat blew one last time, and Michael shouted. "Quitting time!"

Jacob lifted himself up onto the bank and handed the screwdriver to the carpenter. The man nodded, pushing his spectacles up his nose. *"Vielen Dank."*

After the carpenter thanked him, Jacob fell backward into the water, swimming under the dipper before he climbed up a small ladder and into the boat.

"I need my money today!" the Honorable Charlie Caldwell shouted into the phone. He followed his demand with a tirade of words not fit for Chicago's politer society.

Frank's head throbbed and his ear ached from Caldwell's ranting. Even when he pulled the phone away from his ear, the man's words echoed around him. Frank wiped a band of sweat from his forehead and fanned himself with an envelope. The office was sweltering this morning, and as Caldwell verbally lashed him and his bank, memories of another hot day stole back, uninvited—memories of the Great Fire that swept through Chicago twenty years ago.

As flames had ravaged the businesses and homes around him, he'd locked the bank's cash reserves in the vault and fled down the street. The fire had swallowed up his records, but the vault didn't burn. Their business recovered after the Great Fire, and people trusted him to protect their money and valuables at any cost, even if it meant risking his life to lock away their money.

Caldwell continued yelling into the phone, but Frank barely heard his words. They'd lost so much in the fire, but he hadn't lost their cache. Now a fire of sorts was starting to burn again. Not by those terrible flames, but because he'd trusted his customers' money to someone who didn't value his customers as much as he did. Frank had made it through the first fire without losing their reserves but until he found Jacob, there was nothing he could do to recover the money.

Silence pervaded the room, and Frank realized that Caldwell had stopped shouting.

"I can give you a thousand this afternoon," Frank said.

"I need two thousand."

"I'm working on it, Charlie." He wiped another layer of sweat off his forehead. "Most of your savings is invested in businesses and houses around the community."

"That's not my problem, Frank. I've got debts to pay and some unsavory people knocking on my door."

"A thousand today, and I'll have the rest of the money to you within the week."

Caldwell was silent for a moment, contemplating his proposal. The thousand was more than half of what Frank had in the vault; if anyone else came asking for money, he'd be sunk. His wife wouldn't be happy, but he could sell off some of their personal assets. His diamond ring. Some of her jewelry. It would be enough to mollify Caldwell and keep the business afloat.

"I need the other thousand by next week."

"I'll phone you the moment I receive it," Frank said before he dropped the earpiece onto the cradle.

All he needed to do was bandage the problem for now...stop the hemorrhaging long enough to find Jacob and the cash. The missing money would give him enough surplus to ride on until the economy started growing again.

But what if he couldn't find Jacob?

He shook his head. The consequences over not locating the money were too much to comprehend right now. Not only would it mean the loss of his business, it would also be the loss of his reputation. Instead of rising above the corruption, Chicago's Second National Building and Loan would be another black spot on their bruised city.

Someone knocked on his door, and he closed the ledger. "Come in!"

The door creaked open, and Orwin peeked around the door. The distress on his nephew's face startled Frank. "What is it?"

Orwin slipped through the doorway and cleared his throat. "Marshall Vicker is here."

Frank groaned, falling back against his chair. Marshall Vicker was an old friend and a customer…and he was also the managing editor of the *Chicago Daily News*.

Orwin handed Frank the ledger kept in the teller's cage, which had been opened to Marshall's record. In seconds, his finger slid down the list of withdrawals, increments of thirty and forty and sometimes one hundred dollars. Like Caldwell's record, the withdrawals had stopped when Jacob's position was terminated.

His mind spun. Was this ledger a fake as well? If so, how many accounts had Jacob skimmed from? Only one ledger had been found in Jacob's house, spanning surnames from A to E. Were there other duplicate ledgers out there with the real numbers?

He looked back up at Orwin. "What does Marshall want?"

Orwin closed the door, but when he stepped up to Frank's desk, he hesitated before he spoke.

"Spit it out," Frank said.

"Marshall wants to withdraw seven hundred in cash."

Frank slammed the ledger shut. "Tell him I'm not here."

Orwin cleared his throat again. "It's a little late for that."

Frank raked his fingers through his thin hair. He was too old for this. One day he intended to hand over the bank to his nephew and let him run things, but he couldn't give it to him while it was such a mess. At this rate, Frank would be out of a job—and probably tarred and feathered—before he retired.

Through the frosted glass, he saw Marshall's profile and the cigar jutting from his mouth. He would have to think up a reason to withhold the cash from his friend, and he wouldn't let on that his ledger stated that Marshall only had two hundred left at the bank. Somehow, he'd have to get Marshall his money before the man plastered the bank's woes across the front page of his paper.

He closed the ledger. "Send him on in."

*I have shaken your foundation and made you restless,
but there is much that will yet occur.
Be watchful and pray.*

Christian Metz, 1842

CHAPTER 16

*D*ark clouds drifted outside the window as rain beat down on the rooftop. A pillow against her back, Liesel lay stretched out on the woven rug, sipping warm chamomile tea, while Cassie flipped through a picture book of German fairy tales.

When Liesel had been about Cassie's age, her father used to read *Der Struwwelpeter* to her in German, and when she'd started school, her teacher read the fairy tales as well, so she could learn English. They were recited in both languages, and she well remembered the lessons in every one.

Cassie pointed to a boy tugging a cloth off a dinner table. "Who's this?"

"*Zappel-Philipp*. Fidgety Philip." She turned the page to poor Philip, who was buried under a mountain of food and dishes. "He screamed and threw a temper and all the food landed on top of him. His poor parents didn't have anything to eat."

Cassie turned the page and looked at a boy with an umbrella under a storm cloud. "Who's this?"

"Oh, that's one of my favorites." Liesel set her cup on the

table and pulled Cassie close to her. "*Die Geschichte vom fliegenden Robert.*"

Cassie giggled. "English, *bitte.*"

Liesel leaned close, hushing her voice as she recalled the English words she'd memorized years ago. "When the rain comes tumbling down in the country or the town, all good little girls and boys stay at home and mind their toys. Robert thought, 'No, when it pours, it is better out of doors.' Rain it did, and in a minute Rob was in it."

She turned the page. "Here you see him, silly fellow, underneath his red umbrella. What a wind! Oh! how it whistles through the trees and flow'rs and thistles."

Cassie clasped Liesel's arm. "Do you hear it?"

The wind outside their window whistled through the trees like a train weaving its way through the forest. The rain pattered on the roof above them and soaked the glass on their window.

Cassie nudged her. "Keep going."

"It has caught his red umbrella; now look at him, silly fellow, up he flies, to the skies. No one heard his screams and cries."

Cassie gasped. "Where did he go?"

"Through the clouds," she continued. "The rude wind bore him, and his hat flew on before him. Soon they got to such a height, they were nearly out of sight! And the hat went up so high that it almost touch'd the sky. No one ever yet could tell where they stopp'd or where they fell; only this one thing is plain—Rob was never seen again!"

Liesel closed the storybook, pleased that she had recalled all the English words, but when she met Cassie's eyes, the girl looked horrified. "They didn't see him again?"

Liesel shook her head. "The wind took him away."

"That's awful."

Liesel paused, leaning forward to take another sip of tea. "It's supposed to remind us not to go outside in bad weather."

"So we don't blow away?"

"Exactly."

Cassie jumped up and skipped toward the window, and Liesel joined Cassie there, her nose tingling as she pressed it against the cold glass. Outside, giant oak branches rode up and down on the crests of the breeze, and she could almost see Flying Robert and his red umbrella being carried away by the wind.

Cassie shivered. "Is *Papa* going to get blown away?"

She reached out her arm and pulled Cassie tight again. "Oh no, child. He's much too big and strong to be blown away."

"But what if he had an umbrella?"

"Your *Vater* knows to stay inside when it's storming."

Cassie flashed her a look of doubt.

"He's just fine, Cassie."

Cassie followed her back to the sofa. "I wish Papa was here."

Liesel nodded as she tucked a woolen blanket around the girl's feet. "I wish he was here too."

Cassie spread out across her lap, and Liesel brushed the girl's hair out of her eyes. "I wish Mama was here too."

Liesel's hand froze on Cassie's head. "Do you miss your mother?"

Cassie nodded.

"Where is she, Cassie?"

The girl squirmed on her lap, her eyes closed. "She's in Chicago…with my brother."

"Chicago…" Liesel's voice trailed off. She'd thought Jacob was a widower, but Cassie's mother was still in Chicago with their son.

"Where in Chicago?" she asked, but Cassie had already started to fall asleep.

Liesel's head fell back on the cushioned seat. Had Jacob taken his daughter away from the city, leaving his wife behind? That didn't seem right. He'd fought so hard for the life of his daughter. Surely he would fight for the life of his wife as well. Perhaps Cassie's mother had birthed her out of wedlock and had another child later. But if that were the case, why didn't Jacob marry the poor woman?

Her chest felt as if it were about to crack into two pieces, her heart charting forbidden waters. Jacob Hirsch belonged to Cassie's mother, not to her. And she belonged to Emil Hahn, or at least she would belong to him less than six months from now.

Perhaps on the outside it was all right to leave the mother of your child behind, but that was not permitted in their Society. Forgiveness was poured over those who sinned, but the Elders expected them to be faithful as well. Jacob needed to go back to Chicago and find Cassie's mother. He needed to make it right.

There was a knock on the door, and Liesel slid out from under Cassie and rushed to the door.

The doctor's coat and hat dripped rain, but in his hand was a letter. He smiled. "Her culture came back negative."

Liesel sighed. "Thank God."

"If the sun comes out tomorrow, she can go outside."

Liesel rubbed the chill in her arms. Sunshine would be good for both of them.

Jacob's skin was coated with a sticky black, and it was blistering hot from the hours he'd spent shoving wood into the boiler fire. Never in his life had he been this dirty, nor had he worked this hard, but it was good, honest work.

Above him, the pulleys and chains clanked and the boat rocked as the dipper lifted silt from the canal and dumped it onto the bank. Jacob picked up three more logs off the pile and heaved open the heavy door to the fire, but before he threw in the wood, Michael signaled for him to stop.

Jacob dropped the logs on the ground and slammed the

boiler door shut. He teetered on the steps, his body depleted from his afternoon in the sweltering room. Michael handed him a tin of homemade brew, and he guzzled it down.

"Get yourself cleaned up," Michael said.

In seconds, he'd changed into his wool jersey and trousers. Diving off the side of the boat, he plunged into the cool water. The canal rinsed away some of the soot and slowly soothed the aches in his body.

Rain splashed on his face as he climbed back up onto the boat and then down into the cramped hull. Michael threw him a towel, and he mopped up his hair and face.

"You will go with us to *Nachtgebet* tonight, *ja*?" Michael asked as Jacob dried himself.

Jacob stopped for an instant, surprised by the invitation. Three times a day their meals were delivered in a basket, but every night, Michael and the other men walked the half mile back to Amana to attend the prayer service. They'd yet to ask Jacob to go with them.

"I don't know...."

Michael clapped him on the back. "Prayer will be good for you, my friend."

Rain soaked the crew's slickers as they tromped toward Main Amana, the hub of the Colonies' seven villages. The muddy pathway to the village was lined with plump elderberry bushes, golden fields of dandelions, and beds of freshwater oyster shells from the canal.

Stone houses mixed with Amana's brick and wood structures, and in every yard hung a tandem lawn swing with facing benches, shaded by a grape arbor.

The boat crew made their way down a small path between buildings, toward the back door of a large stone home, but instead of going into the house, they waited in the rain with a dozen other men dressed either in slickers and dark hats or huddled under umbrellas. Michael greeted his son with a hug and several other men with a handshake, but the men only nodded at Jacob.

The boat crew frequently laughed together on the dredge boat, but there was no laughter in the courtyard tonight. Some of the men talked quietly in German, but Jacob couldn't hear their words. Perhaps they were asking about him. Liesel had been so kind to him, so gracious, but tonight he felt like an outsider.

In his peripheral view, he saw one of the men eyeing him like a hunter sizing up his prey. Jacob turned, confronting him with his gaze, but the man didn't look away.

Michael elbowed him and whispered in English. "That's Emil Hahn."

The name registered slowly. *Liesel's fiancé.*

Jacob stood even taller as they waited, eyeing Emil again from the side.

"He's a *gut* man, Jacob. Works hard."

"Where does he work?"

"The bakery."

He faced his boss. "Liesel said he had an important job."

"That is an important job in Amana. He and his father bake sixty loaves of bread a day."

Not to discount the importance of bread, but Jacob couldn't believe that this job kept Emil from visiting Liesel when she was quarantined.

The door to the house opened and, with their heads bowed in silence, Jacob followed Michael into a sitting room that was three or four times larger than the one in the doctor's home. Neat rows of benches filled the space with an aisle down the middle to separate the men from the women. On the other side of the room, each woman wore a dainty cap over their hair like the pretty prayer cap Liesel wore.

If only Liesel was there with him tonight. She would

tenderly guide him through what to do and what to expect. Perhaps he wouldn't feel so out of place.

Michael nudged him toward the back row, and Jacob sat down beside two young boys. The rest of the boat crew sat in the second and third rows.

The silence broke when someone spoke out in German from the front, startling Jacob with the strength of his voice. Even though he didn't understand all the words of the prayer, he was extremely thankful for all the blessings that flooded into his life. Cassie's health. His new job. Food. Housing.

Liesel.

His gaze wandered over the small crowd. Emil Hahn sat three rows in front of him, his head bowed in prayer. Jacob had met plenty of women during his life, but few of them gave out of the depths of her heart. Katharine had been like that...and so was Liesel. Liesel needed a man who would care for her in the way she deserved.

The boy next to him opened a hymnal and slid it toward Jacob. From the right side of the room a woman began to sing, and the rest of the group followed a cappella. Reading the words in the hymnbook, Jacob didn't sing, but he tried to mentally translate the words into English.

Mercy. Grace. Faithful through another year.

As a community, they were thanking God for His blessings. His love. In song, they were offering up their thanksgiving.

The past year had been painfully hard for him, yet God had been faithful.

When the final prayer had finished, Jacob filed out of the room with the rest of the men. Outside, Michael pulled him over to the side. "I want you to meet Emil Hahn."

Jacob countered Emil's intense gaze, waiting for the man to approach him.

Jacob had no respect for Liesel's fiancé. She'd been exposed to diphtheria and had been quarantined with a man they'd never met. The fear of what could have happened to her should have sent Emil racing over to Homestead weeks ago to check on her.

Emil lifted his arm, and for a moment Jacob thought he might swing a punch. Instead Emil stuck out his hand. "A pleasure to meet you."

Jacob shook his tight grasp. "Liesel helped to save my daughter's life."

Emil nodded his head once, very slowly. "She is a *gut* woman, *ja?*"

"Yes, she is."

Jacob waited for the man to pull him aside and tell him to stay away from the woman he planned to marry, but Emil didn't ask any questions nor did he threaten Jacob. Instead he nodded and walked away.

Jacob watched him leave, surprised that he didn't even ask about Liesel's health. If a woman like Liesel were his fiancée, he would have made certain that no other man compromised her.

*Why are you so discouraged, you poor children?
Do you not know, have you not learned,
that your Jesus lives?*

Johann Friedrich Rock, 1733

CHAPTER 17

The dirt cooled Liesel's fingertips as she dug a red-crowned bulb out of the garden bed and tossed the radish into her woven willow basket. The *Küchebaas* and her crew would chop the radish and its leaves for a summer salad tonight alongside pork chops, Spätzle, and tapioca pudding.

When she finished the row of radishes, she would pick cabbage and navy beans until their noon break. Come afternoon, she and the other women would weed the beds and pluck the grubs and beetles from the leaves.

Honeybees swarmed over the flowering melon plants next to her, and she shooed the bees away with her skirt until they flew off to sip their nectar some other place. There was plenty of room for both the bees and her in a garden that stretched for acres behind the *Kinderschule* and kitchen house.

In dozens of rows—planted perfectly straight, with a guideline for proper order—the beds teemed with peas, string beans, asparagus, cucumbers, carrots, red peppers, kale, garlic, tomatoes, and onions. Jacob had questioned her about the source of their food supply, but never once had she wanted for food in the Colonies. Her entire life, they'd eaten in abundance—and the

Society sold hundreds of pounds of excess seed and produce to people across Iowa and in Illinois, Missouri, and Minnesota.

Once the summer crops were harvested, she and the six other women on the garden crew replanted for the fall, adding squash, pumpkins, horseradish, and salsify. Only in the winter did the garden beds—along with most of their community—rest.

The sun heated her bonnet and sweat dampened her skin, but even so, she was glad to be back outside in the fresh air, harvesting the summer's bounty with her friends.

Her gaze wandered back toward the weathered building perched on the edge of the garden. The *Kinderschule*. How was Cassie faring today without either Liesel or Jacob to care for her? The early morning had been rough on both of them. Cassie wanted to go outdoors after being quarantined for so long, yet as they walked to school she was reluctant to leave Liesel's side. The moment she saw the piles of sand outside the school, though, her uncertainty vanished. Cassie kissed her and rushed off to dig and play with the other children, and Liesel left her to dig in the garden.

The teachers would care well for Cassie today. She would play outside with the other children, sip milky coffee during break, and begin her lessons on how to knit. Liesel missed playing with her, but Cassie probably wouldn't miss her one bit.

Two rows down from her, Amalie rose from her work in the onion bed and walked toward her. She knelt down behind Liesel to pick the yellow and red tomatoes from the vine, and Liesel was glad for her company.

"We've missed you," Amalie said.

Liesel tugged at another radish, and it slid out of the dirt. "I missed you too."

"The gardens are much quieter without you and Sophie."

She smiled back at her friend as she worked, thinking about all the questions they'd inundated her with at evening prayers.

She'd enjoyed the quiet for a few days herself. "I don't believe that."

"Sophie writes to you, *ja*?"

She nodded. "Almost every day."

"Does she like her new home?"

Out of the corner of her eye, she saw the *Gartebaas* watching her. She'd just picked all the radishes in front of her, so she scooted up the row to resume her work. "She's still adjusting to city life."

Amalie glanced out beyond the gardens, to the fields and hills beyond Homestead. "It must be very romantic for her and Conrad to be out there, just the two of them."

Liesel thought about the long letters she'd received from Sophie, the ink often smeared by tears. Romantic wasn't a word she would use to describe Sophie's feelings. Regret, perhaps. Despair.

"She misses Homestead."

Amalie shrugged as she plucked another tomato off the vine. "I suppose I would miss it as well."

"I know I would miss it."

The *Gartebaas* shuffled away to check on someone else's work.

"There is much for you to miss, Liesel. In a few months you will be married."

"You will marry someday."

"Perhaps..." Amalie moved her basket further down the row. "Have you seen Emil lately?"

She shook her head. "Not since our picnic."

"I thought he would have visited by now."

Liesel loosened another bulb with the tip of her shovel. "The Elders must not have given him permission."

"I can't imagine why not...," Amalie began, before clamping her jaw shut.

"He respects the Elders."

Amalie nodded, her smile forced. "Of course he does."

"I'm sure he will visit as soon as they approve," Liesel said.

"Right."

Liesel rocked back on her feet, sitting on the moist ground. She couldn't convince Amalie of Emil's intentions if she couldn't even convince herself. Still, was this what all the women thought? That Emil didn't want to visit her?

She brushed the dirt off her apron. Surely Emil wanted to see her but for some reason, the Elders hadn't wanted them to visit each other quite yet. Perhaps they wanted to ensure that their love for each other could withstand even the possibility of sickness and death.

Emil was faithful to the Elders' instruction. If he wasn't, he would have come.

The question that scared her even more was not whether Emil would come, but whether she wanted him to come.

Amalie popped a small tomato into her mouth and swallowed. "I'm sure you will be excited when you see him."

"Absolutely," Liesel said, even though the word felt sour on her tongue.

Not that many months ago, Sophie had spent a year in Main Amana waiting to marry Conrad Keller. Her dear friend had pined for her betrothed, crying giant tears whenever he left the village to hike back to Homestead. Even though Conrad was the son of an Elder, he still snuck to Amana almost every week without permission because he couldn't stand to be separated from the woman he loved.

Every time he arrived, Sophie would run from the gardens to greet him. Though she had refrained from embracing him in public, her face had shone with love for the man who wanted to marry her.

Not once during Liesel's engagement to Emil had he snuck away to Homestead to be with her. When she'd left Amana in February, he had hugged her then and told her he would count the days until he saw her again, but during their visits since, he hadn't mentioned day- counting, nor had he said that he loved her.

If one day she looked across the gardens and saw Emil running to her, she wouldn't be ecstatic, but she would be glad that he still cared for her.

She sighed. At least she thought she would be glad.

Tugging her last radish out of the ground, she picked up her basket and moved away from Amalie, toward the bed of cabbage.

Even if she couldn't muster much excitement, Amalie and the other women mustn't guess at her lack of enthusiasm—and affection—toward Emil Hahn. No matter her feelings, she would be faithful to her promise.

Her mind wandered, and she wondered what it would be like to look across the gardens and see Jacob smiling at her. Waving. She would run to greet him and then he would pull her into his arms....

She grabbed a head of lettuce and yanked it so hard that the leaves shredded in her hands.

Stop it! She shouldn't be thinking about other men, especially not an outsider like Jacob. Even entertaining thoughts about him was dangerous to her soul.

Love was a fleeting emotion. No matter what happened, she would honor her promise and care for Emil the best she could.

A breeze ruffled the leaves of the cabbage, and a low cry rattled over the beds. She glanced back at the fence around the *Kinderschule* as the cry grew louder, and she knew. Cassie Hirsch needed her.

After a quick scan for the *Gartebaas*'s bonnet, she found the woman ten or so rows down, staring back at her.

"Go tend to her," Helene said with a wave of her arm. Liesel rose from the ground and rushed toward the school.

Through the haze of smoke, Marshall Vicker stared back at Frank, his eyes as clouded as the air in the saloon. Frank hadn't wanted to come to a wretched saloon, nor had he wanted to meet with Marshall, but he had no choice if he wanted to avoid the lawsuit Marshall was threatening to slap on him.

Marshall had sold his sailboat and wanted to purchase a bigger one to sail with friends on Lake Michigan before summer's end. Last week, Frank had explained to Marshall that it would take a few days to get his money, and the man refused to wait any longer. When Frank fudged on giving him the seven hundred, he demanded the entire amount in his account.

Three thousand dollars.

Frank rolled his shoulders, trying to purge the knot lodged in his neck.

He had no choice but to tell Marshall the truth. The man could take him to court along with Caldwell and the others, but the cost to hire an attorney would deplete the little money left in the vault. If they proceeded to court, his customers would get the bank's assets instead of cash—assets they would have to pay taxes on until they could sell the property...and no one knew when property would start selling again.

Perhaps Marshall could help him contrive a way to find Jacob and his stash. If not, the entire bank—including Marshall's savings—would go under.

Marshall's eyes narrowed. "You're saying this Jacob Hirsch stole my money."

"Your money and multiple others." The bottom of Frank's mug trailed wet ringlets as he pushed it across the table. "I don't know how much is missing."

"The money vanished. Right out from under your nose." Marshall snapped his fingers in Frank's face, and he jumped back.

"I was checking the books, every day. Nothing looked amiss."

"You didn't check close enough."

"Jacob hid the original set of books."

"I trusted you, Frank." Even in the dim light, he could see anger contort Marshall's face. "There's not another bank in this blasted city that I'd trust with my money, but I thought you would watch over it like it was your own."

Frank looked down at the rough table, wiping up the watermarks with his sleeve. His friend was right. He should have caught this scheme long before he let Jacob go. He should have wondered why several of his faithful customers were withdrawing small amounts instead of depositing their cash as they'd done for years. But since times were hard, he hadn't questioned it.

Marshall cleared his throat. "You used to have a surplus."

"We handed out fifty thousand in the panic last summer."

"And your capital?"

"Invested in businesses and mortgages."

"So Jacob Hirsch stole from your reserves."

"Apparently."

Marshall squeezed his hands together. "We have to find him."

Frank leaned back against the booth. He hadn't planned on telling anyone about the bank's loss yet, but perhaps Marshall could use his reporter's instincts to help him sniff out the man who'd robbed them both. He'd have to use his instincts, though, without writing an article. A news story would nail his coffin closed.

"I've been trying to find Jacob," Frank said. "But the police refuse to help."

"Someone has to know where he went."

"I haven't been able to locate any family in Chicago."

"Then talk to his friends."

Frank shook his head. "No one's giving us information."

Marshall slapped the table. "So you hire a private detective."

"I can't afford one."

Marshall tapped his mug on the table, lowering his voice. "Then we have no choice. We'll have to use the free press."

Frank shook his head again, harder this time. "I don't think so."

"It's our only option."

Frank closed his eyes for an instant as he envisioned all of his remaining customers outside the bank, waving the *Daily News* in their hands, demanding their money.

"An article will ruin the bank."

"Your bank is already ruined."

"But we can recover, Marshall. We can track him and our money down, and when the economy starts growing again, I'll sell off the property and homes the bank owns."

Marshall picked up his mug and drained it. "You really think you can recover?"

He squared his shoulders. "Eventually."

"And my money?"

"I'll pay you back every cent."

"So maybe we compromise." Marshall rested his chin on his hands. "I write an article and talk about the theft from one of the city's most prestigious banks."

He sighed. "Then every bank will have a run on their capital, including me."

"You're certain that Jacob Hirsch was your thief?"

"Absolutely," he retorted. "The ledger was in his house."

"Okay." Marshall leaned closer. "So maybe we don't mention the bank. Instead we write an article about Jacob Hirsch."

"You'd have to mention the bank."

"I'll report he stole from a local company and then disappeared."

Frank twisted his mug again. "Someone could trace him to my bank."

"How would they do that?"

Frank blinked, thinking of the ramifications of such an article...and the ramifications if he refused to cooperate. Marshall would sue for his money and so would Caldwell and the others.

If he opted to let Marshall write the article, though, someone could figure out that Jacob once worked for him. Then again, Marshall could write the article without permission and headline the bank's name for revenge.

If he worked with Marshall, anonymously offered some sort of compensation, someone might give them information to lead them to Jacob. Even if Jacob had fled the city—and he was likely in Florida or California by now—perhaps a friend or relative in Chicago could tell them where he had gone.

"I'll put up a reward to find him," Frank said. "Three hundred dollars."

Marshall's eyes narrowed. "You don't have money for a reward."

"I will when we find him."

*Who can stop the wind that My Spirit stirs
as it rushes from the profound depths of Love Itself?*

Johann Friedrich Rock, 1720

CHAPTER 18

Liesel's sunbonnet bounced on her shoulders as she skipped through the forest, her fingers clasped around Cassie's small hand. It was glorious, skipping over the stones and branches in the woods, with no one but Cassie watching her.

Cassie didn't care if Liesel pulled up her skirts and hopped like a bunny or twirled in circles under the canopy of silvery leaves. Her toes ached in her narrow boots, yet she felt more alive than she'd felt since she was a child herself, chasing her friends through the forest.

A tapestry of bluebells shimmered in the sunlight, and a Baltimore oriole dipped in front of them, its orange breast a bright flame against the muted browns and greens. The oriole landed on a branch and cheered them along with his chirping.

Liesel ducked under the branch and the bird trailed behind them, hopping from tree to tree as if he longed to join in their fun. "He wishes he could skip."

Cassie slid her fingers out of Liesel's grasp and flapped her arms. "I wish I could fly."

"Me too," Liesel said, running forward, the breeze ruffling the calico draped over her arms. Strands of hair fell from her hairnet, stringing across her forehead and neck.

Ahead of her, Cassie's auburn hair bounced with curls. Her monster tears from this morning were long gone, replaced by a smile and a song. "A tisket, a tasket, a green-and- yellow basket."

Liesel poked her arm. "What's a *tisket?*"

Cassie shrugged and then twirled around, her arms fluttering in circles. "I sent a letter to my love and on the way I dropped it."

A cloud passed under the sun, and the shimmering light in the forest faded to gray. With one last chirp, the oriole disappeared back into the trees.

Cassie's cries had scared Liesel this morning, but she was glad of them now. Glad that God had softened Helene's heart and that her *baas* had told her to leave her work until tomorrow so Cassie could visit her father.

Ten days had passed since Jacob left to dredge the canal, and every morning Cassie asked to visit her father, but until the quarantine was lifted, she couldn't leave the house. The doctor was concerned about her walking so far this afternoon, so soon after she'd recovered, but his heart had softened as well when Cassie's tears flowed fresh. He, too, agreed that Liesel should take the girl to find Jacob's boat and even added that the long walk might do her some good too. No one argued that it would do Cassie good to see her father.

Sunshine flooded the forest again as they rounded the bend. A narrow bridge stood before them, wooden railings on both sides. It was the only way to cross the wide Iowa River between Homestead and Main Amana.

Liesel hesitated, but Cassie tugged on her hand. "Come on."

She grasped the girl's hand as they stepped onto the bridge together. Below them the current rolled over the rocks, traveling east, but Liesel kept her eyes focused on the trees in front of her. Only a hundred or so steps and they would be on the other side.

"Look." Cassie stopped on the bridge to point down at the water.

Liesel froze but didn't move toward the railing. With a quick glance, she saw a snapping turtle paddling upstream. The creature's long neck twisted to the side, and he ducked under the water.

Cassie leaned through the wide slats of the railing for a better look, and Liesel tugged her back, away from the edge. Cassie struggled against her grasp, but Liesel pulled her off the bridge and onto the safety of the bank.

Cassie stuck out her lower lip. "I wanna watch the turtle."

"Can you swim?"

Cassie shrugged, her neck craned to catch another glimpse of the turtle. "A little."

"Well, I can't," Liesel said. "If I jumped in after you, you'd have to rescue me."

Cassie tugged on her arm to go back to the river.

Liesel bent down, eye to eye with the girl. "Nothing is as calm and peaceful as water, Cassie. In a basin or a glass it heals and it quenches our thirst, but in large amounts, it can cause tremendous damage and even death."

"I'll be careful."

Liesel sighed. No wonder Heinrich Hoffmann wrote *Der Struwwelpeter*. Young children didn't listen well to reason. "Do you want to see your papa today?"

Cassie eyed the river for another moment before she nodded.

"Then we have to hurry to Amana."

Cassie broke her gaze from the river and skipped forward, toward the fields in the distance.

A new thought settled over Liesel as she watched Cassie, one that startled her. She loved being Cassie's friend, but at this moment, she didn't feel like a playmate. She felt more like a parent. And she wasn't sure she wanted to be a parent.

On the other side of the trees, they emerged onto one of the fields that supplied food for the Amana people. The pathway cut through maroon-tinged cornstalks and over a grassy field spotted with dairy cows. Amana's *Glockenhaus* rose above the rooftops to their right, ready to call out to the other villages if there was an emergency.

The woolen mill stood east of town, and the waterway that powered the mill carved a channel through the field in front of them. Liesel stopped walking to watch the lofty trees sway in the village where she'd been raised.

As the village carpenter, her father would be in his woodworking shop this afternoon, building a piece of furniture or a tool for the gardens. Emil's work in the bakery would have finished hours ago, and he'd probably joined her father to help in the shop.

Since Liesel had been a schoolgirl, her desire was to work in the *Kinderschule*, and Emil had had a desire as well for his profession. Instead of following his father's path as a baker, Emil wanted to work as a carpenter.

When they were children, Emil always seemed to be carving something from the scraps her father provided. One summer, for her birthday, he'd carved her an ark with a dozen wooden animals. She'd played with it for years, and her father had been impressed with his work.

Main Amana didn't have need for another carpenter, but one day they would. The Elders knew that Emil hoped for that position—coveted it, even—more than any other man in Amana did.

Liesel took another small step—westward to follow the Mill Race instead of toward Amana. She wished she could go visit her own father this afternoon, but she didn't want Emil to think she'd come to see him. And even if she did want to go, they wouldn't have time for a long visit. The sun would set in five hours, and they'd need to back in Homestead before dark. A piece of her longed to go to Amana, but even more, she wanted to see how Jacob fared on the dredge boat.

Cassie tugged on her hand, and the two hurried along the pathway. Willow leaves draped over the slow-moving canal, and clusters of grapes grew wild along the path. She plucked a white grape and popped it into her mouth, the sour tang overpowering the sweet. Cassie bit into one and her eyes crossed as she spit the grape onto the ground.

Liesel reached above Cassie's head and pulled down a vine of deep purple grapes. She broke off a cluster of the fruit and handed a grape to Cassie.

Cassie waved her hands in front of her face. "No, thank you."

Liesel ate the fruit instead. "The purple ones are sweet."

Cassie eyed her warily, like Liesel might be pulling a trick on her, but she reached forward to take the cluster. Testing a grape on her tongue, she swallowed and reached for another piece of fruit.

The two of them gobbled the dark grapes, nature's sweetness refreshing them after their long hike. Quietly Liesel thanked God for the abundance of His gifts on this fertile land. The richness and beauty never ceased to amaze her. Everywhere she went, there was evidence of God's care for them.

Cassie tossed her stem back into the tangled vines and raced down the pathway, so Liesel lifted her skirts and followed.

On the other side of the canal, under the folds of a weeping willow, she heard whispering. Cassie stopped to gape at the cascading leaves like the tree was speaking to her. The tip of a canoe poked through the willow leaves, and the whispering turned to giggles. A man hushed the woman with him, and she laughed again. A couple in love.

If the Elders found out about the canoe, the man would be reprimanded for spending valuable time building a luxury item and the canoe would be confiscated—but for the couple's sake, Liesel hoped the Elders didn't discover their secret.

She smiled as she hurried Cassie along the pathway. The colonists laughed often in their villages, usually over a *seidel* of homemade ale, but there was little time and space in the Amanas for privacy. Affection between married couples was reserved for a few private hours in their rooms at night.

The couple must have snuck out of one of the villages, stealing away for a few hours alone. The Elders wouldn't have approved, but when a couple was in love, they would do anything they could to be with each other. They even moved away from all they held dear, to a lonely city like Cedar Rapids, when one decided to pursue a law degree.

Which brought her back to the questions that haunted her—why didn't Emil insist on coming to Homestead to visit her? Why didn't he want to be with her?

And why didn't she want to go to him?

On the other side of the canal, the willow trees broke away to reveal the glory of the Amana Colonies' coronet, Lily Lake. Thousands of yellow blooms enveloped the surface on the shallow lake. God's garden.

His gifts never ceased to amaze her.

Smoke puffed over Lily Lake, and Liesel saw the hulking frame of the *grosse* boat in the distance. Cassie dropped her hand and ran.

"Papa!" she called out.

Liesel lifted her skirts and ran behind Cassie, toward the monster of a boat. What would the crew think of her, running up the path like a crazed child? And what would Jacob think?

She wiped her sleeve across her forehead, and hair tangled in the sweat on her face, sticking to her eyelashes. She pushed her hair away from her face as she ran, trying to tuck it back in the hairnet, but it was futile.

"Papa!" Cassie yelled again.

Panting, Liesel reached back and pulled the sunbonnet over the mess of her hair and retied the lace under her neck.

Cassie was yards in front of her, shouting louder and louder for her father. Liesel saw the white hull of the boat, the giant dipper hanging in the air...and then she saw Jacob standing on the stern.

With a loud splash, Jacob dove into the water and swam swiftly toward them.

Seconds later, he hopped out of the water and gathered Cassie in his wet arms. Together they spun, father and daughter, and Liesel stepped back.

Perhaps she would go to Main Amana for the remainder of the afternoon and let Cassie and Jacob enjoy their time together. She could return in a few hours to escort Cassie home.

Stepping back a second time, she intended to leave, but Jacob turned as well and his smile slowly encompassed her. Her heart quaking, she smiled back at him.

Maybe she did belong after all.

Jacob couldn't believe his ears nor could he believe his eyes. Cassie was out of quarantine, and she was here at the Mill Race. He twirled her around again and again, savoring the melody of her laughter. She was whole again. Healthy. He could ask for nothing more.

When they stopped spinning, he glanced back and saw Liesel there. Her face was splotched with red, and her blue eyes dipped when he met her gaze, but he couldn't take his eyes off her.

He'd known before that Liesel was pretty, during those days

and nights that she nursed Cassie back to health, but he hadn't realized until now exactly how beautiful she was.

Cassie tugged on his arm, and he shook his head, breaking his stare. "I want to swim, Papa."

He tweaked his daughter's chin. "Not in this water, sweetheart."

She knelt down, cupping water in her hand. "What's wrong with it?"

He held out his stained hands, and for the first time he felt self-conscious, standing here in his wool jersey with dirt encrusted on his neck and arms. Even with soap, the murky water along the Mill Race did little to wash off the soot.

He guided the women toward the boat, and Michael tossed him a towel. Drying off, he wrapped the towel around his waist, and then his *baas* handed over a basket filled with food.

The three of them sat on the bank of the canal and watched the pipe on the boat chug out the last of its smoke for the day. He put his arm around Cassie. In spite of his damp suit, she snuggled close to him.

"I missed you, Papa."

He kissed the top of her head. Words couldn't express how much he'd missed her. "You are all better?"

She nodded. "Liesel took good care of me."

His gaze traveled over to the woman beside his daughter. "I'm sure she did."

Liesel blushed. "Cassie was a stellar patient."

"The laboratory results came back?"

"Yesterday," Liesel said. "The diphtheria is gone."

He kissed the top of Cassie's braids. "Thank God."

"Indeed."

Liesel had promised to care for her while she was at the doctor's house, but her *baas* probably needed her back in the gardens for the summer harvest. Would another woman in

Homestead take over the care of his daughter? No one could possibly care for her as well as Liesel had.

He leaned toward Liesel. "What happens now?"

She smoothed her fingers over her lap. "I spoke with Niklas Keller yesterday, and if it's all right with you, Cassie can stay with me for the remainder of the summer."

"But your work..."

"Two older women work in the *Kinderschule,* caring for the younger children while their mothers are working." Liesel stopped, blushing again. "Not that I'm her mother."

"I understand."

"She can play at the school while I work in the gardens." Her cheeks remained flushed, and he wanted to reach out and pull her close to him. "I will care for her in the evenings and at night."

As she peeled back the cloth covering the basket of food, his eyes were on her face. "You've been so kind to Cassie and me."

"The Bible says that pure religion is caring for the fatherless in their affliction."

He braced himself. "Cassie isn't fatherless."

"I only mean..."

He cocked his head. "What do you mean?"

"I enjoy being with her, Jacob."

He nodded slowly. "I'm grateful."

She glanced away from him, back toward the village. "Have you visited Main Amana yet?"

"The crew took me to *Nachtgebet.*"

She looked back at him. "Really?"

"They thought I needed to pray...and they were right."

"I'm glad for you, Jacob." She handed him a piece of bread. Its hard crust crumbled in his fingers. "What did you think of it?"

Cassie engulfed her piece of bread, and Liesel handed her another.

"The men were different than the men in Homestead." He hesitated. "Not as welcoming."

She unwrapped a round of soft brick cheese and held it out to him. "They are wary of strangers."

He didn't take the cheese. "As they should be."

"None of them spoke to you?"

"One man did." He paused, watching white clouds mingle with the blue sky. "Emil Hahn."

She breathed in so quickly that Cassie turned her head.

"Are you all right?" the girl asked.

Liesel coughed, slapping her chest. "*Ja.*"

"Emil's an interesting fellow," he continued. "Seems to know what he wants."

"Most of the time…" She took a bite of the cheese, an uncomfortable silence resting over them before she spoke again.

"Did he ask about…" She brushed away her words. "Never mind."

"He didn't ask me anything."

She tossed her food back into the basket. "I see."

"I thought he might slug me."

Liesel shook her head. "Violence is not our way."

"What is your way?"

"We talk about our problems. Pray about them."

He broke off another piece of bread, which had probably been made by Emil that morning. "And they go away?"

"Not always, but we ask God how we should respond in love." She brushed her hands over her skirt. "I wanted to ask you a question."

Jacob put his arm around Cassie's shoulders and whispered, "See that giant tree down there?"

She shaded her eyes, looking up the canal. "That one by the lake?"

"The very one. How about you run all that way and tag it?"

Cassie didn't wait for him to start counting. She untied her shoes, kicking them off, and picked up her skirt.

Jacob looked back at Liesel and the ringlets of blond hair that had tumbled out of her bonnet onto her shoulders. "What's your question?"

She plucked a piece of grass from the bank and began twisting it in her hands. "Cassie told me her mother was in Chicago."

The bread fell out of Jacob's hand, onto the grass. He didn't know what he had expected Liesel to ask, but it certainly wasn't about Katharine. "Her mother is buried in Chicago."

Liesel wouldn't look at him. "I see."

"She passed away last year, after the birth of our son."

Liesel's voice shook. "How long were you married?"

"Five years."

"You loved her?"

He nodded. "Very much."

"When Cassie said that…I wasn't sure."

"I'm not hiding anything from you, Liesel."

Her blue eyes were tender. "Nor I from you."

Cassie raced to his side, tackling him. "How long was it, Papa?"

He turned to face his daughter, but he didn't want this moment to end. "Less than a minute, I believe, but I'm not certain. Should we try again?"

Cassie collapsed on the ground. "No, thank you."

Katharine would have loved to see her daughter playing along the banks, and she would also want her to know the love and affection of another woman. His wife would want *him* to know love as well. Katharine had been faithful to him for five years, and it felt like he was being unfaithful to her to even think about loving someone else…yet he knew she would want him to love again.

He couldn't think about that now.

He hopped to his feet instead, picking up Cassie in his arms, and he pointed toward the canal. "Have you ladies ever been inside a dredge boat?"

Cassie sat up. "Not me."

Liesel shook her head. "Me neither."

Grinning, he took the basket from Liesel's hand. "Allow me to give you a tour."

Whosoever cannot endure storms, rain, sunshine, cold, and heat; whosoever cannot allow the Lord to guide the ship of his faith in the great and stormy ocean of life and death; will not safely enter into the harbor of eternal rest.

Christian Metz, 1833

CHAPTER 19

With gray clouds hovering over the *grosse* boat, Jacob tried to release his hold on Cassie, but she clung to his neck. He understood. He didn't want to let her go either. Still, the storm clouds were building on the horizon, and if she and Liesel didn't rush through the forest, they would be drenched before they reached Homestead.

Reluctantly, he pried Cassie's hands from his neck and kissed her forehead. "Walk quickly now, Pumpkin."

Her nose scrunched into a pout. "I'm not a pumpkin."

He hugged her again. "You're my pumpkin."

"We want to stay with you tonight. Don't we, Liesel?"

Liesel blushed and shook her head.

How he wished they could stay—but Michael wouldn't allow either woman to sleep on the boat.

He met Liesel's eyes. "Perhaps you should stay in your father's home."

She shook her head. "My *baas* is expecting me in the morning."

"You're going to get wet."

Her smile warmed him. "The rain will feel good."

That it would.

Cassie leaned over to tie her shoelace, and he took Liesel's hand, gently squeezing it.

She was intended for another man, but she was also his friend. And his guardian angel.

"Thank you," he whispered.

Her eyes met his, awash with confusion, and he searched her face. Both of them were confused.

She pulled her hand away, her voice shaking. "We'd better hurry."

"Liesel…"

She reached down, her hand reaching for Cassie's, and together they turned.

He wanted to run after them. Run after her. But he had no choice but to let them go.

He stood on the bank, watching them until they reached the woods. Michael had promised he would be able to return to Homestead for a visit next Sunday, less than a week away. Still, he didn't know if he could wait that long.

Dark shadows consumed the sunlight in the forest, and the wind swept up leaves and swirled them around their knees. Cassie didn't skip through the trees, nor did Liesel need to urge her across the bridge. The girl understood. They must hurry back to Homestead or they would be drenched when the clouds emptied themselves on the Colonies.

Thunder cracked in the distance, and Cassie froze on the pathway. Turning toward Liesel, her eyes were wide with fear. "Are we going to blow away?"

"What?"

"The wind…will it blow us away?"

She pressed down her skirt as she knelt on the ground near the child. "Of course not."

"But Robert blew away."

"Robert?"

"Robert and the red umbrella."

The fairy tale in *Der Struwwelpeter*.

She hadn't thought twice about reading Cassie the silly story of Robert. After all, it was what her *Vater* had read to her when she was a child—what most German parents read their children. Yet out here in the wind, she clearly remembered reading the story of little Johnny Look-in-the-Air when she was a child. Johnny's head was always in the clouds, like hers used to be. She was always dreaming, watching the sky more than she watched her feet. In the story, Johnny fell right into a deep, swollen river and almost drowned.

"Robert blew away, but...," Liesel said as Cassie leaned closer. Try as she might, she couldn't think of a reason why the wind wouldn't steal them away like poor Robert.

Thunder shook the trees again, and Cassie trembled as well. "But what?"

"The umbrella," Liesel blurted. "The wind picked up Robert's red umbrella and took them away."

She held out both of her hands and took Cassie's hands in hers, turning them over. "See, no umbrella."

A slight smiled reemerged on Cassie's face. "God will protect us tonight."

The girl nodded, but she tugged on Liesel's hand to hurry, and they ran through the blowing leaves. The wind whipped her skirt around her knees and her feet ached, but the first raindrops didn't fall until they crossed the railroad tracks into Homestead.

The rain fell hard and swift, stinging her eyes and cheeks, but they were close to the safety of her home now. Close to warm wool blankets and a dry change of clothes.

Mud weighed down the hem of her skirt as they ran up the steps to the kitchen house. She flung open the door and Cassie raced into the hallway. Inside, out of the storm, they both burst into laughter.

Liesel flung her soaked bonnet and shawl on the floor, water dripping off her skirt and hair. Cassie clutched her stomach and curled up like a pretzel. Together they laughed and laughed until a black-cloaked man stepped out into the hallway.

The laughter vanished from her lips.

Two other Elders joined Niklas Keller in the hallway and Cassie curtseyed at the men. Niklas gave her a small nod.

She nudged Cassie toward the staircase. "Go change into your nightclothes."

Cassie hesitated, eyeing the three men.

"Hurry now," she said. "You don't want to get sick again."

Cassie turned and jogged up the steps.

She stared back at Niklas. Afraid for Sophie. Afraid for her father. And even afraid for Emil.

Her voice cracked. "What is it?"

Niklas pointed toward the sitting room and waited as she hurried into the room and sat on a cane chair. The Elders lined up on the divan in front of her. Part of her wanted to shake the news out of them, while the other part never wanted to hear why they were visiting her.

Niklas spoke first. "You left the village."

She glanced across their grim faces. "What?"

"You left Homestead, Liesel. Without permission."

She sighed with relief. Sophie and the others were fine. "I took Cassie to see her father."

Niklas looked at the other men before catching her eye again. "Who told you to take Cassie to Amana?"

She twisted her hands on her lap. Never before had she left Main Amana or Homestead without first asking an Elder, but today...today, she'd been so excited when Helene and then Dr.

Trachsel told her she could take Cassie to Jacob. Not once did she consider petitioning Niklas or any of the others. She assumed they would want Cassie to visit her father.

"It was my decision," she said quietly. "I thought Cassie needed to go."

"What if something had happened to you?"

She glanced up. "My *baas* knew where I went, as did Dr. Trachsel."

"They both thought you received permission from an Elder."

"Please forgive me." Her voice quaked as she spoke. "I had the best intentions."

Niklas looked at the other men again as if he were getting a silent concurrence. "We are all concerned about your intentions."

She pushed herself up on her chair. "You have no need to be concerned."

"We think it best that an older woman take over Cassie's care."

"But she is attached to me…and I to her."

"This is what concerns us."

"I won't be so careless next time," she insisted. "I will ask permission."

"We believe…"

She interrupted him. "Cassie has gone through so many changes in the past year. Too many changes for a child. She lost her mother and then her home, and now her father has gone away from her too." She leaned forward, pleading. "Another change will wound her even more. She needs to feel secure, at least for a while."

"Only God can give her security."

"Please…," she begged.

When Niklas asked her to leave the room, she paused at the doorway, turning back toward the row of Elders.

"Jesus loved the children," she whispered, before stepping into the hallway.

It wasn't until she was on the other side of the doorway that she realized her hands were trembling. Even though her clothes were drenched, she knew the shivering wasn't because she was cold. She was scared. Scared that they would take this precious girl away from her care.

Each Amana village was governed by a board of Elders, and it was their job to watch over her and all the men and women in their community. The Elders were godly men, each one of them noble and kind. They wouldn't turn away a needy child, but they would act swiftly if they thought one of their younger women was losing her heart to an outsider. It was their job to protect the people in the Amanas as well as their way of life, set apart from this world.

She strained her ears, trying to listen to the men's words, but all she heard were whispers. In the dim hallway, she whispered herself, lifting up prayers to God.

The Elders thought she was too immature—too much like a child herself—to work in the *Kinderschule*, but she could care for one child when she wasn't in the gardens. And then perhaps she would prove to the Elders that she was mature enough, responsible enough, to watch over a group of children.

Minutes passed, and the clock chimed in the hallway.

She didn't want Cassie to go to another home, not yet. She had no illusions that Cassie would stay with her past October, but for now, her company was yet another gift from God. Was there something else she could say to convince the men that she was the right one to take care of Cassie? That God had placed the desire in her heart to care for children and being with Cassie filled her heart with joy?

They would argue that God should be her only fulfillment, and He did fulfill her, yet He'd given her friendships with women like Sophie and even children like Cassie.

Relationships she treasured with all her heart.

Footsteps crossed the sitting room, and Niklas stepped out into the hallway. He waved her in to join them. She sat back in the stiff chair, her hands trembling again. She would have no choice except to comply, no matter what they decided, but she prayed they would say that Cassie could stay with her.

Niklas leaned toward her. "We have talked and sought God's wisdom."

She nodded. These men had no selfish motives, of that she was sure, but she hoped they listened well to God's voice...and she hoped God blessed her with the privilege of being Cassie's guardian.

Niklas glanced one more time at the other men, who nodded back at him. "We have decided to allow Cassie to remain in your care."

Her breath rushed out of her in relief. "I will do the job well."

Niklas nodded. "You have blessed Cassie with your kindness, Liesel. God is pleased."

She tried to smile, but her lips trembled. "Thank you," she said, starting to stand.

He motioned for her to take her seat again, so she edged back into the chair and waited for him to continue.

"We have also decided that it is unwise for you to take Cassie to the Mill Race."

"But the girl needs to see her father."

He held up his hand. "We all agree that she needs to see him, but my wife or another older woman in our community will escort her."

His words echoed in her mind, and her heart began to sink. *Not take Cassie to the Mill Race?* That meant she wouldn't be able to see Jacob. Perhaps ever again.

Niklas spoke one last time. "Guard your heart, Liesel."

She stood up slowly, her wet clothes weighing down her shoulders. "There is nothing for me to guard against."

*Learn that Love instills peace and hates
all fleshly and spiritual defilement.*

Johann Friedrich Rock, 1724

CHAPTER 20

Rain pounded the roof above Jacob's head, and thunder shook the hull. The crew gathered around a small table, drinking dandelion wine and chattering about their families and the work that awaited each of them when they finished dredging the Mill Race in the fall. Jacob barely heard their words. His ears were honed on the clamor of rain pouring from the skies.

Two hours had passed since he'd said goodbye to Cassie and Liesel. They should be in Homestead by now, out of the rain. He would have to trust that Liesel had hurried back to the village before the downpour, and he would have to trust that God and His mighty force of angels was watching over them along the way.

God had watched over Cassie and him from the moment they'd arrived in Homestead. It was almost as if these Colonies hidden deep in Iowa's farmlands had been anointed by the Almighty. The people here served God, and He blessed them with His power and protection. And He blessed Jacob by healing his daughter and giving her Liesel as a friend and guardian.

Liesel had sacrificed her own health and well-being by joining him at Cassie's sickbed. He was certain she would do anything to keep Cassie well.

A smile played on his lips.

Tonight was one of the best nights he'd had in a very long time. Cassie always seemed to be giggling as she found humor in the smallest, strangest ways, but he'd never been able to appreciate her laughter. Not like he had tonight. He'd forgotten what it was like to have fun.

He would treasure the memory of their picnic along the bank. Even when Liesel asked about Katharine, the darkness hadn't returned. He'd been honest with her, and she respected the memory of his deceased wife.

Michael elbowed him. "You've been smiling since you got back on the boat."

He tried to swallow his smile, but it wouldn't go away. "It was good to see my daughter."

Michael took another swig of his ale. "I think you also enjoyed seeing someone else."

He straightened his shoulders. "What do you mean?"

Michael shook his head. "You've obviously lost your heart to Albert's girl."

"And he's lost his mind too," David said.

The others laughed as they waited for his reaction, but there was nothing for him to say. He admired Liesel for her graciousness to Cassie and him, and he certainly appreciated her beauty —what man wouldn't appreciate it? But like Liesel said tonight, she'd befriended Cassie and him because God commanded His followers to help people in need. It wasn't personal.

Michael reached for a sausage, cutting it into two pieces with his knife. "You must be careful around her."

Jacob took the meat, but he didn't eat it. "I've been nothing but careful."

"The Elders worry about outsiders stealing our women."

"I'm not here to steal anyone."

Michael nodded. "I'm only warning you, Jacob, as a friend. If they think you're sweet on Liesel, they'll ask you to leave, and frankly, I need your help."

Jacob pushed away from the table and walked over to his bunk. He climbed up and lay down on the pillow, staring at the ceiling. If they thought he cared for Liesel, they might kick him out of the Amanas. And if the Elders kicked him out…

He wanted to spend time with Liesel, but he couldn't do anything to jeopardize his work on this boat. Not until the fall, at least. If he worked hard and didn't give them reason to worry, perhaps the Elders would let Cassie and him stay through the winter.

Cassie breathed softly on the small mattress they'd placed on the floor for her, but Liesel couldn't sleep. Niklas and the other men almost took Cassie away from her, and she couldn't say goodbye to this girl, not yet. One day she would have to say goodbye, just as she'd done with Sophie, but if they had taken Cassie away tonight, without any warning to prepare her heart, she didn't know what she would have done.

She'd seen this child through the grueling nights of her sickness and played with her during the long days of their quarantine. The Elders would be watching her even more closely now, to make sure she cared well for Cassie and to make sure she stayed away from Jacob. She wouldn't give them a reason to doubt her faithfulness.

She stared at the ceiling, replaying Niklas's words. *God is pleased.* That was the deepest desire in her heart, even more than her work in the *Kinderschule* or being close to her friends or even staying in the Amanas. More than anything, she wanted to please God.

But why wouldn't God be pleased with a man like Jacob? A man who had loved his wife and loved his daughter. A man who had committed his life to serve Him.

The Elders were elected to keep the colonists accountable and safe, but Jacob wasn't dangerous. In the past month, he'd become a friend.

Tonight he'd lingered as he held her hand. He'd lingered and smiled. He'd been glad to see her today, so much happier than Emil had been at their picnic. In fact, she couldn't remember a time when Emil had been that happy to see her. It was almost as if Jacob had welcomed her into his little family with Cassie.

Now Niklas and the other Elders had forbidden her from seeing him again. Any friendship they'd shared was over.

Cassie stirred below her, whispering in her sleep. Rain pattered against the window, and she wondered about Jacob tonight, on the dredge. Was he missing her as much as she missed him?

She couldn't see Jacob again, not even when he visited Cassie. She wouldn't give the Elders any reason to doubt her loyalty to God and to her faith.

When Jacob was finished with his work on the Mill Race, Hilga Keller would take Cassie back to him. They'd leave the Amanas, and she wouldn't even be allowed to say goodbye.

She punched the feathers in her pillow and turned on her side.

Perhaps it was better that she wasn't permitted to say goodbye to him. It was too hard to watch someone she cared about leave. Even though she'd only known Jacob for three weeks now, they'd walked through the fire together. She'd known him during a dark hour, and she admired his strength through it. His strength and his faith even when it wavered under the thought of losing the daughter he adored.

The months would move on, she would marry Emil, and…

Thunder cracked, and she shot up in her bed.

She couldn't marry Emil.

The thought flashed through her mind, and she pulled her nightdress close to her chest. Tiptoeing toward the window, she looked down at the village and the darkness that enveloped the town of Homestead, its inhabitants asleep in the storm.

Amana's Elders had sent her to Homestead as a test to ensure her and Emil's love was strong. But her love wasn't strong, nor was it true. She may never see Jacob again, but her heart longed to know him more, to be with him. She'd failed the test.

Not once, in the months and years before Emil asked for her hand in marriage, had her heart leaped at the sight of him. Not once had she longed to be at his side. Her father believed that her and Emil's shared heritage would ensure a strong marriage, not the fleeting whims of youthful love. And her father knew—because the vows of his marriage had been fleeting.

Emil had never told her that he loved her, but when he proposed, he said their marriage would be strong. Even then, the moment he asked for her hand, she'd wondered at his motives. Marrying the daughter of the town carpenter and an Elder would improve his chances of becoming the next carpenter and an Elder as well.

And she wondered at her motives. She'd said yes to please her father and because no other man in the Amanas intrigued her. One day she wanted children. A houseful of them. Emil Hahn would give her children and lead their family along the path of righteousness.

She didn't need a husband in the Amanas to be respected, but she longed for a family.

She only wished she longed for Emil as well.

She couldn't marry Emil to have children, and she couldn't allow him the heartache of marrying her in order to become the town carpenter. If he wouldn't end this farce of an engagement, she would do it.

Lightning illuminated the street below her window. She may never see Jacob again, but she would care for his daughter. And when Emil decided to call, she would release him from their engagement.

Consider the matter which causes you the greatest conflict.... Man is always happier when a relentless concern can, through Love's leniency, be set aside.

Johann Friedrich Rock, 1728

CHAPTER 21

Frank bought the *Daily News* from a newsstand and clutched it in his hands. He didn't dare open it. Not until he was back in the safety of his office. A trolley clanged by him and sprayed mud on his trousers. Stepping back from the crowded street, he cut through an alleyway of tents to Clark Street.

Last night Marshall Vicker had called him to say the story would run today. Now they needed someone who knew Jacob Hirsch to read it and respond to the three-hundred-dollar reward. It would be worth every penny to find Jacob and get the money back.

Jacob may have spent a chunk of the cash by now, but Frank refused to admit defeat. He would find Jacob, and the police chief would send someone to arrest him. And whatever was left of the bank's surplus would be returned to the vault.

Orwin wasn't in the teller cage, but Frank's office door was opened. When he walked inside, he found Orwin waiting by his desk with a copy of the newspaper in his hands.

Orwin waved the paper. "Did you see this?"

Frank threw the paper on his desk. When he sat down in his chair, he opened the front page. "I haven't read it yet."

"But you knew about it...."

"Marshall told me yesterday."

Orwin leaned against the desk. "How much did Jacob take?"

"I don't know yet."

Frank opened the paper and found the article on the third page. Marshall reported that Jacob had taken approximately twenty thousand dollars, but with all the fraudulent bookkeeping, he may never know exactly how much the man stole from him.

Orwin scooted even closer, his eyes narrowing. "What if they can't find him?"

Frank couldn't say the words, but his nephew understood. Orwin turned and stomped out of the room, the window of his office shaking with his slam. Both of their careers would be ruined if Jacob didn't return their money.

Frank looked back down at the headline.

REWARD OFFERED FOR EMBEZZLER

Marshall had kept his word. Nowhere in the article did it mention Jacob's place of employ. Most of his customers didn't know Jacob's last name, and he hoped they wouldn't equate this man with the clerk who used to handle their money at the bank. If someone really wanted to find out the source of this article, it wouldn't take them long to discover where Jacob had worked. Hopefully by then, Frank would know where Jacob had gone and have managed to recover the money.

He closed the paper and glanced over at the telephone on his desk. Marshall promised to call the moment someone contacted him with information on Jacob's whereabouts. Now all he had to do was wait...and hope that no one else would want to withdrawal a sizeable sum from their bank account before they found the man who'd stolen their money.

Rain fell in the Amanas for well over a week. Sometimes it would mist, dusting the *grosse* boat with water, and sometimes it would pour. It had been too wet for the men to even journey into Main Amana for evening prayers and much too wet for Jacob to return to Homestead.

Today, however, the sun finally broke through the clouds, and Jacob lifted his face to the light, soaking up the sun as he helped Michael drive the oaken beams into the bank to secure the boat before they operated the dipper for the afternoon.

More than a week had passed since Liesel and Cassie had surprised him with their visit. Every afternoon, when he worked outside, he found himself looking to the east, hoping they would come running down the path again. Yet the rain didn't cease, and his daughter and Liesel didn't come.

Michael promised Jacob that he could go home last Sunday, but a torrent of lightning and thunder accompanied the rain clouds last weekend and ruined his opportunity to return to Homestead. The crew spent the entire day of rest playing cards in the hull, a pastime Michael begrudgingly allowed on the dredge boat although it wasn't permitted in the villages. Jacob kept going up the steps, checking to see if the skies had cleared, but the rain never ceased.

Perhaps today Liesel and Cassie would come. Or tomorrow. He could only hope to see them soon.

Laughter rang out on the canal, and he shaded his eyes to scan its surface. A man paddled a canoe boat toward him and a woman sat across from the man, her head hidden under her sunbonnet.

Michael grunted behind him. "Stupid *Kinder*."

Jacob squinted at the couple. They were seemingly oblivious to the much larger boat blocking their path. "They don't look like children to me."

"Only children would get this close to us." Michael eyed the boat again, but the man hadn't stopped paddling. "Go tell them not to come any closer."

Jacob crossed the plank and hopped onto the path. The man stopped paddling and leaned forward to kiss the woman, and she giggled. When Jacob was alongside them he called out a greeting, but instead of returning the greeting, the woman ducked, her face hidden behind her sunbonnet. Emil Hahn looked up, his eyes locking on Jacob, and Jacob flinched.

"Liesel?" he whispered.

Liesel didn't turn around, so he said her name again, but still she wouldn't face him. Emil paddled to the far side of the canal, and Liesel slipped out of the boat, into the willows.

He called her name one last time, but she was gone, hidden in the tall grass and leaves on the other side of the water.

Should he go after her? His swimming outfit was back in the boat, but he could jump in the Mill Race with his trousers and work shirt to ask her what she was doing here. And why she had betrayed him.

Emil eyed him, and Jacob wanted to knock the smirk off his face. He stuck his hands in his pockets instead. "Michael needs you to stay back from the dredge boat."

"Of course." Emil tipped his hat as he ducked under the trees. Seconds later the man pulled his canoe up onto the bank and was gone.

Jacob stepped back onto the pathway in a daze.

He could catch up with Liesel and demand answers, but what good would that do? He had no right to her, and she had no obligation to answer his questions. She'd told him clearly that she was engaged to Emil, and nothing had changed in the past month. For her, at least. She had a right to be here, spending an afternoon with the man she planned to marry.

But if she was here, visiting her Emil for the evening, who was taking care of his daughter?

Eyeing the forest in the distance, he wanted to take off running toward Homestead. But if he left his post Michael would relieve him of his job, and he couldn't sacrifice the work because he was angry at Liesel.

Surely she had left Cassie in good care. She wouldn't have gone off with Emil unless she was certain Cassie was being cared for.

He pounded the tree trunk beside him. It was so hard, being here, so far from his daughter. He was glad for the job. Glad to be in the Amanas. And he trusted Liesel to take good care of Cassie.

But still…

Liesel hadn't betrayed him. He'd been a fool, betraying his own heart instead. Liesel loved Cassie, of that he was certain. She wouldn't leave her unattended. The only reason he was angry was because Liesel was with Emil Hahn.

Despite what the men on the boat had told him, he couldn't stop thinking about her. He needed this job, yet he also couldn't stop from wondering what might have been if he'd met Liesel in Chicago. Or if he'd come to the Amanas before she was engaged to marry.

His stomach churned. He couldn't imagine Liesel being married…at least not to Emil Hahn.

Therefore, fear not when pain and tribulation loom before you, when the wild ocean waves threaten to turn and engulf your little ship.

Christian Metz, 1825

CHAPTER 22

Liesel chewed the tip of her pen as she stared at the words on the writing paper. Ink dripped from the nib, spreading a muddy puddle across the lines. She'd started this letter to Emil days ago, but the right words still escaped her.

At last he'd written her a letter to inquire about her health, even apologized for not coming sooner to visit. His work in the bakery kept him from an overnight visit, and he hadn't been able to secure permission as of yet to borrow the buggy for an afternoon.

When she'd read his words last week, she couldn't help but wonder if he'd even asked for permission to use a buggy. She knew for a fact that he didn't deliver bread to the kitchen houses on Sunday mornings, so he could easily walk the three miles over for a visit after church if he'd wanted to see her. It was clear that he didn't want to come, and it was even more clear to her that she didn't want to see him. His inattentiveness had wounded her pride, but her heart was intact.

She glanced down again, deciphering his scribble once more under the kerosene lantern. She'd read it over and over, wondering if she'd missed something. Perhaps somewhere in his letter he longed to see her again.

Amalie's words from the garden echoed in her mind. There was no reason why the Elders wouldn't let him come visit, especially since they hadn't seen each other in almost three months. Even more so because her father was one of Main Amana's Elders and he wanted her to marry Emil.

Nothing in Emil's letter even hinted at missing her.

She glanced over at the bed. Cassie was still sleeping this morning, but Liesel's thoughts had awakened her an hour before breakfast and wouldn't let her rest.

She balled up the spotted paper and placed a fresh piece on her writing desk, but her thoughts returned to her visit with Jacob and the heat that had rushed through her skin when he'd enveloped her hand in his.

There was no hope for a marriage with Emil, nor was there any hope for her and Jacob. He would finish his job in two months and go back into the world where he belonged. No matter how much she wanted him to make his home in the Amanas, Jacob would never stay.

She blinked, thinking again about his hand in hers. He'd held it twice now. On the bank by the Mill Race and back in the doctor's office on his first day here. He probably wouldn't remember that first time, but he'd grasped her hand while he was in pain. And she had borne his pain. Gladly.

She could never go into a marriage with another man when she would spend her life thinking about Jacob, wondering what it would be like to marry a man who loved her....

Not that Jacob loved her—or even felt a hint of the longings that stirred in her heart— but it wasn't fair to Emil. She would rather remain single for the rest of her life than live each day with a man who didn't love her. And a man she didn't love.

She held out her pen, ready to being writing again, but no words came to her mind. She sighed. This was a conversation she should have with Emil in person, not on paper. If only she knew when she'd see him again.

The bell outside tolled, and Cassie stirred. Liesel pushed aside the letter and bent down to kiss the girl's head.

"Good morning, sleepyhead." Cassie slurred her good morning.

Liesel helped the girl dress in a new calico dress, and as she tied Cassie's shoelaces, the girl ran her fingers across Liesel's hairnet. Then she patted her own auburn braids. "Can I have a net?"

Liesel smiled. "Maybe one day."

Cassie reached for a handkerchief and strung it over her hair. "I want one just like yours."

What would it be like to teach Cassie how to make a net? Perhaps teach her how to quilt and tat? It would be a privilege to watch this girl grow into a woman who loved their Lord.

Taking Cassie's hand, the two of them trotted down the stairs for breakfast, and when they'd finished eating, they walked out into the muggy air. Hilga Keller tapped her shoulder, and Liesel turned, greeting the woman with a nod.

Instead of greeting her, Hilga held up a newspaper in response.

Liesel looked back and forth between Conrad's mother and the newspaper. "What is it?"

"Take Cassie on to the school." The older woman placed her hand on Liesel's shoulder. "And then we need to talk."

The hours ticked by, but no matter how hard he tried, Jacob couldn't sleep. Even though his body was exhausted from the hard labor, his mind raced with pictures he wished he could erase. Emil and Liesel in the boat. Liesel leaning in to kiss her betrothed. He called out to her, but she hadn't given him the courtesy of greeting him back. Instead she'd ducked, like he didn't know she was sneaking away with Emil.

He didn't have any hold over Liesel. No promise or even a hint of promise. He never should have expected her to be interested in anything other than a friendship with him. He was clearly an outsider…and a foolish one to think that Liesel might care even a bit for him. She'd done her duty, nursed both him and Cassie back to health, and she'd made it clear she'd done this to honor God. She was faithful to God first; he was only a product of her faithfulness.

He rolled over, but sleep evaded him. He was still tossing on his bunk when an Amana boy delivered hot coffee and biscuits for breakfast. At the small table, Michael pushed a tin of coffee toward him. "You look terrible."

Jacob blew the steam off the hot drink. "I couldn't sleep."

Michael reached for another tin and poured a cup for himself.

"I need to go to Homestead," Jacob said.

"You can go in two days. On Sunday."

He shook his head. "I was supposed to go last Sunday."

Michael set the coffeepot on the table. "I need you here."

Jacob knew he was risking his position on the dredge boat, but without a wife, his responsibility was to care for Cassie as well as provide for her. How was he supposed to do both…and do them well? The Homestead Elders had promised him that he would be able to see Cassie at least once a week if he took this job…and he needed to see her.

He leaned forward. "I must take care of my daughter as well."

Michael glanced around, seeming to size up the other men in the cramped room. "You won't receive your pay for today."

He rubbed his hands together. "I understand."

Michael took a long sip from his cup. "And I'll expect you to be back at work in the morning."

He reached for his hat and placed it on his head. "I'll return by nightfall."

Shovels and pails were piled in a crate beside the *Kinderschule*, and Cassie kissed Liesel on the cheek before she pulled out a shovel to dig in the sand. The girl no longer fought when it was time for school, nor did she cry during the day. She adored the teachers at the school, and she was even speaking some German now. And she'd knitted her first pair of stockings.

Jacob would be proud at how Cassie had not only adapted to life in Homestead but how she'd thrived. If only she could take Cassie over to visit so Jacob could see how well his daughter was. None of the older women in town had been available to escort Cassie to the dredge boat.

Liesel glanced one last time at Cassie playing in the sand before she turned to find Hilga Keller. A gaggle of geese honked overheard, shadowing the sun for a moment as she waited on a bench for Hilga. She tugged at the fabric already sticking to her arms and chest. Her bonnet kept the sun from burning her scalp, but the sunrays were hot on her skin, almost unbearably so.

Hilga rushed around the corner, the newspaper flapping at her side, and her eyes showed worry mixed with something else. Anger, perhaps.

The woman fixed her bonnet as she sat on the bench. Liesel glanced down at the newspaper in Hilga's lap. *Chicago Daily News* was plastered across the top of the paper. What could possibly concern her in Chicago?

Hilga shifted the paper between her hands. "The Elders asked me to speak with you."

Liesel gulped. Something must be terribly wrong. "All right."

Hilga opened the front page and pointed to an article

halfway down the page. A story about a reward for an embezzler.

She glanced up at Hilga. "What is an *embezzler*?"

"It's someone who steals money."

She looked back at the paper, wondering why the Elders had sent Hilga to show her this article. She knew very little about money, certainly not how to steal it.

Then, in the first paragraph, she saw his name. *Jacob Hirsch.*

The trees around the bench swirled, and she couldn't breathe. Why was Jacob in the newspaper? He couldn't have stolen any money.

She forced herself to focus on the article again, trying to make sense of it, but she didn't understand. According to the writer, Jacob had taken at least twenty thousand dollars from a Chicago company, and the company was offering three hundred dollars for information about his location so they could recover the missing money.

She fell back against the wooden slats of the bench and closed her eyes. Was Jacob Hirsch a thief? That didn't seem right at all. He was too moral of a man to steal money. Too kind.

Or at least she'd thought he was.

Hilga placed her hand on her arm, forcing her out of her thoughts. "The Elders will confront him."

Her mouth felt dry, her mind clouded as she replied. "Of course."

"They will have to report him to the newspaper."

Liesel tried to nod, but she couldn't move.

"They won't accept the reward, but it is the right thing to do."

The clouds in her mind broke. "What about Cassie?"

Hilga shook her head. "I don't know."

"She could stay here, with me."

Hilga's eyes were sad. "Cassie belongs with her father."

"But what if—what if he goes to jail?"

"He will find her a place to live."

Liesel stood, glancing at the trees in the distance. She wanted to run and run and never return. This story had no good ending for her, Cassie, or Jacob.

"I have to go to work."

Hilga nodded and picked up the newspaper.

After their days and nights caring for Cassie, she thought she knew Jacob Hirsch, but how much did she really know? Maybe he'd screened what was truly inside his heart.

Perhaps he was a fraud.

She felt as if she were in a trance, wandering back to the rows of garden beds. Had Jacob deceived her? Used her and her community to care for his daughter?

Perhaps he was planning to take this stolen money and run from here.

But why would he take a position on the dredge boat, one of the hardest jobs in the Colonies?

So many transients used their community for food or lodging or even to escape their problems in the world. Was Jacob hiding out in the Amanas? Maybe he thought law enforcement wouldn't find him here, secluded from the outside.

The government may not find him, but God was everywhere. The verse in Numbers rushed through her mind—*"Be sure your sin will find you out."*

No one could hide from the presence of God. Not even in the Amanas.

The writer of the article may claim that Jacob was a thief, but even so, she couldn't reconcile the words in her mind. He was a good father. A good friend. And he'd never stolen anything from her.

She stopped before the bed of carrots, frozen. He'd never stolen anything from her…except perhaps her heart.

*The pure and peace-loving souls arise
from their unworthiness and escape
the wilderness of their own hearts.*

Barbara Heinemann, 1820

CHAPTER 23

All morning Frank worried that someone would ask him about Jacob Hirsch, but no one seemed to guess that Second National was the scene of the embezzlement crime.

Marshall Vicker had fielded a couple dozen calls in the past three days, all of them crank calls. Not one person had given them viable information to begin tracking down Jacob.

Standing behind the teller's cage, Frank recorded the deposits of two customers, and when his customers left, Frank eyed the lobby doors again. Orwin was usually at the bank before nine, often unlocking the door before Frank arrived, but it was almost eleven and his nephew had yet to arrive. He hadn't bothered calling to tell Frank when he would come to work either. Frank had already phoned Orwin's house twice, but no one had answered.

He'd hired Orwin on the request of Alice, his only sister. Alice lived in Pittsburgh, but when he agreed to take Orwin on as his apprentice, Orwin and his family had relocated to Chicago. Over the past year he'd questioned Orwin's competency, but he never questioned his devotion to the work. As the hours ticked by this morning, though, he was beginning to doubt his nephew's devotion.

The telephone bell rang in his office, and he rushed into the other room to take the call. When he heard Orwin's wife crying, he collapsed into his desk chair. "What is it?"

"Orwin...," she started.

"Where is he?"

"He's caught it."

He leaned forward in his chair, trying to understand. "Caught what?" he pressed.

"Diphtheria."

The breath drained out of him, words escaping him.

"The doctor came last night," she said. "We are all under quarantine."

"What about your children?"

"They are all right so far, but I'm keeping them away from him."

Frank's gaze wandered back to the window. Orwin had been sick for the past week, coughing and complaining of a sore throat, but never once had he thought it was anything serious. Diphtheria was reserved for the people in the street tents, not respectable bank clerks.

"What can I do for you?" he asked.

"There's nothing...."

"He's not going anywhere, Lydia," he said, though his assurance sounded hollow. Diphtheria was unpredictable. None of them could control it, and Frank hated anything he couldn't control.

As he hung up the phone, he realized he, too, had been exposed to the disease, but he couldn't close the bank, especially not now.

∼

Jacob wanted to be angry at Liesel—she shouldn't have left Cassie in Homestead for a rendezvous with Emil Hahn. Even so, he couldn't help his smile when he saw her across the brightly colored garden beds, plucking tomatoes from a vine. A dozen eyes followed him as he crossed through the vegetable rows, but Liesel didn't see him until he was a few yards away. When she turned, her face broke into a grin.

Her smile faded quickly though, and his smile fell as well as he reminded himself that she belonged to another man. And the only reason he was here was to check on his daughter.

He glanced around; the entire crew was watching him. "Where is Cassie?"

"In the *Kinderschule*," she replied, pointing her trowel toward a fence behind him. "Why are you here?"

"To see my daughter."

Liesel nodded, but she looked wary. Guilty, perhaps.

"Come, then." She motioned him toward the small school building, and he followed her through the garden. She reached to open the school door, and he caught her arm.

"Wait," he whispered.

Her face was partially hidden under her bonnet, but he could see her eyes, and they looked scared.

He stuck his hands in his pockets. "You could have acknowledged me yesterday."

"What?"

"At least given me the courtesy of saying hello instead of sneaking off."

She shook her head. "I don't know what you're talking about."

"Come on, Liesel." He pointed her toward the shade of an apple tree. She didn't owe him an explanation, but he hoped she would be honest with him. "Who took care of Cassie yesterday?"

She glanced back at the weathered walls. "She was right here."

"You left her here all evening?"

"Of course not. She came home with me."

"I saw you, Liesel." The jealousy was potent in his voice, but he didn't care. "You know I saw you."

"Jacob…"

"If you and Emil want to spend your hours amusing yourselves on a canoe, that's your business, but you promised me that you'd care for Cassie."

"Amusing ourselves?" The color drained out of her face. "What did you see on the canoe?"

"You and Emil…" His voice trailed off. "You were with him."

Her voice shook when she spoke again. "I haven't left Homestead since we came to visit you well over a week ago."

His mind spun with confusion. If Liesel wasn't with Emil, who was the woman in the canoe?

Relief quickly replaced his confusion. It didn't matter who was with Emil. Liesel wasn't on that boat, kissing Emil, nor was she reneging on her promise to care for Cassie. He wanted to pick up and twirl her around like he did his daughter.

Liesel pinched her lips together. "You thought I neglected my duty?"

His hands dug farther into his pockets. "I didn't know."

"Because I promised I'd stay with Cassie."

"I'm sorry, Liesel."

"I wouldn't leave her here without me."

She looked over his shoulder again, and he felt like a heel, telling her that he'd caught her fiancé with someone else. He should have known he could trust her.

Someone tapped his shoulder and he turned around. Niklas Keller was behind him, his face grim. "We have a problem, Jacob."

~

Liesel fell back against the bark of the tree and wiped the beads of sweat off her brow as she watched the two men walk toward the brick church. She'd hoped Jacob would come for a visit soon, but she hadn't been prepared for him to come today. Not after reading that newspaper article.

She removed her bonnet and fanned her face with it. The words of the article rolled through her mind, but even so, the accusations didn't match the honorable man she thought she knew.

Her heart quaked—she couldn't help it. Jacob was in Homestead, and she could only guess as to what Niklas and the other Elders would say to him. He would be asked to leave the community, and Cassie would go with him.

Stepping toward the school, her hands trembled. She had to get Cassie out of school and prepare both of them for the changes to come. There was no time to ask permission from Helene or the Elders. Whatever the consequences, she would face them after Cassie was gone.

A branch cracked under her foot, and she kicked it away. Jacob and Cassie were leaving her, and Emil...

She stopped walking. Jacob saw Emil on a canoe yesterday... with another woman.

What was he doing with someone else? An Amana woman.

The image of Emil courting another woman played in her mind, but the thought didn't upset her like she thought it would. Like it should. Perhaps that was the reason Emil hadn't come— he'd fallen in love with someone else and couldn't tell her. Who had caught his eye while she was away?

It didn't matter, she supposed. The Elders set up the year of separation for this very reason. It was much better for her and Emil to fail now than to fail after they married.

She skirted around the piles of sand and reached for the doorknob on the *Kinderschule*. It was time to let Emil go, but Cassie and Jacob…she didn't know if she could bear to say goodbye.

Let My followers who have remained true and loyal step forth, and I shall speak to them tenderly and ease their suffering and tribulation.

Johann Friedrich Rock, 1748

CHAPTER 24

A dozen rows of simple hand-carved benches ran the width of the church building, facing the pale blue walls on the left of the room. The glass on the windows was clear instead of the stained colors that decorated the church Jacob had attended in Chicago, and the only furnishings were a woodstove and an oak table that stood at the side with a green cloth draped over it.

Niklas pointed toward a bench at the back of the room, and Jacob sat on the smooth wood. The older man took a seat on the bench in front of him.

"You've been with us a month now," Niklas began.

"Yes, sir."

"How is your work on the dredge boat?"

"Very good. Thank you for entrusting me with this job."

"Trust." Niklas said the word slowly. "Trust is a fragile thing."

"Yes, it is."

Niklas passed a newspaper over the back of the bench, and Jacob took the wrinkled copy of the *Daily News*.

"You told us you came from Chicago."

"That's correct."

"What did you do in Chicago?"

Jacob blinked, glancing between Niklas and the paper. Niklas said there was a problem, but until Niklas told him what it was, he supposed he would need to answer his questions since he didn't have a clue why he was here.

"I was a bank clerk."

"What happened to your job?"

He hesitated at the simple question. The answer was easy, yet it seemed that there was much hanging on it.

"The bank lost a lot of money last year when the economy collapsed. They couldn't afford to keep paying all the clerks."

"So you lost your job."

He nodded. "The president dismissed me and another clerk in April."

Niklas tapped his knees, the silence between them begging to be filled. "How did you provide for your family after you lost your position?"

"I had a little money set aside to get us through the first few months."

"But not enough to stay in Chicago."

"No, sir. I'd already spent a good deal of money when my wife was ill."

Niklas paused again. "You were angry when she passed."

Annoyance pricked like needles across his back. "What does this have to do with my work in Amana?"

Niklas paused. "The Elders and I are wondering why you decided to come here."

"I didn't intend to come here.... I purchased train tickets to Washington State."

"Yet you stopped in the Amanas."

"Cassie was sick," he insisted. "I had no choice."

"Even when she was better, you chose to stay."

Jacob shifted on the bench, the newspaper still in his hand. "I was searching for work, sir. You and Adam offered me a job."

The sanctuary door opened, and five other men—Homestead Elders—shuffled into the room. Jacob glanced between the Elders and Niklas. The men didn't approach Niklas and him, instead waiting by the door as if they were guarding it. Something was very wrong, but apparently he was the only one who didn't know what it was.

"Did something happen?" Jacob asked.

Instead of answering his question, Niklas asked him another. "Was there any other reason why you stayed in the Amanas?"

Jacob focused on Niklas. "I don't understand what you're asking."

Niklas stared at him. "Were you intending to hide out among our people?"

His eyes caught the stares of the other men, but none of them acknowledged him.

Puzzled, Jacob said, "I'm not hiding from anyone."

Niklas reached for the newspaper and opened it. In the center of the page, he pointed to a headline—a headline about an embezzler.

Jacob froze when he saw his name.

Stunned, he scanned the article and then read it again, trying to comprehend the words. Was Second National accusing him of embezzlement? That couldn't be. When Frank Powell had removed him from his position, he hadn't taken anything.

He slumped back against the bench. The truth didn't matter. Niklas believed he'd stolen the bank's money, and so did Liesel. That was why her face clouded when she saw him in the garden. She thought he was a thief.

How could she doubt him? They hadn't known each other long, but she should trust him…just like he should have trusted her.

Over his shoulder, he watched the barricade of men move toward them. Were they planning to haul him off to prison until he proved his innocence?

He shoved the newspaper away, and its page scattered on the floor. "This is a lie."

"Why are they accusing you of this crime?"

"They aren't accusing me. There must be another Jacob Hirsch in Chicago."

The men were behind Niklas now, like he needed protection. Niklas picked the newspaper off the floor and found the article again. He read out loud. "Hirsch disappeared on July fifth, and he may be traveling with his daughter, Cassie, a four-year-old with long, auburn hair."

Jacob reached for the paper, and Niklas pointed at the paragraph that clearly accused him of stealing from the bank.

"I don't know why they're accusing me."

Niklas stood up beside the other Elders. "We cannot let you stay in the Colonies any longer, not until we know the truth."

"I understand." He pushed himself to his feet. "I will clear my name."

Niklas bowed his head in resignation. In his eyes, Jacob was a transient who'd landed in their town with a deathly ill daughter. They thought he'd used them to care for Cassie and to escape from his crime. Cut off from most of the world, the Amanas would be a good hideaway, but he hadn't been hiding. He'd been working. Hard.

Did they really think he would be feeding the boiler on the dredge boat if he had twenty thousand dollars to his name? He could think of plenty of other things he'd rather be doing with that kind of money.

He didn't have thousands, but he'd saved fourteen dollars from his work on the dredge. Enough to purchase a train ticket back to Chicago.

"Can Cassie stay with Liesel while I'm in Chicago?"

Niklas sighed, his eyes heavy.

"God knows I am innocent, Niklas."

Niklas looked up at him. "Then He will answer our prayers."

~

As she pushed Cassie on the tree swing, Liesel quietly petitioned God for answers. And she pleaded with Him not to take Cassie—and Jacob—from her life. Not yet.

Cassie stretched out her feet, kicking at the branch above her, and she laughed with delight as the tree rained twigs on her head.

Liesel pushed her again, but her own joy was dampened. Oh, to feel so carefree right now, relief from the burden pressing down on her. If Cassie left her today…

She would miss the girl's hugs after school. Her laughter. And she would miss knowing that Jacob was nearby, that he might come to visit at any moment. She would miss *him*.

He couldn't possibly be guilty of this crime. Even if he was an outsider—and people in the world did things she didn't understand—it didn't mean he'd stolen money.

She glanced back at the church building again. How long did it take to confront a man and seek resolution? The men had entered the side doors at least a half hour ago, and Liesel wished she could climb up a window and steal a glance inside. Cassie fluttered her legs in the air again, oblivious to the tension on the other side of the brick wall.

Cassie's toes brushed the branch again, and as she swung back, Liesel pushed her once more.

The church doors creaked as they opened behind her. Her heart pounded, but she didn't turn around. Seeing Jacob's face right now…it was almost more than she could bear.

"Liesel," Niklas called out.

Slowly, she turned toward him.

The other Elders were gone, but Jacob stood beside Niklas, the pallor on his face gray. He looked like the man she'd found along the railroad track so many days ago. In spite of what she'd read, in spite of what he might have done, her heart broke for him.

Cassie broke the silence with her squeal. "Papa!"

Launching off the swing, the little girl tumbled into the grass and ran toward Jacob. He lifted her, clutching his daughter close to his chest, but he didn't twirl this time. Nor did he laugh.

Cassie placed her hands on his cheeks, forcing him to look in her face. "What's wrong, Papa?"

"I...," he started, but his voice faltered.

"What is it?" she repeated.

"I have to go away," he said simply.

Cassie's lower lip quivered, and as Liesel stepped toward her, Niklas cleared his throat. She faced him.

"I need to speak with you," he said.

She glanced back toward Cassie, aching for the child, but she followed Niklas toward the greenhouse. They passed several women, friends of hers from the garden, but no one spoke to her, not even Niklas. He motioned her inside the empty greenhouse and closed the door.

"Jacob is leaving for Chicago in the morning," he said.

She felt her own lips shake, but she didn't speak.

"He says he is innocent of the crime."

In front of her was a table filled with gardening tools, and she steadied herself on it. "Is he innocent?"

"We don't know," Niklas said with a shake of his head. "Adam Voepel is traveling with him."

"And Cassie?"

"Jacob asked that she stay here...with you."

She breathed deeply of the sweet aroma flooding the air. "I would like that. Very much."

"Liesel..." Niklas cleared his throat. "The Elders and I are concerned about one other thing."

"What is that?"

He hesitated. "What if Jacob doesn't return?"

*When you are inspired by His Spirit to follow
in His footsteps, He shall turn
into a quiet and gentle Lamb and His roar
shall become a holy and mysterious rushing.*

Johann Adam Gruber, 1717

CHAPTER 25

Grasping his satchel in one hand, Jacob clung to Cassie's fingers with the other. Leaving her had never been an option, at least not leaving to travel two hundred and fifty miles back to Chicago, but now he had no choice.

If he didn't go to Chicago, the Elders would notify the newspaper of his whereabouts, and he had no doubt that they could detain him until the Chicago police appeared on their doorstep.

It didn't matter either way. He was innocent, and he would prove it.

The train whistle blasted from the west, the rail rattling. Only moments now before he would be traveling back to Chicago to face this accusation.

Adam was busy saying goodbye to his family beside the station so Jacob stepped toward Liesel.

She stood on her toes to whisper in his ear. "You asked me once what I was afraid of."

He stepped back and looked at the tears in her eyes. "What is it?"

Her voice shook. "I believe I'm afraid of you."

Slowly he lifted her chin. He didn't care who was watching him. "I didn't do it, Liesel."

"I know you didn't take the money." She whispered again, "And that wasn't me on the canoe."

Her gaze arrested him, and more than anything, he wished they were back in the quietness of the doctor's house, alone.

"Are you going to marry Emil?"

She slowly shook her head. "I can't marry him."

The train pulled up beside him, but he didn't move. "I won't be gone long."

"I'll take good care of Cassie."

His daughter tugged on his arm, but his eyes lingered another moment on Liesel's face before he bent down beside his daughter. "You listen to Liesel."

"Of course."

"I'll miss you, Pumpkin."

Tears filled her eyes. "I'm not a pumpkin."

He kissed the top of her head.

"You're my pumpkin," he said, before he forced himself to embark the train.

Cassie slept through the noon hour, but Liesel's eyes wouldn't close. Quietly she shuffled to the desk in her room and sat down in her chair.

Dear Emil, she scribbled with her fountain pen. *We have tested our engagement over the past seven months, and I believe we've failed the test. It is not fair to either of us to continue this facade. I release you from this commitment and ask that you release me as well.*

The words came easily now. They wouldn't be married. Couldn't marry. He loved another, and even if he didn't, she didn't long for him—not as she should. Her gaze wandered out the window. She longed for another man.

Crumpling the paper, she threw it on the floor, on top of the growing pile of attempts to end her engagement. Her thoughts were clear now, but perhaps the words shouldn't come in a letter. Perhaps she needed to communicate them in person.

Cassie stirred on her bed and rubbed her eyes. "I'm not sleepy," she said with a yawn.

Liesel smiled. "I'm glad you didn't get any sleep then."

The girl opened her eyes. "Is Papa in Chicago?"

Liesel looked back out the window and saw two horses pulling a wagon down the street. "Oh, I think he's probably crossed into Illinois by now."

"Do you think he misses me?"

She walked over to the girl and knelt by her bed. "Without a doubt."

Cassie patted her chest. "I miss him too."

The words played like a song in Liesel's mind. "Tomorrow is Sunday."

"Will Papa be back by then?"

"No, not yet." She chewed on the end of the fountain pen. None of them knew how long it would be before Jacob returned. "Would you like to go to Main Amana with me, to visit my father?"

"Oh, yes." Cassie swung her legs over the side of the bed. "I want to meet your papa."

For a moment Liesel hesitated. Her father was wary of any outsider, but even he would be kind to a child. She would visit her father while she was in Amana…and she would talk to Emil.

Niklas may not want her to visit Jacob, but since it had been almost four months since she'd seen Emil, surely Niklas would give her permission to visit the man she'd agreed to marry.

∼

Jacob flung open the doors to the Second National Building and Loan and marched inside. Adam Voepel's heels clicked across the polished floor behind him, but the older man didn't say a word.

"Who's there?" Frank called out from his office, and when Jacob stormed through the door, the color drained from the man's face. His old boss muttered something, his eyes volleying between Adam and him, and then Frank fumbled for his telephone. Hurrying to the desk, Jacob took the earpiece from Frank's shaking hand and hung it up.

Jacob sat in the chair beside Frank's desk, but Adam stood waiting by the door.

Frank's eyes were on Adam.

Jacob leaned forward. "I didn't embezzle your money."

Frank broke his gaze away from Adam. "You took thousands of dollars."

He shook his head. "It wasn't me."

Frank reached over and unlocked the safe near his desk. Shuffling through the paperwork, he picked out a ledger and shoved it toward Jacob. "How do you explain this?"

Jacob opened the book and thumbed through it. It was the ledger they'd used to record transactions when he was working at the bank. His initials, as well as the initials of the other clerks, were scattered across the pages.

At one time this had been his livelihood, recording all these notes. Even during last year's panic, he'd thrived on numbers and serving the people who came to deposit and withdraw their savings. But his days at the bank seemed like a lifetime ago. He'd gone from a comfortable job, working behind a cage, to the backbreaking work on the dredge boat. Still, it was honest work, and he did it honorably...just like he'd worked honorably during his years at Second National.

He pushed the ledger back toward Frank. "I don't see anything in here to explain."

Frank didn't blink. "You can explain why Orwin found the journal in your house."

"My house?"

"He found it under your bed."

Jacob glanced behind him at the window. "Where is Orwin?"

Frank's face paled again. "He's out today."

"Why would I take your ledger, Frank?"

"To cover your steps."

Jacob dug into his inner pocket and pulled out four dollars, the remainder of his earnings. "This is all the money I have to my name."

Frank's lips shook again. "Where did the rest of it go?"

"I didn't embezzle your money." Jacob stuffed the bills back into his pocket. "I've been working on a dredge boat in Iowa to earn a living."

"A dredge boat?"

Jacob reopened the ledger. "Nothing seems amiss here."

"No, this book is just fine." Frank lifted another book from his safe and flipped the pages until he found a specific record. "This is the problem."

Jacob glanced down at Charlie Caldwell's account. The page was riddled with withdrawals from January to April, many initialed by him. Jacob had been at the bank every day, but he didn't recall seeing the judge except on the occasion when he won some money gambling and wanted to keep it in a safe place. Of course, he'd handled hundreds of transactions this spring and couldn't remember everything, but he certainly didn't remember Caldwell withdrawing that much cash either.

He reached for the first ledger, the one Frank had initially showed him. The ledger listed surnames from A–E. Opening the cover, he turned pages until he found Charlie Caldwell's record. In this book, not a single dollar on Caldwell's account had been drawn out.

Glancing back up at Frank, he swallowed hard. "What does this mean?"

"Someone was recording the withdrawals, but instead of giving Caldwell the money, he pocketed it."

"Does Caldwell know?"

"He came in a few weeks back, asking for his money." Frank rapped his fingers on the desk. "I've given him most of it."

"And the bank's surplus?"

Frank shook his head. "It's gone."

Jacob tapped his foot on the floor, turning the pages of the ledger, although he wasn't really reading. Someone had planned well for this, pilfering the surplus a little at a time so Frank wouldn't notice the money slipping out the door. Still, they must have known that Frank would discover the missing money eventually. They probably prepared well for that inevitability.

Jacob slammed the ledger shut. "Why exactly was Orwin in my house?"

"I asked him to try to find you," Frank said. "You were gone, but he found the ledger instead."

"I need to speak to Orwin."

Frank shook his head. "You can't."

"Why not?"

Frank cleared his throat. For a moment, Jacob didn't think he was going to answer. "He's contracted diphtheria."

"Diphtheria?" Jacob stood up and slapped his cap onto his head. "I'm going to speak with him anyway."

"But he's been quarantined…."

"I won't get too close to him."

Frank stood up on the other side of the desk, the earpiece in his hand again. "I can't let you leave."

Jacob heard Adam's boots click behind him as the man joined his side. "I will go with him."

Frank's eyebrows narrowed. "Who are you?"

"Adam Voepel." He stretched out his hand. "I'm an Elder of the Amana Society."

"The what?"

"The Amana Society," Adam repeated. "We are a religious community in Iowa."

Frank's fingers ran down the phone cord. "A commune?"

"We live faithfully together."

Frank kept his eyes on the man. "I can't trust you—"

"Yes, you can, Mr. Powell. I answer to the Almighty." Adam turned toward Jacob. "You're not going to run away again, are you?"

Jacob shoved his hands into his pocket. "I never ran away."

Frank hung up the phone before the police precinct answered his call. Part of him had thought he might track down Jacob Hirsch eventually, but he'd never expected the man to walk through his door. And he certainly wouldn't let him walk away again.

He liked Jacob, and he hoped Jacob was innocent of the crime, but that didn't explain who had stolen the bank's money. If he was going to keep the doors of Second National open and keep himself from being sued, he needed to find out what happened. Perhaps Jacob would lead him to the truth.

As he walked into the lobby, he buttoned his morning coat and slipped his tall hat off the rack. He stopped to lock the bank doors and then motioned for a hansom cab. As Frank clung to the side of the cab, the driver and horse whisked him through the hectic marketplace, toward Lake Street.

What did Jacob hope to accomplish at Orwin's house? If his nephew had known anything about the missing money, Orwin would have told him. After all, the entire bank would become his after Frank retired. There was no reason for him to hide it.

The driver pulled up half a block away from Orwin's small house. Jacob and Adam were already there, opening the picket fence that wrapped around Orwin's neat lawn. Instead of getting out, Frank waited in the cab and watched.

Jacob knocked on the door and then knocked again, but no one answered the door.

Despite their determination, the self-exalting and self-empowered shall fall. Like water, they will not remain stable during times of trial and trouble.

Christian Metz, 1842

CHAPTER 26

The Iowa River bubbled and swirled under the bridge as the rain-soaked horses plodded toward Amana. Cassie leaned over Liesel's lap, looking through the small buggy window to watch the water rush below them, but Liesel forced herself to focus on the trees ahead. The draft horses' gait slowed along the muddy bridge, and Otto Müller clicked the reins. The hooves moved a bit faster, but not fast enough for her.

Water dripped down the glass window, and she was grateful that Niklas not only gave them permission to come to Amana but insisted that Otto take them in the buggy after the morning service. She and Cassie never could have come in this downpour without it.

She glanced down at the river and scooted forward so Otto could hear her from the rear seat. "Does the water seem high to you?"

He clicked his tongue. "The highest I've seen in my lifetime."

Otto had come with the Society from New York in the 1850s, so he'd driven wagons and buggies across the Iowa River for a good forty years now.

"Is it safe to cross?" she asked.

"*Ach,*" he said, as he flicked the reins again. "It's a little too late for us to wonder now."

Seconds later, the horses trotted off the bridge and into the forest, and Liesel eased back against the cushioned seat. They wouldn't be swept away by the river, at least not today.

Cassie scooted closer to her, looking up. "Does the river scare you?"

"No...," Liesel began—but that wasn't true. The river terrified her. "Yes, it does."

"Papa loves the water."

"Your *Vater* knows how to swim."

Jacob had probably never read *Der Struwwelpeter* as a child either. He didn't know that Johnny Look-in-the-Air almost drowned in the river.

"Does your papa know how to swim?" Cassie asked.

"No."

"Hmm..." Cassie's gaze wandered across the trees as they trotted out of the forest. The flooded land ahead looked more like a lake than a field. "What does he know how to do?"

"Well, *mein Vater* can build just about anything with wood. And he is a really good leader. All sorts of people come to him with questions, and he helps manage the community's money."

Cassie nodded, looking much older than her four years. "My papa *ravages* money too."

She started to correct the girl, but Cassie kept talking.

"What about your mama?" the girl asked. "What does she like to do?"

Liesel looked at the horses as they walked through the water, their beautiful manes drenched by the rain. What did her mother like to do? "I don't know."

"My mama liked to give me kisses," Cassie said. "And she liked to sew. She made me the prettiest dresses when I was a baby."

"I'm sure she loved you very much."

The girl's head bobbed up and down. "That's what Papa says."

"Do you remember her?"

"A little." Cassie reached for Liesel's hand and sighed. "Not so much."

Liesel squeezed her hand. "I don't remember *mein Mutter* much either."

"Is she in heaven too?"

Liesel pressed her other hand against the cold glass. "I don't think so."

"Well...where did she go?"

"No one knows."

In front of them was the village of Amana, cloaked in a mantle of gray. Grapevines laced the trellises at the edge of town, and the woolen mill towered in the distance. On the hilltop above Amana was the smallest village in the Colonies, East Amana. Most of the three thousand sheep needed for the woolen mills were kept in East Amana's immense barns on the village's edge, and their bleating could be heard across the valley.

Liesel's father had been born in Ebenezer, New York, and his family migrated to Iowa in the 1850s. Her mother's parents were from Iowa City, and they joined the Society soon after the migration.

Her parents married in 1862 and Main Amana became their home. They were married almost a decade before she was born, but something had happened to her mother after Liesel's birth. Something her father never discussed. Liesel was born in Amana twenty-two years ago, but when she was three years old, her mother decided she didn't want to live as an Amana any longer. Her mother left the Society in 1875, and Liesel grew up without brothers or sisters or a second parent.

The years passed, her father refusing to speak about her

mother, though he never married again. She suspected that her father still loved the woman he'd married so long ago.

As she grew up, Liesel had heard the whispers of other colonists, and sometimes she heard them today when she was working around the older women. No one faulted her for her mother's decision, but she felt as if she were marked for life, like the others expected her to leave for the world as well.

They were wrong. She would never leave the Amanas.

The buggy wound through Main Amana, and Otto turned onto a side street. Her father lived in a brick home right beside the church. Before Liesel stepped out of the buggy, she opened her umbrella and motioned for Cassie to follow. The girl eyed the umbrella and the storm clouds overhead.

"It's okay," Liesel said, but Cassie shook her head.

Sighing, Liesel retracted the umbrella, and when she held out her wet hand, Cassie clutched it. Rain drenching their hair and dresses, they ran toward Albert Strauss's home.

Jacob curled up the collar on his raincoat and knocked again on Orwin Tucker's front door. A quarantine notice was plastered across the pale green paint, but he ignored the warning. He'd already been exposed to the disease…and he'd taken the antitoxin. God, in His mercy, had spared him from the disease, and now he needed to find the truth to clear his name…and return to the Amanas.

Instead of venturing into the rain this afternoon, Adam opted to stay back in the boarding room he'd rented for a week and pray. Jacob fought his generosity at first, wanting to pay his share for the room, but he'd swallowed his pride and let Adam pay. Even though they were hundreds of miles away from Homestead, the Society continued to provide for both of them.

The Elders may have sent Adam with Jacob to keep him accountable, but since they'd arrived in Chicago, Jacob realized that Adam Voepel was trusting him to do the right thing. The man hadn't expressed it in words, but Adam seemed to believe he hadn't stolen the money. If he thought Jacob was a thief, he never would have let him come to Orwin's house unescorted.

Jacob wouldn't run, and Adam knew it. Everything that was important to him was in Amana. The only reason he had come back to Chicago was to clear his name.

Jacob rapped on the door again.

Yesterday he'd seen someone at the window peeking out at him. All he wanted to do was ask a few questions, like how Orwin had come into possession of a second set of ledgers, because he knew for certain that Orwin didn't find the ledgers under his bed.

The curtain moved in the window beside him, and he saw the face again. A woman. He pointed for her to open the door, and she shook her head. When she disappeared from the glass, he pounded on the door again. She could ignore him, but he wouldn't leave until he spoke with someone inside.

Seconds ticked by, and he lifted his fist to knock again. The lock clicked, and the woman he'd seen in the window opened the door. She couldn't have been much older than twenty-five, but her face looked aged. Hair escaped in frazzled strands from her bun, and her once-fashionable dress was soiled.

She tapped on the notice. "Can't you read?"

"I need to speak with Orwin."

"Go away."

He didn't falter. "I've already been exposed to the disease."

"Go away," she repeated, motioning with her hands for him to leave.

"And I've taken the antitoxin."

She eyed him warily. "Why do you need to speak with my husband?"

"I have some questions about the bank."

"That's no reason..."

"Urgent questions," he interrupted. "About the books. If we don't straighten this out, he'll be livid when he returns to work."

"I don't know if he'll be returning...." Her voice shook, but she slowly opened the door. "It's your life, mister."

Mrs. Tucker stepped aside, and he slipped into the sitting room. Deep red curtains decorated the sitting room along with a table of potted ferns, and above the piano was a portrait of Orwin and his family. A boy and a girl about Cassie's age sat on the rug near the piano, jacks scattered around their feet. Both children watched him intently, but neither spoke.

"Hurry now," Mrs. Tucker said, shooing him away from her children.

It wasn't hard to find Orwin's sickroom; the rancid smells of whiskey and urine saturated the hall. Orwin lay against a pillow, his neck swollen and open sores festering on his cheeks and arms. The man opened his eyes and blinked, staring at Jacob like he'd returned from the grave.

"Hello, Orwin." He twisted around a chair to face the sick man's bedside. "I'm sorry to hear you've been ill."

"You're not supposed to be here."

Jacob sat down on the chair. "I thought you'd want to see me."

Orwin coughed. "What did you do with the money?"

Anger lanced his chest, and he wanted to reach out and shake the man in front of him, no matter how sick he was. "You know I didn't take the money."

"Frank will prosecute you. He will get it back."

Jacob scooted the chair a few inches closer. "Where did you find that ledger?"

Orwin ignored his question. "You can't steal all that money and get away with it."

"This is an opportunity for you to do the right thing, Orwin.

You can pay back all those who've lost their money before it's too late."

Orwin shook his head. "You pay them back."

"The money doesn't belong to you, Orwin. If the bank goes under, it'll put hundreds more people on the street. They trusted you and Frank, and you're failing them."

"Failing them? God is the one who's failing them."

"This isn't about God. It's about man's greediness."

"Do you believe in God?" the man asked.

"Very much."

The man smirked. "He took your wife."

"God has taught me much over the past month," Jacob said slowly. "Most of all, He's taught me to trust in Him."

"Trust? He can take your life too." Orwin tried to snap his fingers. "Just like that."

"Yes, I suppose He can, and when it's time for me to go home, I'm ready."

"You're a fool, Jacob."

"I don't think so." He stood up. "A fool would be someone who steals money and refuses to admit it. And a fool would leave this world without asking God to forgive him of his sins."

"Get out!" Orwin shouted. "You're not welcome here."

He stepped toward the door. "Jesus can rescue your soul, Orwin. It's not too late to make it right."

Silence followed him out into the hallway, followed by a curse. Mrs. Tucker was waiting for him outside the door.

"Uncle Frank is missing money?" the woman asked.

"At least twenty thousand dollars."

"God is a merciful God," she said.

"That He is."

"He can forgive my husband."

He nodded. "If he asks…"

Mrs. Tucker locked the door behind him, and he jogged

down the steps. Perhaps Adam Voepel would let Jacob join him in prayer.

*While I have the power to do all things,
speaks the Lord, I want your will, your faith,
your love and your obedience.*

Barbara Heinemann Landmann, 1880

CHAPTER 27

Liesel carried the kerosene lantern down from the guest room, into the sitting room on the first floor. In the corner, her father was hunched over a writing desk, and she stopped at the doorway, watching the man who'd cared for her since she was born. He loved her like Jacob loved his little girl.

This was the house where she'd grown up, in the small bedroom beside her father's room. Three other families lived on the first and second floors of the large house, the residents in the home changing over the years as some members of their Society had married while others had gone on to meet their Lord.

Except for the cry of a baby above them, the house was quiet tonight. As she tucked Cassie into bed, Liesel began telling her a grand story about a princess who wasn't afraid of the rain, but the child didn't stay awake long enough to hear how the princess rescued Robert and his red umbrella from the sky.

Her father lifted his head. Behind his spectacles, his tired eyes smiled at her. "Come, dear," he said in German, patting the wooden chair beside him. "Sit and keep your poor father company."

She crossed the room and kissed the bald spot on his head. "My father has never been poor."

He took her hand. "You're right, Liesel. God has blessed me in abundance."

"It's time for bed, *Vater*."

He spread his hand across the pile of papers. "Not yet for me."

She glanced over at the papers and books on his desk. "What are you doing?"

"Willhelm asked me to balance the accounts for the village."

"But, *Vater*…," she began to protest.

He held up his hand. " 'Tis only temporary."

"You must sleep as well."

He shook his head. "It's my duty to serve the community."

She set the lantern on the table as he resumed his notations in the books.

Her father already provided all the town's carpentry needs as well as leading church services and prayer meetings at least twice a week. The Council of Elders took turns handling the outside accounts, but it was too much for her father to carry this load as well. He was more worn than she'd ever seen him before, and as he recorded the transactions, he moved like someone had tied shackles around his wrists and ankles.

Setting his pen on the desk, he stopped to rub his temples.

She pushed her chair closer. "What is wrong?"

"It is nothing."

"Your head aches?"

He picked up the pen again. "There's no reason for you to worry, Liesel."

"You are doing too much, *Vater*. It is wearing you down."

"Emil is helping me more at the shop."

"That is good."

"If only I were better with numbers…"

She slid the ledger off the table and spun it around. "Why don't you read me the receipts and I'll record them?"

"You don't have to…"

"Let me serve as well."

Picking up the receipts, he began to read the amounts on each form, and for the next hour they worked side by side, father and daughter. He read the expenses for items like coffee and shoes purchased outside the Amanas, property taxes and new equipment for the mill, as well as the income for the sales of woolen goods to suppliers in Des Moines and Iowa City. She recorded the expenses and income, and together they added and subtracted to total up how much the Amana Colonies had in reserve.

She'd never thought much of how complicated it was to keep track of what they'd earned and what they were spending. Except the Council of Elders who governed the entire Society, no one in the Amanas worried about money nor even thought much about it.

Her father's eyelids drooped, and she nudged his shoulder. Never before had she been so grateful that the Elders shouldered this load for their community.

After her father read the last receipt, she shut the ledger and her father set his spectacles on top. "I will miss you when you are married."

She couldn't stop the shiver that ran up her spine. What would he say when she told him she was ending her engagement to Emil?

"But you will be right down the street, of course," he said. "You will visit me often, *ja?*"

"*Vater…*"

He stopped her. "Emil will make a fine husband for you. He will never leave you, nor will he take you away from here."

"I'm sure he will make a fine husband…" She hesitated. "Just not for me."

The baby cried out again overhead, but her father didn't speak. Instead, his lower lip rumbled, like the dam of a river about to crack. She braced herself for an explosion.

When he spoke again, his voice was quiet. Too quiet. "I've heard rumors about you and the worldly man."

"I don't want to talk about him."

"Several have said you've become too friendly with him."

"They shouldn't be gossiping."

"Sometimes there is a thread of truth in gossip."

Her hands twisted in her lap. "We spent a week together at the doctor's house, *Vater*. We should be friends."

"You shouldn't have stayed at the doctor's house."

"I had no choice." A protest bobbled on his lips, but she spoke again before he did. "You would like Jacob if you met him."

A grunt escaped from his lips. "I have met him, and I can't say I liked him much."

She tapped her foot on the floor. "When did you meet him?"

"He helped me take apart the bridge on the Mill Race." Her father paused. "He's a terrible carpenter."

She couldn't help but laugh. The Elders probably said the same thing when they discussed her cooking skills.

"He may be bad at carpentry, but he has a good heart."

Her father sighed. "*Your* heart is what I worry about, Liesel. This man is being accused of embezzlement."

"The accusations are false."

Her father stood up and stepped toward the window that looked out onto the dark street. "It is not my position to question his goodness or even the state of his soul. What I question is your relationship with a worldly man."

"How can he be worldly if he worships the same God as we do?"

"He may not come back, Liesel." Her father turned, facing her again. "And if he does, he won't stay."

"You don't know that...."

"The Elders met yesterday." He hesitated. "If Jacob returns to the Amanas, they will ask him to leave."

"But Niklas—he promised him work for the summer."

"The Elders will compensate him for what they promised."

The flames seemed to spin inside the lantern's glass, and she felt as if she were falling. "You're going to bribe him to leave?"

"Not bribery, my child. We're helping him…and we're helping you."

"It doesn't help either of us for him to leave."

"It is our duty to protect you."

"Even if you do this…" Her voice broke. "Even then, I cannot marry Emil."

"You don't know that for certain. Not now."

"I do know."

He moved toward her and picked up her hands, pleading with her. "All I ask is that you wait to tell Emil. There is no need to rush."

Her mind rushed back to what Jacob had told her, about Emil on the canoe with another woman. Could Jacob have lied to her about Emil? Maybe he'd been lying about many things. Maybe she really didn't know him.

Shaking her head, she cleared her thoughts. Jacob had done nothing to make her doubt him. He would clear his name in Chicago and come back to the Amanas and then— then her father and the others would ask him to leave.

Even if Jacob was lying about the canoe, the truth was still the same. She no longer wanted to marry Emil, and if the canoe story was true, apparently Emil didn't want to marry her either.

"I have to tell Emil," she insisted.

He put her hand on his heart. "Out of respect for your poor father, please wait a few weeks before you do this."

"You are not poor...."

"I'm not asking you to marry him, Liesel. I only ask that you delay breaking your engagement."

Honour thy father and thy mother: that thy days may be long upon the land which the Lord thy God giveth thee.

She dropped her father's hand. "I will wait for two weeks before I talk to Emil, but it's not fair to him nor to me to wait any longer."

~

The next morning Liesel's father insisted they stay for breakfast before Otto and his horses carried them back to Homestead. And not only did he want them to stay for breakfast, he insisted they walk two blocks south in the rain to eat buckwheat cakes at Schmidt's Kitchen instead of eating in their normal dining hall.

Liesel knew exactly what her father was doing, but she didn't protest. She couldn't help but wonder how Emil would react when he saw her.

Cassie clung to her hand as she trudged along beside her, still groggy from the early morning bell.

Liesel hadn't slept much last night, nor could she stop thinking about Jacob. For most of her years, life had been filled with wonder. She'd marveled in the strength of her friendships and the beauty of God's creation. Every day her schedule was the same, yet within the routine she delighted in the abundance around her.

Some days, however, she longed for fresh joy to well inside her along with a new hope for the future. Ever since Jacob and Cassie arrived in Homestead, predictability had vanished from her life. Even the hours she spent in the garden were filled with anticipation. Purpose. Joy. She loved her hours with Cassie. Loved wondering what it would be like when she saw Jacob again. And she loved feeling his firm fingers intertwined with hers.

Perhaps her father was right. Perhaps she had become too friendly with Jacob Hirsch. She'd allowed herself to care too deeply, and when the Elders asked him to leave, the pain would sting for weeks and months to come. Even so, she wouldn't trade her days spent with Jacob and Cassie. Not for anything.

Her father opened the door to the Schmidt house, and she and Cassie stepped into the hot kitchen. Grease sizzled on the stove top as the *Küchebaas* barked out orders for her crew. The aromas of bacon and maple syrup urging them forward, Cassie tugged on her hand to hurry.

Liesel's stomach grumbled, but she hesitated at the arched entrance into the dining hall. All eyes would be on them when they walked into the room, and she had to be strong.

She tried to bow her head, to walk quietly to her table, but she couldn't help skimming the heads of the men and women waiting for their food. Her gaze stopped on the blond-haired man at the left table. The clamoring and clattering from the kitchen behind her seemed to stop, and all she heard was quiet.

In the briefest of moments, she searched Emil's eyes...and what she saw in them confirmed what she already knew. He wasn't the least bit excited to see her. Instead, he looked almost scared. He broke away his gaze, focusing on the table, but she couldn't take her eyes off him. Why didn't he have the courage to tell her that he cared for someone else?

"Liesel!" Someone squealed beside her, and she turned to see her friend Margrit balancing a huge platter of buckwheat cakes in each arm. Margrit set both platters on a table and embraced her with a hug.

When Liesel stepped back, though, she saw doubt drift across her friend's face. Did Margrit question her relationship with Jacob too? Margrit knew she wouldn't run away with a worldly man…nor would she do anything to compromise her faith or her purity.

"Are you all right?" Liesel asked.

Margrit nodded back toward the kitchen. "I must go."

Liesel stepped back. "Of course."

Margrit bustled back to her work in the kitchen, and Liesel and Cassie slid into the remaining two seats at one of the women's tables. She ate two slices of bacon and a bowl of milky oatmeal, but she couldn't eat the bread Emil and his father had baked that morning.

As she spooned syrup over a helping of the hotcakes, she glanced again at Emil. He didn't look her way.

Oddly enough, she wasn't angry at his indifference. Irritated, perhaps, and even a bit curious, but seeing him confirmed what she already knew. His heart belonged to another…and so did hers.

*Continue the battle, withstand all suffering
and trial, survive until the end;
then you will receive the crown of honor.*

Johann Friedrich Rock, 1741

CHAPTER 28

Jacob turned the page of the ledger, his eyes weary as he compared the numbers on the doctored ledger alongside the original book. Whoever mastered this plot had been frighteningly patient and detailed with their work. The forged initials resembled perfectly his and Bradford's and Orwin's initials. No one would suspect that the men hadn't withdrawn the money. Perhaps, from now on, Frank should have the customers sign when they took money from the bank, instead of relying on the clerks.

Hours passed at an agonizing pace as he searched the books for some sort of answer. He was anxious to find a solution to this debacle, and he was even more anxious to get back home.

The telephone rang in Frank's office, but the man's door was shut, so Jacob couldn't hear what he was saying. Perhaps another customer was attempting to withdraw money from the empty vault.

For the past three days, he and Adam had prayed every morning and evening against the enemy's deception, and as Jacob poured over the ledgers at the bank, he could hear Adam whispering prayers at the desk behind him. Frank had yet to follow through on his threat to call Marshall Vicker at the newspaper, and as far as Jacob knew, he hadn't called the police either.

Jacob was fairly certain he knew who took the money, but without some hard evidence, he couldn't prove Orwin's guilt. Perhaps that was why Frank didn't call the precinct. Perhaps he suspected that Orwin took the money as well.

The door to Frank's office opened and his former boss stepped into the room, but he stopped to steady himself on the edge of a desk. Before Frank spoke, Jacob knew what had happened.

"That was Orwin's wife," Frank said, his voice sounding far away. "Orwin passed on this morning."

Poor Mrs. Tucker and their children. The months ahead would be tough for them. "Are his wife and children still well?"

Frank clung to the edge of the desk. "She and the children haven't showed any symptoms yet, but the department of public health is keeping them under quarantine for another week."

Jacob stared back down at the numbers. Without Orwin's confession, he would never be able to prove his own innocence. Even if Frank didn't have enough evidence to convict him, Liesel and his Amana friends would doubt him. He wanted Liesel to know she could trust him. Always.

He closed the ledger. "What do we do now?"

Frank cleared his throat. "Orwin's wife asked one favor."

"What is that?"

"She wants to speak with you."

"Me? She wasn't too pleased the last time I was there."

"I don't know why, but she said it was urgent."

It was too rainy to work in the gardens this morning and too wet to be wandering around outside as gallons upon gallons poured over their village. If God had cursed the Egyptians with a plague of rain instead of frogs or locust, Liesel was certain it would have been just like this. Homestead's streets swam with mud, and the walkways had turned into streams weaving between the buildings.

Liesel no longer tried to keep her dress clean, nor did she scold Cassie for letting her hem drag in the puddles. There was no washing off the mud until Monday's laundry day and no hope of staying dry either.

Fortunately she and Cassie didn't need to leave their house to eat—but even more than food, they needed to pray, so once a day they ventured outside for *Nachtgebet*. She and Cassie had spent hours this week in the sitting room, playing with Cassie's toys, reading from her Bible, and making puppets and dolls out of paper.

Two other families and an elderly woman fondly named Tante Salome joined them in the sitting room this afternoon. Greta's daughter, Magdalena, had given Cassie one of her dolls when they were quarantined at Dr. Trachsel's, and now Magdalena shared her dollhouse as well. The two girls giggled as they played, and Liesel preferred their laughter to the pounding rain.

In her lap were two letters delivered by the morning train. One was addressed in Sophie's familiar writing. The other handwriting wasn't as familiar, but her heart leaped when she saw the name on the return. Jacob had written a letter, just for her, but she couldn't bring herself to open it quite yet. She was frightened that his news might not be good.

Tearing open Sophie's letter, she read her friend's words about the rain drenching Cedar Rapids as well. Even with the rain, though, Sophie wrote that she was beginning to enjoy the bustle of the city. She'd obtained a recipe book, and with the instructions, she'd learned she could make almost anything she wanted to eat in her stove.

Sophie said she missed the Amanas and all her dear friends, but Liesel would adore the funny variety shows that played in the theater called *vaudeville*. And had Liesel ever heard of a library? In Cedar Rapids, the library housed thousands of books, and Conrad told her she could check out five at a time. Five new books every week.

There was a museum in the city with beautiful art and a park along the river where she could stroll when her baby arrived. A church down the street held quilting bees every Tuesday, and there was a new department store near their boardinghouse with bolt after bolt of fabric available for purchase. Once Conrad began practicing law, she would have the money to dress in the latest fashions instead of her old calico dresses.

Liesel dropped Sophie's letter into her lap, and the smile on her lips slipped away as well. Her friend was happy at last, or at least contented in Cedar Rapids. She should be happy for Sophie, but after reading her friend's words, she couldn't muster happiness at Sophie's enthusiasm for fabric and museums and the library.

How could new dresses and artwork replace the kinship of the Colonies? Here Sophie had family and security and a place to serve God, but nowhere in her letter did she mention evening prayers or worship.

Cassie and Magdalena sang a silly song, dancing together with their dolls. Salome laughed as she knitted a pair of stockings, asking them to do it again. Greta soothed her newborn in the rocker, and the others in the room were reading or talking quietly.

None of them noticed her fingers trembling as she slipped Sophie's letter back into the envelope and stared at Jacob's letter in her lap.

She wanted him to return to the Amanas, yet when he did, her father and the Council of Elders would ask Cassie and him to leave. Perhaps she could write him, warn him of their decision. Perhaps he could think of some reason to change their minds.

Slowly she pulled Jacob's letter out of the envelope. What if, like Sophie, he was writing her to applaud all the luxuries of the city? His delight would only widen the gulf between them, reminding her that Jacob wasn't accustomed to the simple ways of their Society. He was used to the museums and library and department stores. The outside world was where he belonged.

Sinking into herself, she stared at the neat lines of his writing. Even more than reading about the wonders of city life, she was afraid his letter contained a confession of some sort.

Perhaps he was writing to tell her he really had stolen the money like the paper said.

She'd learned how to forgive, but once someone misused her trust, it was almost impossible for her to trust them again. She would love as God called her to do, but she couldn't trust someone who'd lied to her. Someone like Emil…

Emil hadn't actually lied, she supposed, but he certainly hadn't been honest with her. Whether or not Jacob had seen him with another woman, it was clear that Emil had changed his mind about their relationship. He just hadn't bothered to tell her yet.

When she left the kitchen house on Monday morning, she'd expected Emil to wait for her so they could have few moments to talk before she left for Homestead. Instead, all she saw was the cut of his shoulders as he rounded the corner of the street toward the bakery. Even her father had been surprised.

Her fingers brushed over the fold of Jacob's letter. She would never marry Emil, but what if Jacob wanted more from her? What if he asked her to leave the Amanas to be with him?

Never once had she traveled outside the seven villages that made up the Colonies, and while she often wondered about the outside world, she never wanted to leave here. Could she find good on the outside, like Sophie had?

She glimpsed back up at Cassie, now playing on the floor with her friend. God help her, if Jacob asked her to leave with Cassie and him, she didn't know what she would do.

She opened the letter and saw her name at the top.

Dear Liesel.

Heat rose up to her cheeks, and she kept her head bowed, hoping no one saw her blush. Her eyes focused on the first lines of his letter, but before she began to read his words, someone opened the door to their house and stomped into the sitting room. Dr. Trachsel stood before them, his cloak soaking the rug. Liesel wasn't concerned about the rug, but what she saw in the doctor's eyes petrified her.

"What is it?" she demanded.

"Your father…," he began. "He collapsed in his shop."

She bolted out of her chair, both letters falling to the floor as she tried to process the doctor's words. Leaning over, she quickly gathered up the letters and stuffed them into her pocket. "What is wrong with him?"

"I don't know yet," Dr. Trachsel said. "But Dr. Eisenberg is working in West Amana today. The Amana Elders sent a messenger asking me to come."

She didn't have time to seek permission, but Niklas and the other men would have to understand. "I will go with you."

The doctor nodded. "We must leave right away."

Glancing back across the room, she found Cassie still playing at the dollhouse, lost in her own world.

Greta spoke from the rocking chair. "I'll take care of her, Liesel."

"But your baby…"

"Cassie and Magdalena will help me while you're gone."

Cassie turned to Liesel, her own small eyes filling with concern. "Are you leaving?"

She rushed to the girl and knelt down. "My father's ill, sweetheart. I must go to him."

The girl nodded.

"Will you help Greta while I'm gone?"

Cassie eyed the door. "I can help you."

Liesel glanced back at Dr. Trachsel. He gave her a slight but firm shake of his head. "Not this time, but I will come back soon."

Cassie's lower lip trembled, and the girl reached out and hugged her. Liesel's heart tore, wanting to stay and care for Cassie yet needing to go to her father. She stepped backward and when she lifted her umbrella out of the stand, Cassie rushed to her, reaching for it.

"Please, no…"

Rain dripped down the window beside the door, but even so, she wouldn't scare the child. She leaned down, kissing Cassie on the cheek, and slipped the umbrella back into the stand.

"There is no reason for you to be scared, Cassie."

The girl's eyes were wide. "Yes, there is."

Liesel wanted to protest, say that nothing bad would happen to her, but she couldn't assure a child who'd already lost her mother and didn't know when her father would return.

She knelt down beside Cassie. "You are God's child, Cassie. He will take care of you."

"I love you, Liesel."

She hugged her again. "I love you too."

Her heart was full as she walked out the door, and she tried to reassure herself. There was no reason for her to be afraid.

I, the Lord, shall forever bless the obedient children who live in accordance to their faith.... You will have enough and plenty and shall no longer be servants to those who seek only money.

Christian Metz, 1842

CHAPTER 29

The afternoon sun sweltered Chicago's marketplace. Bells chimed on the delivery carts, and vendors shouted out to Jacob.

Fresh fish. Pretzels. Raaaspberries.

The smell of leather, sausages, and coal clung to the stale air and the hundreds of people who crowded around him. Mrs. Tucker had asked him to hurry to her house, but he didn't want to spend the little money he had on a hansom cab. Instead he rushed through the busy streets by himself.

When he left Chicago, he thought he would settle into another city like Spokane so Cassie could enjoy all the modern conveniences while he worked. But after his weeks in the Amanas, city life no longer appealed to him. Now he missed the trees. The rolling fields. The beautiful lake filled with lilies. Even on the hot days he spent feeding the boat's boiler, he could jump into the Mill Race for a cool swim after he finished his job and eat his supper on the quiet canal banks.

As he walked, he could see the white rotunda of the World's Fair on the skyline. Just last year, when the economic status of their country hadn't seemed so ominous, twenty-seven million tourists came to Chicago to paddle the lagoons, gawk at the exhibits, and ride the giant Ferris wheel—but the gaiety met an abrupt end when Carter Harrison, the city's mayor, was assassinated.

A wave of solemnity washed over the city with the death of their mayor. It was almost as if the gluttony of entertainment left the entire city with a bellyache...not just from the fair, but from the prosperous years before the fair as well.

"Italian i-cees," a vendor yelled in Jacob's ear.

He missed the tranquility of the Amanas. The solemn stillness that allowed a person to contemplate. He couldn't imagine a single man or woman in the Amanas shouting at another to buy their vegetables or meat. They viewed each other as friends instead of customers. None of them were pressured to stand out on the street and yell louder than their neighbor to make a living.

Not all the people he'd met in the Amanas had befriended him, but they'd been honest with him from the day he arrived, and they'd valued both Cassie and him. He felt more at home in the Amanas than he'd ever felt in Chicago.

He'd never known his father, and his mother had died before his fifth birthday. The German language and traditions reminded him of his comfortable childhood years he'd spent with his grandparents.

He wanted to give Cassie the gift of a home. Security. He'd experienced that security when he was a child and again during the five years he and Katharine were married. When his grandparents passed on, followed by Katharine's death, he never expected to regain this sense of place again. But in the Amanas he felt rooted again in his faith and in his hope for the future. He'd made his peace with God.

Jacob turned onto a side street and made his way into a neighborhood with small homes and even smaller yards. At the end of the street, he stopped in front of the white painted house

Katharine and he began renting months before they welcomed Cassie home. The grass was overgrown and curtains were closed, just as he and Cassie had left it a month ago. A monarch fluttered by, and he watched the butterfly hover over Katharine's prized rose bush and disappear around the side of the house.

Someone else could have moved into his home by now, but it didn't matter. Chicago held memories of his loving wife, Cassie's birth, and their years spent here as a family, but he didn't belong here anymore.

Water splashed along the sides of the buggy as Dr. Trachsel pressed the horses forward. Closing her eyes, Liesel prayed in earnest for her father and silently scolded herself for not doing something earlier to help him.

When she'd seen how tired he was, she should have usurped his authority on Monday and asked the head Elder to relieve her father of his financial duties. He would have been furious at her for embarrassing him among the other Elders, but she could handle his wrath. What she couldn't handle was losing him.

"Hold on," Dr. Trachsel said beside her, and she clasped the side of the buggy as they crossed the bridge above the churning waters. The river had swollen even higher in the past forty-eight hours. Another foot or two and it would crest over its banks.

Homestead was built on a hill, safe from the river, but Amana was in the valley. What would happen to their main village if the river broke over the bank?

The draft horses hauled their passengers through the flooded field, and after an hour of slow travel, the buggy arrived at her father's home. Emil dashed out the front door to take the horse reins from the doctor, but she didn't acknowledge him. Picking up her skirt, she rushed into the house.

The village midwife scooted out of the way, and Dr. Trachsel threw his drenched cloak and hat over a hook and rushed to her father's bedside.

"All this fuss," her father said with a valiant smile. "And there's nothing wrong with me."

While the doctor listened to his chest and checked his pulse, Liesel felt as if her own pulse was about to explode. She couldn't watch her father slip away, not even to enjoy eternal life. His soul was ready to meet His Maker, but she wasn't ready for him to go.

Emil was beside her now, and she could see the worry mirrored in his face. "Is he going to be okay?" Emil asked.

"Shh…," she whispered. He waited beside her in silence until Dr. Trachsel motioned them into the hallway.

"What's wrong with him?" she asked.

The doctor stuffed his stethoscope back into his black bag. "He's exhausted, Liesel."

"So he needs a few days of rest…."

"Not days." His eyes were sad. "It may be weeks or even months before he can return to work."

"He won't stay away from the carpentry shop for weeks."

"He doesn't have a choice." The doctor eyed the door. "Ruth can care for him until Dr. Eisenberg returns, but we must leave for Homestead before the river overflows."

"We can't leave yet," she insisted. "We should spend the night."

He shook his head. "I have patients I must care for in Homestead."

"I will stay here, then."

"It may be days before you can return."

"*Vater* needs me to care for him."

"Are you certain?"

"Greta is watching Cassie, and as long as it rains, I won't be needed in the gardens."

"I will tell the Elders you are here." Dr. Trachsel removed several small boxes from his bag. "Albert will need a grain of quinine every hour in a teaspoon of brandy, and the potassium bromide will help him rest."

She held both boxes to her chest. "Will he be okay?"

"As long as you can keep him in bed…"

"I won't let him move."

"And I will help her," Emil said, stepping up beside her. "He won't get past both of us."

"Very good," Dr. Trachsel said. "When Dr. Eisenberg returns, he can assist you with further medication."

The doctor slipped his hat on his head, and rain blew in through the open door as he left the house. The lantern flickered in the hallway, and she turned to face Emil looking down on her.

"It isn't necessary for you to stay," she said.

"I will sleep in the sitting room…in case you need me to go find help."

Three families lived on the second floor of the house—any of those men could go for help if she needed it—but she didn't protest Emil's words. Not because she wanted him to stay, but because she knew he would argue and she had no energy left to fight.

If he wanted to, he could sleep in the sitting room. She would stay vigilant by her father's bed.

"Liesel…," he said as she stepped toward her father's door.

"What is it?"

"We need to talk soon."

"Yes." She patted Jacob's letter inside her apron. "Yes, we do."

∼

Mrs. Tucker answered the door before Jacob knocked. Her red-splotched cheeks were stained with tears, and her voice was strained when she invited him inside. He didn't ask about the children but assumed they were playing in another room.

Mrs. Tucker sat on the couch and pointed for him to sit across from her. "I'm sorry for your loss," he said as he squirmed in the uncomfortable chair.

She blew her nose in a handkerchief. "Orwin told me that your wife passed on last year."

"She did."

"And you still mourn?"

"I'm still sad when I think of her, but God has been faithful to my daughter and I."

"*Aye*," she said. "I pray for His faithfulness…and I pray that God will forgive us too."

"God always forgives."

"I'm not sure this time…." Her words trailed off.

He thought back to his train ride out of Chicago and his anger toward God. He'd practically cursed His Creator and even still, God hadn't let him go. "I haven't deserved God's love, but I've learned that nothing is outside God's span of forgiveness."

"I don't know, Mr. Hirsch." Leaning down, she slipped a large metal box out from under the sofa. Then she reached into her pocket and held out a key.

He stared at the key for a few moments before looking back at the box again.

Could it be?

His hands shook as he took the key from her hand, and he looked over at her face again. Tears fell fresh down her cheeks.

He didn't reach for the box. Not yet. "Where did you find this?"

Instead of answering the question, she told him a story. "My husband never trusted in himself and his abilities. His mother, you see, planned most of his life. He wanted to become a teacher, not a banker."

She blew her nose again. "He couldn't refuse his uncle's offer at Second National. With his mother's urging, he packed up and moved us to Chicago, but he was never happy in his work."

"So he stole money?"

"I don't believe he meant to. At least, not at first."

"All the entries were from last winter and spring."

"He began…" She sighed, fanning herself with her hand. "He began to go see a psychic in January to ask for advice."

"For his work at the bank?"

"That's how it started. He didn't know if he should stay at the bank or pursue another career. He didn't believe in the power of prayer, but the psychic, well, she gave him tangible answers."

"The woman recommended he embezzle the money?"

"She told him his life was short and he needed to prepare for the future."

"Aah…so he prepared by taking other people's money."

"I'd like to think he was doing what he could to provide for his family."

"And you knew about this?"

"Oh no, not about the money. I told him the psychic didn't know what she was talking about. He would never die." She blew her nose again. "But I was wrong."

A psychic could predict Orwin's death but could do nothing to offer him life.

"It doesn't excuse what he did." She sniffed. "But it helps me to understand."

"A man will do about anything for his family," he said, and she responded with a small smile.

"Orwin kept the key around his neck, but I never knew what it was for. Before he died, he gave me the key and told me to look in our linen trunk for a box." She wiped the tears off her face. "He said the money was supposed to take care of us."

Time seemed to stop as Jacob slid the key into the lock and slowly turned it. He knew what was inside, yet he couldn't help but gasp when he saw the stacks of U.S. notes in denominations of twenty, fifty, and a hundred. He lifted one of the stacks from the pile and fanned it. There were thousands of dollars' worth of notes in here. Perhaps twenty thousand.

At the bottom of the money were two ledgers, and he lifted them out and flipped through one of them until he found Marshall Vicker's record. According to this ledger, Marshall Vicker hadn't taken a cent out of his account.

He looked back up at the woman. "This could have taken care of you for the rest of your life."

She shook her head. "It doesn't belong to me."

"Did Orwin set any other money aside for you?"

"A little at the bank."

He sat back in his chair, the metal box heavy in his lap. He couldn't fault Orwin for wanting to provide for his family after he was gone, but it didn't make it right to steal from men like Stanley Roberts who'd saved for hard times. Or even men like Marshall Vicker who wanted a new boat.

"Can you take it back to the bank?" she asked.

He nodded as he stood up. "What will you do now?"

"We'll be going back to Pennsylvania to stay with my brother."

He was relieved that she had someplace to go. "Do you have enough money to get to Pennsylvania?"

Her fingers drummed on her lap. "My brother will send me extra if I need it."

He opened the ledger in his hand and found the record for Orwin Tucker; his former colleague had twenty-five dollars in savings at the bank. Opening the metal box, he took out a twenty-dollar note along with a five and handed it to Mrs. Tucker.

"Bless you," she said.

He thumbed through the money again, removing three hundred additional notes, and held the money out to her. She jumped back in her seat like he'd offered her a vial of arsenic.

"I can't take that."

"It's the reward money," he explained. "Frank offered it to whoever recovered the money."

She stared at the money but didn't extend her hand.

"You don't have to spend it on yourself." He glanced over at the doorway and saw her two children peeking through the entryway. "Use it to take care of them."

Her gaze traveled over to her children before returning to him. "Are you certain about the reward?"

"God blesses honesty, Mrs. Tucker." He held it out to her. "And I'm certain Frank Powell would keep his promise to reward you for your honesty as well."

*In this time, when temptations are great
and subtle reason sits upon the throne,
do not let your power of discernment be taken away.*

Johann Friedrich Rock, 1745

CHAPTER 30

Frank almost leaped out of the cab when he saw the box under Jacob's arm, but Adam blocked him from stepping into the street.

"Let Jacob finish his job."

"But what if he…"

Frank couldn't bring himself to finish the sentence. If that box contained what he thought it did, his livelihood—and his reputation—rested in the arms of Jacob Hirsch. His former employee had proved himself trustworthy, but the temptation of that much money would weigh heavy on the strongest of men. It might be unbearable for an unemployed man with a child.

"We will watch him, *ja?*" Adam said. "Make certain he finishes well."

Frank tried to sit back against the padded seat, but his chest felt like it was about to explode. During his many sleepless nights, he'd imagined what it would be like to recover the bank's money, but as the weeks passed, he'd lost hope that he would ever find Jacob or the money.

Now the money appeared to be found, but Jacob hadn't

stolen it. Frank had been swindled by his own nephew—the man to whom he'd planned to leave his business. Instead of raising an heir, he'd trained a thief.

At least he had discovered the truth before it was too late. Or, rather, Jacob had discovered it.

Jacob climbed into a black cab in front of them, and Frank shouted up to their driver, telling the hackman to hurry.

He breathed deeply, trying to stay calm, but a new thought bubbled in his mind. What if Orwin and Jacob were in collaboration? Orwin may have passed on, but even now Jacob could take the money. Or maybe Orwin wasn't even dead. This could be the next step in their scheme to steal from the bank.

He glanced over at Adam. The man's face was calm, though his lips moved in earnest and his eyes were focused on the hansom cab in front of them. Frank hoped God heard the man's prayers…and he hoped Adam wasn't in on a plan to take his money too.

Jacob's cab turned right, and their hackman followed.

No matter what happened, Frank wouldn't let Jacob out of his sight. The money belonged to Caldwell, Marshall, Stanley, and the rest of his customers. They'd hired him to protect it, and he'd do everything he could to get it back into their hands.

An elevated transit rattled over the trestle above Jacob's cab. The buggy vibrated with the clatter of the railway, and he clutched the metal box with both hands so it wouldn't drop to the floor. As soon as he was back at the bank, handing the box over to Frank, he would be a free man again. His name would be cleared, and he could hop on the next train toward Iowa so he could surprise Cassie and Liesel with the good news.

Minutes later a commuter train blocked the road in front of his cab, and he tapped the lid of the metal box as they waited for the train to pass. No one knew how much was in this box except Orwin. Mrs. Tucker hadn't counted it, and Frank didn't know yet that Orwin had stolen the money.

He slid his hand across the cool metal lid. He didn't need thousands of dollars, but five or six hundred would help him purchase a nice home in Iowa. When the economy returned, he could obtain a position at another bank.

Reaching up, he fingered the key around his neck. It was almost as if God had delivered this gift right into his hands. Justice. He could pocket a thousand dollars and Frank would never know. Or two thousand.

He closed his eyes, his imagination wandering. What would happen if he jumped on the next train out of town with the entire money box? It might be hours before Adam even knew he was missing, and then there would nothing the man could do about it except catch the morning train home. He could sneak Cassie out during the night...and convince Liesel to come with him too.

He raked his fingers through his hair.

Adam was right—the enemy was real, and it was in moments like this that the opposition was strong. It would be so easy to steal this money and disappear.

Emil went out in the rain to fetch hot coffee along with some cheese and bread. Though her father was too weak to get out of bed this afternoon, he was awake and hungry. Liesel insisted that he rest, like the doctor said, but he listened to her as well as he'd listened when she told him to find someone else to balance Amana's books.

He kept trying to stand up even though his legs wouldn't support him, and each time he tried, she had to lift him back into the bed.

Albert wiped his glasses on his nightshirt. "Bring me the ledgers," he grumbled. "At least I can do that in bed."

Her fists flew to her hips, and she shook her head. "I will most certainly *not* get you those books."

"I can't be idle, child. I'll lose my mind as well as my strength."

"There are other ways to occupy your mind, *Vater*."

"My mind is not easily appeased."

Liesel reached for one of the old leather books and opened to the printed words of their leader Christian Metz's testimony in 1834. Sitting back in the chair, she began to read.

"The name Jesus is indeed a mighty fortress to all who seek His protective care. He is a soothing power wherever He speaks and whenever He makes His presence known. The name of Jesus is a healing balm to all who come to Him.

"He is the true Healer for all who, unreservedly, entrust all pain, injury, and illness to His care. To them He will administer the good medicine which, though bitter to the taste, has the power to penetrate body, soul, and spirit, dissolving all hardness of heart."

The inspired words of their *Werkzeuge*—the men and women God used as instruments to communicate to their Society—lingered, and for a moment she thought she'd upset her father with the choice of her testimony. His gaze wandered from the raindrops on the window back to her face.

"Thank you, Liesel," he said. "It is good to hear about our true Healer, *ja?*"

"Yes, it is."

"You are very much like your mother. She loved to read."

"My mother?" she said quietly. Her father never talked about the woman who'd left both of them so long ago.

Liesel closed the dusty book and placed it on the nightstand. "What else did Mother like to do?"

"Aah...so many things." He sighed, the lingering sadness

woven into his words. "Rachel loved walking by the river and singing the hymns. She loved pretty things...and loved to dream about wearing fancy dresses and hats. The Elders warned me about marrying her because she longed so often for worldly things, but I wouldn't be convinced otherwise."

Liesel leaned closer, her mind longing for the truth. "Why did she leave us, *Vater*?"

"Her parents didn't join the Society until Rachel was twelve years old."

"*Ja*, I know."

His voice sounded weak as he wrestled with his next words. "She was old enough to remember the world and its entrapments. And she longed for them."

"Why didn't she leave when she was of age instead of waiting until..." Her voice cracked, but she was determined to hear the truth. "Until after I was born?"

"Rachel didn't want to leave back then. She loved her parents, and I like to think she loved me as well. Our first years of marriage were good. She was content in her work at the mill, and she seemed happy in our home too."

"And then you had me."

"We were blessed with you, Liesel."

"She didn't want to have children, did she?"

"She thought she wanted children...." He cleared his throat. "You were a good baby, but she didn't know what to do with you."

"So one day she decided to leave...."

"She didn't just decide, Liesel." Her father's face paled. "There was a man who came to Amana. A salesman."

She set the book of testimonies into her lap. "Oh, *Vater*."

"He was a handsome man and he told such wonderful stories about the outside world. She couldn't seem to help herself."

"So she ran away with him...."

"Not right away." Her father's voice sounded small. "He left months before she did, but I found their letters, and when I did....she packed up and never returned home."

Liesel blinked. "Why didn't you tell me?"

"I thought one day she would return, asking for forgiveness. I would forgive her and we would resume our life as a family. The community knew she left, but no one knew she went to live with an outsider. I didn't want them to know that when she came back either."

"Do you still hope?"

"I have hope in God but no hope that Rachel will return. A decade ago someone sent me a letter with no return address. Inside was an obituary for a Rachel Barington, born in Iowa City on August 12, 1842. The day your mother was born."

"So she's gone forever."

"*Ja*, she is, but I try to recall the good memories with her instead of the bad ones."

Liesel gently squeezed her father's arm. He'd carried this burden for so long, protecting both his daughter and the wife whom he'd loved. Rachel Barington had left him alone in this world to raise their child, and even so, he'd been willing to forgive her. That was true love.

"Not all outsiders are bad, *Vater*."

"Perhaps not, Liesel, but you and I—we don't belong to the outside world."

A protest formed on her lips—Jacob Hirsch was different than other outsiders and very different from this salesman who had seduced her mother. But what could she say to convince her wounded father that their community should welcome an outsider into their fold? Few joined their Colonies over the years, but most of those who did join served faithfully until their deaths. Her mother was an outsider at birth and chose to leave this world on the outside as well.

She'd relished the words in Jacob's short letter while her father slept last night. He had assured her again that she could trust him and that he would return soon. She wanted him to hurry back to her, but she was also scared that her father was right...and when Jacob came back to town the Elders wouldn't let him stay.

The front door opened outside the room, and someone stomped across the hallway. Emil stood at the doorway seconds later, panting. His dripping slicker left a puddle on the floor.

Liesel stood up. "What is it?"

Emil took a deep breath before he spoke. "Schmidt's basement is flooding."

He, the Lion of Judah, roars mightily to awaken and invigorate all who have sunk into a deathlike sleep. Stirred to jump to their feet, they no longer choose the anxieties of this world over God's peace.

Johann Adam Gruber, 1717

CHAPTER 31

Frank swore as the hansom cab turned the corner and dumped them onto another frenzied street. Cabs scurried in every direction, their drivers dressed in identical black cloaks and hats. Cyclones of paper swirled over the cobblestones as horses scuttled through the trash-filled streets, vendors shouted at the hurried crowds, and bicyclists wove through the throng.

If Jacob hopped out into this street, they'd never find him. There were a million hiding places for him and the money.

The horses on their cab turned left on Clark Street, toward the bank, and Frank held his breath as they neared Second National. There was no other cab waiting on the street, nor was Jacob standing outside the locked doors. Adam didn't speak, but he was scanning the sidewalk too.

Frank pounded his fist into his palm. He'd had Jacob in sight along with the bank's money, and he'd let him walk away.

Did Jacob know he was being followed? Perhaps Jacob and Orwin had collaborated all along. Now that Orwin was gone, Jacob had control of their cache...or was Orwin really gone?

Maybe his nephew was waiting someplace for Jacob and the two would escape together.

Frank's head spun as he paid the hackman and stepped out before Adam, onto the wooden sidewalk. He unlocked the bank's doors, but he left up the nickel-plated sign stating they were closed so that none of his customers could watch him break down.

Inside the lobby, his heels clapped as he paced the floor. He should have overpowered Adam and taken the box when he had the opportunity. Everything he'd worked for, everything men like Stanley Roberts and others had worked for, it was all gone. He'd sell everything he had to cover his losses, but it wouldn't be enough to save the bank. One of the most respected banks in Chicago would disappear, and then who would people trust with their money?

The bell clattered with the opening of the door, and he held his breath until he saw a man's cap. And his face.

Jacob had returned, the metal box in his hands.

Frank stammered over his words. "I—I didn't think you were coming back."

Jacob took a key from his neck and held it out to Frank. "It's not mine."

The metal seemed to tingle in his hands as he slid the key into the lock and turned it. Inside the box were stacks of bills. Money that belonged in his vault.

He clasped the box to his side. "You've—you've saved the bank."

"Mrs. Tucker saved it by returning the money."

Frank set the box on a desk, pulling out the notes. "I owe you the reward."

Jacob shook his head. "I gave the reward money to Mrs. Tucker."

Frank blinked, marveling at the honesty of the man he'd thought was a thief. "That's commendable, Jacob."

"It was the right thing to do."

Frank motioned for Jacob to take a chair beside Adam, a plan formulating in his mind. Orwin was gone, and he needed someone to take over the bank when he retired. Someone he could trust with his accounts…and his customers.

He sat down behind the metal box. "I've been working at this bank for almost fifty years."

"Yes, sir."

"My father passed the bank on to me, but I have no son to take over my family's work and follow me as president. I had hoped my nephew would…." He twisted the key in his hand. "I'm planning to retire next year, and I need to train someone to take my place. Someone with integrity."

Jacob scooted forward a few inches, listening to him.

"You know this bank, Jacob, and you've proven yourself to be someone I can trust." He closed the lid of the box and locked it. "I would like to extend the offer to come back to Second National with the intention of taking over as president next year."

Jacob rubbed both ears as if his hearing had failed. Frank smiled back at him with a mix of relief and desperation before repeating the offer. He wanted Jacob to move back to Chicago and take over management of Second National Building and Loan.

Both Frank and Adam watched him, expecting him to accept the offer, but the affirmation froze on his lips. This was what he'd wanted for his career—a viable position with the promise of promotion. And now Frank was offering him an opportunity for security and success. His worries about money would be over. As president of Second National, he would be able to provide for Cassie for the rest of her life.

But he didn't want Cassie to just have a nice home; he wanted her to have a heritage. To grow up in a place like Homestead where people rallied around and supported each other. A place where people loved God and expressed their love for God by caring for each other.

He lowered his eyes. In his mind he saw the pristine blue of Liesel's eyes, and he could almost feel the touch of her hand in his. She would never move to Chicago, and he—he couldn't move back here without her. He didn't want to move anywhere without her.

He blinked and sat tall in his chair. "Thank you for the offer, Mr. Powell, but Chicago is no longer home for me."

Frank stared at him in disbelief. "I'm offering you my bank, Jacob."

President of Second National Building and Loan. The title echoed in his mind as he contemplated the offer one last time, an offer he would never receive again. His grandfather would have been proud.

"I'm honored that you would trust me with this responsibility, and a few months ago I wouldn't have hesitated to accept this position—but much has changed since I left Chicago."

"You're turning down my offer?"

Jacob nodded. "I am."

Frank cocked his head. "Who is she?"

"What?"

"There must be a girl in Iowa."

Adam was beside him, listening to his words, but Jacob was tired of pretending. "My daughter is in Iowa…and so is a woman I've come to love."

"Aah…" Frank sighed. "I can't argue with love, no matter how fleeting."

"This isn't fleeting, sir."

Unlocking the box again, Frank opened the lid and counted

out three hundred dollars before handing the money across the desk. "You are still entitled to the reward money."

Jacob tucked his hands behind him. "I can't take it."

"For heaven's sake, Jacob, you don't have to use it for yourself. Use it to buy something...for both of your girls."

With God's help, he'd resisted taking the money in the cab, but three hundred dollars would give him the freedom to stay near the Amanas for the winter and perhaps longer. He glanced over at Adam, but the man didn't say anything.

"There is more than enough here to give Caldwell and the others what I owe them," Frank said.

So Jacob took the money—more money than he'd ever pocketed before—and stood up.

"I wish you'd reconsider my other offer."

He slowly smiled. "I'm sorry, Mr. Powell, but I've got to go home."

"The basement of Schmidt's Kitchen is flooding," Emil blurted from the doorway. Liesel looked out at the rain pounding the streaked window. It had hammered them relentlessly during the past twenty-four hours.

Albert flung off the comforter. "We've got to help."

Liesel picked the bedspread off the floor and put it back over him. "You're not going anywhere, *Vater*."

Her father pushed away the comforter a second time and slid his feet off the bed onto the wood floor, but when he tried to stand, he stumbled again. Emil rushed forward and caught him before he hit the floor.

Her father tried to stand again, but he was too weak. She patted the quilt softly. "Come back to bed."

He tried to resist, but he was too weak to walk on his own. Emil helped him ease back onto the bed.

Still, her father refused to lay back against the pillow. "They will need every hand to get the water out of the basement."

"There are already a dozen men bailing out Schmidt's," Emil said. "We need to get you upstairs."

Liesel glanced around the room. "The water won't come in here...will it?"

"No one knows."

"I'll be fine," Albert insisted, but Emil didn't listen to him and neither did she. Leaning over, Emil tucked his shoulder under one of Albert's arms, and she ducked under the other to lift him back up. Her father protested as the three of them walked toward the steps, but he didn't struggle. If he did, he would fall back to the floor.

A door opened above them, and Wendel Faber, the town butcher, rushed down the stairs. He stopped in front of Emil. "Do you need help?"

"Of course not," Albert said, but the butcher ignored him, waiting for an answer from Emil instead.

"We can help him," Emil said. "They need you over at Schmidt's."

The man nodded and jogged down the rest of the steps.

Albert groaned. "They need me at Schmidt's too."

"You'll be better in no time." She squeezed her father's hand. "Then you can help."

They escorted Albert to a guest room on the third floor, at the far end of the hall, and Emil helped him settle into the bed.

Her father pushed his glasses back up his nose and patted Emil's arm. "You're a good son-in-law."

Liesel's head lurched up, wanting to scold her father.

Emil avoided her gaze. "I'm not your son-in-law, sir."

"*Ja*, but you will be soon, and that will make me a happy man."

Liesel stood frozen by the bed, trying to ignore the contented smile on her father's face along with the silence that pervaded the room. How was she supposed to end her engagement with Emil while her father egged him on?

Emil flashed an apologetic smile at her. "You are already a happy man, Albert."

"*Doch*," he replied with a wave of his hand. "I will be much happier when Liesel marries you."

"*Vater!*"

"She will be much happier too."

It seemed as if someone had sucked the air from the room, and she felt like she might faint. Emil's plastered smile looked like it was about to crack as well.

"Your daughter doesn't need me to be happy."

Albert grumped at him, and Liesel needed to do something...say something. At that moment, she wanted to remind her father that she couldn't marry Emil—but looking into his tired face, she knew she should wait until his strength returned.

She wiped her sleeve over her forehead. No matter what happened, she couldn't marry a man she didn't love, not even for her father.

Footsteps pounded down the hallway, and Wendel Faber stuck his head through the doorway. "We need you, Emil."

Emil backed toward the door. "I'm coming."

Through the window, Liesel watched Emil and Wendel wade through the rising water. And she prayed that God would have mercy on their town.

*In order for a soul to find its origin
in the true place of peace and rest,
a pure-intentioned heart is required.*

Christian Metz, 1834

CHAPTER 32

*J*acob clamped his hand over his jacket pocket as he and Adam elbowed their way through the crowded street. He couldn't remember the last time he'd carried so much money—money he was entitled to spend. "Can we catch the train tonight?"

Adam tugged on his watch chain to check the time. "We're too late," he said, tucking the watch back into his pocket. "But the Rock Island leaves at six in the morning."

Jacob was tempted to jump on another freight train instead.

"We'll be back in Homestead tomorrow afternoon," Adam said.

Jacob's heart leaped at the thought of seeing Cassie and Liesel. He would be back in the Amanas with the women he loved, and he didn't want to leave again. Ever.

Michael said it took years for someone new to be accepted into the Amana Society, but he had years. He already embraced the Amana work ethic. Their faith. If they let him stay, he would work hard to earn his keep.

Someone bumped into Jacob, knocking him off the curb. He didn't see the horse behind him, but Adam reached for him, grabbing his elbow to pull him back up as the animal passed. He took a deep breath of relief before he thanked the man.

As they waited to cross Monroe Street Adam fiddled with his pocket watch, and Jacob knew the man was just as anxious to get back to Homestead as he was. Adam didn't have to come to Chicago with him, yet he came willingly to help Jacob clear his name.

Unlike many of the leaders in the world who were intent on serving their own needs, the Amana leadership served their community. They didn't hoard money for themselves or build larger homes or buy finer horses. Instead of seeking power, they sought after God.

He crossed the street beside Adam, but on the other side of the street, a display window caught his attention and he stopped in front of it. Necklaces and bracelets glittered in the sunlight, and a braided silver ring with diamonds lay swathed in blue velvet.

His fingers rapped on the glass, and he knew exactly what he was supposed to do with a portion of the reward money.

When he started for the door, Adam stopped him. "What do you need in here, my friend?"

"I just want to look."

"Jacob." Adam reached for his shoulder, his eyes sad. "You can't marry her."

A horse stomped in a puddle beside them, spraying mud across their clothes.

"You will break her heart," Adam said.

"I would never do anything to hurt her."

"Perhaps not intentionally." The man hesitated. "Mr. Powell offered you a good opportunity with the bank."

"I can't move back to Chicago. Not without Liesel."

Fear flickered through Adam's eyes. "One of the women could bring Cassandra to Chicago tomorrow."

"You don't want me to return to Homestead?"

"I don't want you to take Liesel away from us."

Jacob met the man's intense stare. "I'm not going to take her away."

Sweat poured off Frank's forehead as he climbed the steps in the tenement building. The stairwell smelled like sewage and rotten meat, and the banister was coated with black coal dust. He wanted to turn around and ride back to the refined walls of his bank, but before he could plan for the future of Second National, he needed to mend what he could from the past.

At the top of the steps, he unbuttoned his collar and fanned himself with the envelope in his hand before he knocked on the door marked EIGHT. A child with a sagging diaper and a crusted nose peeked out from behind it. The boy's chest was bare, and in this heat, Frank was tempted to shed his own vest and shirt as well.

"Is your father home?" Frank asked. The child scurried away, leaving him to swelter in the hallway.

A full minute passed, during which Frank felt like he could dissolve onto the dirty floor, when the door opened a bit wider. He hardly recognized his former customer and friend. Stanley Roberts's cheeks had sunk into his bones, and his clothing hung off his body like a rag doll.

"What do you want?" Stanley asked.

"I wondered how you were doing."

A child cried in the background. "My hundred dollars may not have seemed like much to you, Mr. Powell, but it was everything we had."

Frank shifted the envelope into his other hand.

"Something happened at the bank yesterday," he started. "I discovered that one of my clerks was embezzling money."

Stanley blinked, but no emotion registered on his face. "Embezzling?"

Frank held out the envelope. "He stole your money, and I want to give it back."

Stanley didn't hesitate. He reached for the money, clutching it to his chest.

"You trusted me for years," Frank said. "Please forgive me for not trusting you as well."

Stanley opened the envelope, and his eyes welled up. "There's a hundred and fifty dollars in here."

"Is that all?" Frank dug in his pocket and pulled out fifty more dollars he had rolled up inside. Jacob had given Mrs. Tucker the reward money, and he would give this man extra for what he'd endured over the past month. "It's supposed to be two hundred."

Stanley stared at the cash in his hands. "But..."

Frank didn't wait for Stanley to protest, but he heard the man thank him as he climbed back down the steps. Hopefully, the money would be enough to get the Roberts family out of this rat hole and buy Stanley a suit so he could find a new position.

Outside, Frank climbed into the waiting cab and told the hackman to hurry back to the bank. With the exception of his nephew's death and his sister's denial over what had occurred, the past was settling nicely behind him. It was time to look to the future, and Bradford Pendleton was coming in an hour to discuss how to regain Second National's reputation and reserves as president of the bank.

Gray light wisped through the wet leaves and branches outside Jacob's window, rain splattering across the glass. Adam snored in the passenger seat beside him, worn out from the six-hour ride, but Jacob couldn't sleep.

Only a month ago, he'd arrived in Homestead hopeless and broken. So much had changed since his last journey from Chicago. Through the simple life and faith of the Amana people, God healed his spirit and Cassie's body and welded the broken pieces of his life. He felt like a new man on this trip. The old one had passed away.

As the train slowed its pace, his pulse quickened. They were almost to Homestead, and he didn't care what anyone else thought. In minutes, he would gather the two women he loved into his arms, and he may not ever let them go. This was where he belonged.

Reaching into his pocket, he pulled out a small cloth bag and emptied its contents into his palm. He didn't have enough to purchase the diamond ring, but he'd purchased two other rings. The larger silver one was engraved with a wreath of flowers that reminded him of the flowers on Lily Lake. The Amana women may not be allowed to wear jewelry, but he hoped Liesel would keep it in her trunk or somewhere else to remember how much he cared for her.

The smaller ring was silver as well, embedded with a tiny heart—and it held a promise to his daughter. Even though he may have to leave for days or weeks to work, he wanted her to always remember that he would never leave her alone.

The brakeman opened the door of their compartment and shouted, "Homestead!"

Adam jumped, and Jacob hid the rings in his pocket as the train's wheels squealed against the tracks. Squinting into the storm, he looked to see if anyone was outside, but even the animals seemed to be hiding from the rain.

Adam shuffled into the aisle. "Niklas will be waiting for a report."

"Could I see Cassie first?"

Adam nodded. "Of course."

Jacob reached for his satchel overhead and pulled it down. "Jacob…"

He faced the man. "Yes."

Adam put his hat on his head. "I never thought you were a thief."

"You doubted my word."

"I hoped you were telling the truth, but I had to be certain. Outsiders have failed us before."

The train braked, and Jacob steadied himself on the seat. "I want to earn your trust."

Adam nodded. "We must trust each other…and the people who stay with us."

Jacob clung to his cap as they stepped out into the storm, his satchel flapping in the wind. The sheep bleated from the barn, and rain dumped on his head. Adam turned toward Niklas's home, but Jacob ran to see Cassie and Liesel.

Several women worked in the kitchen below Liesel's room, and he greeted them as he rushed by. At the top of the stairs, he pounded on the door to Liesel's room, but no one answered.

"It's Jacob," he said as he knocked again.

A door across the hall opened and he heard Cassie call out to him. "Papa!"

He dropped his satchel as he turned, his arms stretched open. Cassie bounded into his arms, and he held her close, smothering her with kisses.

From the doorway where Cassie ran, a young woman emerged with a baby in her arms. "You have a fine daughter, Mr. Hirsch."

He ruffled Cassie's messy hair. "Yes, I do."

He looked back at the woman. "Is Liesel with you?"

"Oh, no. She went to Amana."

Amana? Jacob squeezed Cassie a little closer. Had Liesel gone to visit Emil while he was gone?

"Why is she in Amana?"

"It's her *Vater*," the woman said. *"Er ist krank."*

"Do you know what's wrong with him?"

"Nein."

He set Cassie on the ground. "Can you get your coat and hat on quickly?"

She smiled. "Faster than lightning."

"I don't know…lightning's pretty fast."

She raced toward the open door.

*The wind blows where it will,
and while you hear its rushing, you do not know
where it comes from, nor where it goes.*

Johann Friedrich Rock, 1732

CHAPTER 33

Cassie clung to Jacob's hand as they stepped inside the sitting room in Niklas's home. Adam was in a chair beside the woodstove, and another Elder sat beside him.

Niklas shook his hand. "We've been anxious for you to return."

"I've been anxious as well."

Niklas nodded toward the two Elders. "Adam told us your good news...and he told us about the offer you received to return to your position in Chicago."

Jacob squeezed Cassie's hand. "I'd prefer to return to my work here instead."

"Chicago is home for you, *ja*?"

"Not anymore."

"You are a hard worker, Jacob, and we've appreciated your contribution to dredging the Mill Race. And we've enjoyed getting to know your delightful daughter as well. I believe she's stolen the heart of every woman in Homestead."

Cassie stood up on her toes and grinned at the men, but Jacob's stomach started to sink. They weren't going to let him return to the Amanas.

Niklas turned to his wife. "Hilga, could you show Cassie one of our puzzles upstairs?"

Hilga stepped toward his daughter. "Certainly."

As Cassie walked out of the room, Jacob clutched his hands in front of him. It felt as if his wrists were tied to the railroad tracks. He would have to beg this man to save his life. "I'd like to stay in the Amanas, Niklas. I've been faithful with my work here, and I will continue to do so."

"Jacob…"

"My name is cleared," he persisted. "Adam can tell you that the accusations were false."

"The embezzlement charges no longer concern us."

"I thought you needed someone to work on the dredge boat."

"Right now, we are most concerned about your friendship with Liesel Strauss."

Jacob looked over at Adam, but the man wouldn't meet his eye. Had the Elder told them about his stop at the jewelry store?

"I have treated Liesel like a sister."

"You've been honorable, Jacob, and we commend you for it…but you must understand, it is our position to protect her and the others in our community. Many of us worry that if you stay much longer, you will take Liesel with you when you leave."

"I wanted to speak with you about that…."

"There are better places for you and your daughter to live, Jacob. If you don't want to go back to Chicago, perhaps it is time for you to travel on to Spokane."

"I don't want to leave the Amanas."

Niklas ignored him. "We are asking you to leave right away, before you see Liesel again."

"But…"

Niklas held out a small canvas bag. "We will give you your unearned wages for the remainder of the summer."

Jacob stuck his hands in his pockets. "It's not about the money."

"Our Society exists because we have strict faith in God and in each other. We pray and work to keep evil at bay and those vices that tempt our young people to long for the world."

"I'm not a vice, Niklas."

"Perhaps not, but you will take Liesel out to the world with you."

"I don't want to take her away. I want to stay here."

"It will never work," Niklas interrupted, holding the money in front of Jacob's face.

He didn't take the bag. "You can't pay me to leave."

"There is no place for you to live in the Amanas."

"No...but I could live over in Marengo or Iowa City. You can't stop me from seeing her, Niklas."

Niklas sighed. "I guess you will have to hear it directly from her."

His heart sank. "Does Liesel want me to leave?"

Niklas lowered the money back to his chest. "She..."

The faint toll of a bell rang out in the distance, interrupting his words. The room grew quiet, and Jacob listened as Adam counted each successive ring. *Two. Three. Four.*

Adam reached for his coat and hustled toward the door.

"Hilga?" Niklas called out—but his wife was already there, Cassie beside her.

"What is wrong?" she asked.

"The emergency bells are ringing in Amana." Niklas looked out at the dark clouds. "The river must be rising."

Jacob pulled his slicker back over his arms. "How do you know they're ringing in Amana?"

"Those are the only bells we can hear."

Jacob kissed Cassie on the head again. "Can you stay with Mrs. Keller?"

She grabbed his arm. "The storm, Papa."

"I'll be all right."

"You can't go out in the storm."

The tears on her face almost made him change his mind, but Liesel was in Amana. He had to go help her and the others. "Please, Papa."

"Pray for us, Cassie," he said. "God hears your prayers."

Niklas stepped in front of him. "You're not coming with us, Jacob."

Jacob didn't stop buttoning his slicker. "Yes, I am."

"No—"

Jacob looked over at him. "How are you going to cross the river?"

"I—I don't know."

"I can get you across."

A resigned look replaced the worry in Niklas's eyes as the man thought for a moment and then waved him forward. "Come along."

～

Her father was napping when Liesel crept out of the room and down the hallway to find a lantern. She could hear the Faber children playing in their room, but other than their laughter, the hall was quiet. The kerosene in her lantern was gone, and she didn't want to risk going out in the storm to refill it at the general store. There were at least two other lanterns down in the sitting room filled with kerosene. No one would mind if she borrowed one until she could refill hers.

The bucket brigade hadn't been able to get the water out of the Schmidt's cellar, but they'd moved most of the stored food to a higher level. Now Emil and the other men were at the church—or at least they had been three hours ago when Emil brought food for her and her father.

As she stepped onto the first floor, her boot sank into the soaked rug. She jumped back onto the step and looked across the entryway in the dim light. Had someone left a window open?

Stepping onto the drenched floor, she crossed the sitting room and snagged a lantern. Before climbing back upstairs, she lit the lantern and her stomach plunged when she saw water seeping underneath the front door, pooling in the entryway.

Rushing into her father's room, she grabbed several sheets and towels and stuffed them into the base of the doorway. Then she gathered a stack of the Society's ledgers into her arms and hurried upstairs. Thankfully, her father was still asleep, oblivious to the rising water.

She set the books on the dresser and rushed back down the steps to rescue the *Inspirations-Historie* from the rising water. She had stayed as far away as possible from the river, but now the river was coming to her.

The rowboat was exactly where Jacob remembered it. He pushed back the overgrowth and tugged the boat out by its rope handle. Below him the Iowa River spilled over her banks and rushed through the trees, toward Main Amana. The bridge at the bend was submerged under the flooding.

Jacob held up a paddle to the eight men who'd ridden with him from Homestead. "Who wants to cross the river with me?"

Niklas slipped off his horse and handed the reins to the man next to him. "I will go."

Adam got off his horse next. "Me as well."

Another man started to dismount, but Jacob stopped him. "The boat can't hold more than three of us."

"Can it even hold three of us?" Niklas asked.

Jacob patted the wood. "We will hope."

Adam pulled his hat closer to his eyes. "And we will pray."

The four bells rang out again from across the river, pleading with their fellow brothers and sisters for help.

"Let's hurry," Niklas said. The men along the bank helped them carry the boat down to the river, the current racing past their feet.

"Do you know how to swim, Niklas?"

The man shook his head, and Adam did the same. "If we capsize, you need to hang on to the side of the boat until we get back to shore."

"You think we can make it across?" Adam asked.

"If we paddle hard." He handed Niklas a paddle. "Paddle with everything inside you."

Adam's lips were moving, and he hoped the man was praying for all of them.

Several Elders attempted to steady the bow of the boat while they climbed aboard. When the Elders released the boat, Jacob plunged his oar into the swirling waters.

"Paddle!" he yelled, and Niklas's oar thrust into the river on the other side of the boat.

Rain doused Jacob's head, water whipping into his face, as he tried to direct the boat across the river. Behind him, Adam pleaded with God in prayer, asking Him to shelter them and their families in this storm, praying for protection over their brotherhood on the other side of the river.

Niklas and Jacob paddled together in unison, and Adam dug his hands into the river to paddle against the current trying to steer them toward the submerged bridge. The wind drove against them like Triton himself was conspiring to sink their boat. It may have seemed that the Greek gods were battling against them, but he could hear Adam praying to the one true God—the only one who could guide them safely to Amana.

Jacob plunged his oar into the water again, his arms burning and his lungs screaming for air. But he wouldn't stop now. Over and over he and Niklas paddled until their boat crept over the flooded banks.

The current surged them forward now, through the trees. Jacob ducked under a branch and shoved the boat away from a gnarly trunk with his oar. Seconds later, the boat slipped out of the forest and into the valley.

Niklas gasped when he saw the swamped field in front of them. The river had turned the pastures and farmlands into a lake, the water already a good foot deep and rising. The current swept them steadily toward Amana, and as they drew closer to the village, the bottom of the boat scratched across the mud.

"We should walk from here," Niklas said, as he set his paddle in the boat. "Well done, Jacob."

Jacob nodded his head as he stepped out of the boat. Water crept up to his knees, soaking through his trousers. The bells rang out again, and Niklas and Adam ran on ahead while Jacob tied the rope handle to a tree.

*Heaven and earth can be moved,
but My Word is firm.*

Barbara Heinemann, 1822

CHAPTER 34

The water rose rapidly around Jacob's ankles—it wouldn't be long before it was too deep to wade through. A group of men passed him with leather buckets in hand, and Jacob saw the dredge boat captain leading the charge. As the other men ran past them, Michael stopped and clapped Jacob on the back. "A fine time for you to return."

"Give me a job."

"We're moving the food and supplies out of the basements and helping our elderly find shelter on higher floors."

"It may be days before the water goes back down." The older residents would be stranded alone if they had to evacuate the entire village.

Michael shook his head. "There are no other options."

Jacob glanced up at the smaller village of East Amana above the town. Perhaps they could get the elderly up there until the water subsided.

"If I could get a boat out here, I could take them to the edge of town. Someone from East Amana could drive them up to their village."

Michael glimpsed up at the village on the hillside. "*Ja,* but where are you going to get a boat?"

Jacob wiped the rain off his face. He could retrieve the rowboat at the edge of town, but they'd waste precious minutes getting it into town. A canoe would be faster—and easier—to push through the streets, and he knew exactly where to find one.

"Have you seen Emil Hahn?"

"Last I heard, he was with Albert and Lie…" Michael stopped himself before he finished saying her name, but the damage was done.

Jacob braced himself. "Where does Albert live?"

Michael pointed to a brick house on their left, and Jacob stepped back. "I'm going to find a boat."

Michael nodded. "I'll find a buggy to drive them up to East Amana."

Jacob swung open the heavy door where Albert Strauss lived and trekked across the wet floor. Emil was spread across the settee, asleep.

Jacob pushed the man's arm. "Wake up."

Emil's sleepy eyes grew wide when he saw Jacob. "What are you doing here?"

"Didn't you hear the bells?"

"Of course I heard them." Emil edged up on his elbows. "I was up all night battling the water."

"I need your help."

Emil rubbed his eyes and reached for his slicker. "What do you need?"

"Your canoe."

Emil left his coat on the hook, turning slowly instead. "Canoe?"

"This is not the time to play dumb, Emil."

"I don't know what you're talking about…."

"Your canoe, Emil. The one you secretly paddle up the Mill Race."

Emil glanced toward the doorway like he was afraid someone was eavesdropping on their conversation. "We're not supposed to have boats in Amana."

"I know you have a canoe, Emil, and so do the men on the dredge boat. We need to borrow it to get some of the older residents out of town."

Emil lowered his voice. "The Elders will wonder where you got the boat…and who you saw on it."

"I won't tell anyone where I got the boat, but I already told one woman who I saw on it."

The color drained from Emil's face. "Liesel knows…."

Jacob nodded. "I thought she was with you that day."

"I didn't want to hurt her," he said. "But I didn't know how to tell her either."

"You can talk to her later, Emil. Right now, we have to evacuate this town."

The bells rang out again as Emil reached for his coat. "Follow me," he said.

The ringing bells had awakened her father an hour ago, and Liesel couldn't console him. The Elders were calling out to the other six villages for help, but instead of joining the other men in the streets, her father was fretting in his bed because his body wouldn't cooperate. She didn't know why the Elders were ringing the bells—in this weather it would be treacherous for anyone to travel across the valley to assist them.

Even though it was still afternoon, the sun had long ago been swallowed by the dark clouds, and her father was hungry, which made him all the grumpier. Emil had brought them breakfast early this morning, but she hadn't seen him since. Her stomach rolled as she glanced out at the flooded lawn and streets of Amana that had turned into a maze of rivers. There was no way she was stepping outside.

As she listened to her father moan beside her, she chided herself for her childish fears.

A good daughter would ignore the rain and retrieve dinner for her father. He needed his strength, and going without food would only exasperate his weak condition. If Emil didn't return soon, she would have no choice but to fetch some food on her own.

She opened the book of testimonies and began to read to him, but the bells chimed out again. Why didn't Emil or someone else come and tell them what was happening outside?

As the bells faded, her father slid to the side of the bed. "I will find out what is wrong."

"You can't, *Vater*."

"I must go."

He tried to step onto the floor, but his legs collapsed under him again, and she rushed to his side. He shook his head, angry at his weakness, and she didn't have the words to comfort him. Albert Strauss had spent his life fighting against evil in their community, fighting for the good of those he loved. Today, however, his body was his greatest enemy.

She kissed his warm forehead as she helped him back into bed. "You must rest."

"Rest will not come," he said. "Not until I know what is happening."

She looked back at the rain again. *Der Struwwelpeter* was only a silly collection of fairy tales, just as she'd told Cassie. The wind wouldn't carry her away on a red umbrella, nor was she going to drown in a couple inches of water.

She would find food for her father and she'd find out why the Elders were continuing to ring the bells.

The carpentry shop was located south of the village, by the Mill Race. In the cellar of the shop, Emil and Jacob pulled back a large canvas and carried the canoe upstairs. Emil steered the boat through the watery streets, and Jacob walked behind it, pushing it toward a stone house where an invalid couple lived.

Emil went inside the house and minutes later walked back outside with an elderly woman huddled under a black umbrella. Jacob helped the woman step into the canoe while Emil returned for the woman's husband and a younger woman with a baby.

Together, Emil and Jacob sloshed through the water to guide the canoe east of town. Michael was waiting at the base of the hill along with a buggy and driver from East Amana. They helped the women, man, and baby into the buggy, and then Emil and Jacob went back into town. The task before them seemed daunting, but if the rain didn't stop them, they would be able to move dozens of children and elderly out of town.

Emil knocked on another door, and they loaded the canoe again with three children and their grandparents. As they floated the canoe back to the east of town, Jacob looked over and saw another boat drifting toward them. Niklas and Adam were pushing the rowboat with three other people inside.

Jacob waved at them, and as the men waved back, hope rose within him. Together they could evacuate everyone who needed a refuge in this storm.

Women and older children waded through the high water beside them with loads of clothing tied to their backs. Men helped the children who were struggling to walk, carrying them on their shoulders until they got to dry ground. Then, instead of climbing to dry ground themselves, the men turned back to help others.

The railroad strike in Chicago flashed through Jacob's mind

—all those men yelling and banging against the trains, destroying property and injuring people, because they were angry with George Pullman and his company.

Yes, the Amana people were much different than the outside world. They bonded together to protect and care for each other, young and old. They didn't fight for themselves, only for the good of those around them.

Isn't that what Christ called them to do—love thy neighbor as thyself? It seemed like the Amana colonists loved other people better than they loved themselves.

Jacob lifted two children from the canoe and into the buggy, wiping water from his eyes before he and Emil started back to Amana. For the next hour, they worked side by side as they made their way from the west of town going east, stopping at each house to rescue those who couldn't get to higher ground on their own.

They were only three houses away from the Strauss house, and if Liesel and her father hadn't gone to East Amana yet, she would be there. Even as he pushed the canoe through the water, his heart raced at the thought of seeing her again.

Emil jogged into another house and Jacob squinted his eyes, peering through the rain as a petite woman crossed the street in front of him with a basket looped over her arm. With her skirt hiked above her knees, she waded through the water, and Jacob smiled as he watched her open the door to Albert Strauss's home.

An orange light flickered suddenly in the window above him, and Jacob stared at the light for a moment.

"Liesel!" he shouted, running toward the house—but she didn't hear him call.

If you draw near to the Lord,
He will shield, shelter, guard, and keep you always.

Barbara Heinemann Landmann, 1880

CHAPTER 35

Water soaked over her boots and chilled her ankles, but Liesel didn't care. Even though she'd trembled the entire way, she'd braved the murky water to the kitchen house and hadn't drowned in it. The women were gone from the kitchen house, but they'd set out baskets of salted pork and hand cheese for anyone who stopped by to eat, so she retrieved food for her and her father.

The bells, she'd been told, were ringing for more help to bail water out of the flooded basements, but even with hundreds of people working, there was no stopping the rising waters from this storm. Her father was too weak to travel up to East Amana, so she would stay here with him for the duration of the storm.

Pulling off her drenched bonnet, Liesel opened the door and stepped into the entryway. Walking up the steps, smoke wafted across her face and she coughed, waving her hands in front of her face to clear it.

Had someone lit a fire? Perhaps someone was smoking a cob pipe or one of the women was attempting to cook on the woodstove that heated their room. But as she climbed the steps the smoke grew thicker, and she rushed toward her father's room, swinging open the door.

Fiery trails of kerosene snaked around the nightstand, and her father was on his knees, collecting accounting books and testimonies in his arms. She dropped her basket and picked up a rug, trying to beat back the flames, but she couldn't stop the fire.

She grabbed her father's sleeve, tugging on it. "We must leave."

He looked up at her, holding out the stack of books. "Take these first."

Her arm recoiled. "There's no time."

The fire ignited the hem of the bed comforter and slowly devoured the material. She must get her father out of this house.

Reaching for her arm, he clenched it. His plea was urgent. "We can't let them perish."

"Oh, *Vater*. I can't let you perish."

"These are the Almighty's words for our people."

"There are other copies."

"But they might get burned in the fire."

She tried to lift him to his feet, but he wouldn't help her. With no time to argue, she swiped the stack of books from his hands and raced for the door. If it would help him cooperate, she'd get the books out of the house and go right back in again for him.

Jacob slammed into Liesel as he rushed through the door toward the flames. Books scattered across the floor, but Liesel didn't reach for them.

Emil rushed in behind Jacob, but she didn't look at her intended.

"Jacob," she whispered, her eyes filled with tears.

He wanted to envelop her in his arms and tell her how much

he loved her, but that would have to wait. "I told you I'd come back."

"My father's upstairs." Her voice shook. "I can't get him out."

He ran past her, following Emil up the steps to the smoke pouring out of Albert's room. Jacob covered his mouth with his cap, rushing through the doorway, and he saw Albert unconscious on the floor, clinging to a book.

Heat singed Jacob's skin and the ceiling groaned above them, the fire popping and sparking as it ravaged the wood. In seconds the attic would cave in on them.

Emil knelt down and lifted Albert by his shoulders, and Jacob recognized the aloof carpenter who'd taken down the bridge with him. No wonder the man didn't like him.

Jacob leaned over, heaving to pick up the man's heavy legs, but when he lifted him, the book in Albert's arms fell to the ground. Albert awoke with a start, his arms flailing as he searched for the book.

Then Liesel was there beside him, picking the book off the ground before he lost consciousness again. "I've got it!" she shouted.

"Get out of here!" Emil hollered at her—but she didn't move. Instead she turned, meeting Jacob's eyes.

"We've got him," Jacob said, and she hurried toward the door, Emil after her, lugging Albert Strauss into the hallway.

The moment Jacob stepped out the guest room door, the ceiling crashed down behind him and the floor rocked underneath his feet. Heat blistered his back as he hurried down the stairs after Emil, carrying Liesel's father into the cool rain.

A crowd of men gathered on the flooded lawn, debating how to stop the fire. It would be too difficult for the men to haul the hand pump through the waterlogged streets, and it was far too late for a bucket brigade. A ball of fire darted around the roof, and Jacob prayed the rain would continue to fall on them. Once the roof caved in, the storm could extinguish the flames.

Jacob and Emil lay Albert in the canoe, tilting his face to the side.

"It will be too hard on him to travel to East Amana," Jacob said.

Liesel glanced over, her face filled with worry. "We need to get him out of this rain."

Emil looked back over his shoulder. "I know exactly where we can take him."

Liesel held the books close to her chest, trying to protect them from the rain by hiding them under her cloak. Emil was wading in front of her, Jacob beside her, and her father was floating down the street.

Thank God these men had showed up at the house when they did. She never would have been able to get her father out of the house before the ceiling collapsed.

Her arms trembled as she held the door open to Schmidt's Kitchen. If Jacob and Emil hadn't come to the house, her father would be gone.

Emil and Jacob carried her father into the flooded kitchen house and up the stairs. The hallway and most of the rooms were crowded with barrels of food brought up from the kitchen and cellar. Liesel moved a crate off a bed, and the men lay her father on it.

Her father woke again as she stretched a warm blanket over his shivering body. "The lantern...I knocked it over."

"It was an accident, *Vater*."

"I was trying to get one of the journals."

"I know."

Alarm rose in his face again. "Did you get the books?"

"I got all of them."

Hi sighed. "I can rest now."

Her father closed his eyes again, and then Jacob was beside her, his arm around her waist.

"I almost lost you," he whispered in her ear.

She collapsed into his chest, his strong arms pulling her close to him. This was what she wanted. To be with Jacob Hirsch and no one else.

Out of the corner of her eye, she saw Emil watching her from across the room, and she backed away from Jacob.

"I'm sorry," she muttered. What was wrong with her? Her brain felt fuzzy and confused. So much had happened in the past hour alone. The fire...and then her father. And now Jacob was here. Emil knew their relationship was over, but they hadn't ended their engagement. And here she was, already rushing into the arms of another man.

She stepped forward, tucking the blanket under her father's arms again. Her hands needed to stay busy, as did her mind.

Then she heard a woman shout Emil's name from the doorway, and Emil raced across the room—to Margrit.

"I was so worried," she said, clinging to Emil's neck—but the moment Margrit's eyes met hers, she released Emil and stepped back. "Liesel…I didn't know you were back."

"It's all right, Margrit." She glanced over at Emil, who looked a bit like a toddler who'd been caught stealing candy. "You will make Emil a much better wife than I."

Margrit stuttered her response, but Emil stepped forward.

"I wanted to tell you," he said. "Margrit and I both wanted you to know, but we didn't know what to say."

"Do the Elders know you've been courting?"

He shook his head. "Not yet."

She looked over her shoulder at Jacob filling a basin of water for her. "*Alles ist gut*, Emil….and for you too, Margrit."

Emil Hahn reached for Margrit's hand, and the two of them hurried out the door together, obviously in love. Had they started caring for each other when she left for Homestead, or had it been even longer? It didn't matter, she supposed. Emil and she weren't meant to be together, and she was glad she didn't have to convince him otherwise. He was clearly not lamenting the end of their engagement.

Jacob was by her side again. "Will you be okay?"

She glanced over at her father, who was sleeping soundly on the bed. "We will."

"There are others who need to get to East Amana tonight."

She pushed him toward the door. "You must help them."

Instead of leaving, Jacob gathered her in his arms again, the heat from his body warming the dampness on her skin. She lifted her face to him, her lips longing to feel his.

"I'll be back, Liesel."

She nodded, trying to suppress the disappointment that rose inside her when he let go. "I'll be waiting for you."

*Why do we never look up to the Star
which has appeared for us and which would very
gladly shine in our hearts, like the morning star?*

Johann Friedrich Rock, 1732

CHAPTER 36

Someone kissed Jacob's forehead, and he woke to the warmth and beauty of Liesel's face and the aroma of bacon escaping from the basket in her hands. The warm sun shone through the windows of the barn, and he rubbed his eyes before he pushed himself up from the hay barrel.

"What happened to the rain?" he asked.

"It stopped this morning."

He reached up, touching the soft blond hair that cascaded out of the braided knot onto her shoulders. "You are beautiful."

"The sun is blinding your eyes."

"My eyes are just fine."

She brushed dust off her apron, but the smile on her face was radiant. "How did you get up here?"

"Emil brought me in his canoe an hour ago." She held up the basket. "I walked up to the East Amana kitchen to get breakfast for you and *Vater*."

He glanced over the heads of the twenty or so sleeping men for the one man who'd worked alongside him through the night. He'd thought Emil a cad, but the man was actually a hero.

Jacob had been jealous because of Emil's relationship with

Liesel; he could admit that now. His jealousy had skewed the reality of Emil's strength and honor. Emil should have told Liesel that he'd fallen for someone else, but Jacob couldn't fault him for that. He probably hadn't wanted to hurt Liesel's feelings.

"Where did Emil go?"

"He and Niklas left early this morning for Homestead," she said. "They are going to let Cassie and the others know that we're safe."

"How is your father?"

"Tired, but he doesn't have any severe burns."

"Thank God."

"If it weren't for you and Emil…" She reached out and took his hand, and he weaved his fingers through hers. "If it weren't for you and the others, we would have lost much more than one house to the fire." She squeezed his hand. "I'm so glad you came home."

Home. The word sounded sweet on her lips, welcoming him back. He sniffed the air, and he smelled coffee beans along with the bacon. He pointed at her basket. "What do you have with you?"

She flipped back the lid and held up a tin of coffee. "Do you think you might want some?"

"The whole pot, please." He stood up, taking her hand. "But let's get out of this barn first."

They walked across the soggy field and found a large rock overlooking the flooded streets of Amana. Liesel spread out a cloth and placed on it an assortment of bread, blackberry jam, bacon, and cheese. "The kitchen crews in East Amana were up early making breakfast for the Amana villagers as well."

He picked up a slice of crispy bacon and ate it before he took a sip of the coffee. "Food tastes so much better here than in Chicago."

"Did you…" She cleared her throat. "Was it a good trip?"

He searched her face and saw the worry in her eyes. Niklas hadn't told her yet. "We found the person who stole the bank's money."

A smile played on her lips. "You've been cleared?"

"I never have to go back to Chicago again."

"But the Elders…they aren't going to let you stay in Amana."

"I will try to change their minds."

"They won't listen."

"Cassie and I won't have to leave Iowa. I can find work in Iowa City, maybe, or in Marengo."

She shook her head. "That's too far away."

Jacob paddled Liesel down Main Street in the rowboat, toward Schmidt's Kitchen. Branches and crates and leaves cluttered the watery streets. It would take days, maybe weeks, to clean up the debris. But even with all the damage, no one had lost his or her life to the water or the fire.

The floods had come, but God had protected and provided for the Amana people once again. He had no doubt they would recover together and their community would grow even stronger as a result.

Jacob helped Liesel climb out of the boat, and she retrieved the breakfast basket she'd brought for her father. Albert was awake in his new room, reading from one of the testimonies they'd rescued from the fire. With some rest, her father would recover as well and be even stronger than he was before the flood.

"Good morning." Liesel kissed her father. "I thought you might be hungry."

"It is a good morning indeed. Do I smell bacon?"

"The East Amana women packed extra slices just for you."

"Perhaps I will move up to East Amana." Albert looked over at Jacob. "I'm told you carried me out of the fire."

"Emil and Liesel and I helped you out together."

"I owe you my life."

"You don't owe me anything, sir."

Liesel spread the food on a tray and placed it on her father's lap. He reached for the bacon and engulfed two slices before he continued talking. "Niklas says your name was cleared in Chicago."

"It was."

"He also said he asked you to leave the Amana Colonies."

Jacob glanced over at Liesel, sitting on a chair near the bed, before he spoke to her father again. "Niklas and the other Elders didn't ask me, sir. They told me to leave right away."

"*Ja*, as they must. Where do you plan on going now?"

"I'm hoping I don't have to go far." His gaze traveled back to Liesel, and she smiled at him.

Albert cleared his throat, and Jacob stopped staring at his daughter. "Don't the men need help with the cleanup this morning?"

Liesel stood up. "*Vater*. Jacob worked most of the night, taking people to East Amana."

"It's all right," he told her. "I was planning to work with them today."

Even as he left the room, Liesel wanted to run after him. Now that she and Emil were no longer engaged, why couldn't she be with Jacob? He'd proven himself over and over again. In his work. In his commitment to God. And even in his commitment to their community.

"You've fallen for him, *ja*?"

She turned around and faced her father. "He wants to join our Society."

"We can't let everyone who wants to join become an Amana, Liesel. Only the faithful."

"Jacob has been faithful."

Albert shook his head, pushing the tray away from him. "But he will leave one day, go back to the world."

"Or he might stay, *Vater*. None of us know."

"Your mother..."

"My mother didn't join the Society on her own. Her parents joined for her. When it was time for her to choose, she decided to go back to the world."

Her father rested against the headboard. "I wanted her to stay."

"Not even those who grew up in the Amanas always stay." Liesel sat down beside him, holding his arm. "But I want to stay here for the rest of my life."

Pain filled his eyes. "What if he asks you to go away with him?"

Liesel trembled, knowing her answer yet not wanting to say it. It would tear her apart to leave her father, her community—yet she couldn't imagine staying here without Jacob.

"He hasn't asked."

"But what if he does?"

"Oh, *Vater*. How can I refuse him when the Elders won't let him join?"

Her father's voice was resigned. "You love him that much?"

"I love him and his daughter."

Albert reached for her hand and clung to it. "It will break my heart."

She kissed his forehead, her stomach in knots at the thought of leaving the man who had loved her for so many years. "I don't want to break anyone's heart."

Jacob gathered an armful of branches with his gloves and threw them onto a growing mound on the muddy lawn. Seven other men worked around him, collecting debris from the subsiding water and piling it up so they could burn it later. The clouds had blown away overnight, and the bright sky was a welcome change from the pouring rain.

Every muscle in his body ached from his labors, yet his soul was content. God had protected him from the fire last night, and God had protected him from himself in Chicago.

He'd wanted to take that money, the answer to his problems. And part of him even wanted to take the job Frank offered him. The idea of success and money would have been intoxicating at one time, rising above the other bank clerks at such a young age, yet God had changed his idea of success and directed him here, to the Amanas. There was no place else he'd rather be today.

It would be weeks before the villagers could return to their normal lives, but there was no rush in this unhurried society. Working as a team, they'd evacuated all the young and elderly alike last night, and, working as a team, they would clean up the aftermath. They'd get rid of the debris and return to their daily routines of doing whatever task they'd been assigned.

When everyone put aside their selfish ambitions, it was amazing what could happen. No one was more or less important in their community. Everyone's work was respected, as was their life even when they were too old or ill to work.

He only wished he could return to his work with them.

If the Elders forced him to leave the Amanas, it wasn't right for him to ask Liesel to go with him. This was her home, and no place in Iowa City or even over in Marengo could compare to what she had here. The Amana Elders were worried that he might leave her for the outside world, but if he took her away, he worried that she might leave him one day to return to the Amanas.

Picking up another bundle of leaves and trash, he tossed it onto the pile. No place else in the world shared and loved and served like these people. It wouldn't be fair to take her away.

Several men began streaming toward the kitchen house, and Michael clapped him on his back. "Are you hungry, my friend?"

"Very."

"Come along, then."

Muck and debris clogged the back door of Schmidt's Kitchen, so Jacob followed the men up the steps, into the front door. The water had subsided from the wooden floor, leaving behind a sticky mess on the rugs and furniture that hadn't been stored upstairs. Liesel and several other women were sweeping the mud off the rugs and floors and back outside.

Liesel looked over, catching his eye, and his heart raced like it had done when she'd woken him this morning. Her ivory face was smudged with dirt, but her smile was a balm to his weary body.

As he sat with Michael and the other men, eating the hot chicken soup and salad in silence, his eyes kept wandering over to meet hers. More than anything he wanted to be with her, but that would be an incredibly selfish act on his part. Even if she agreed to go with him, he couldn't ask her to leave this place.

My children, young and old, from now on I shall call you my blessed children. Step into the light!

Christian Metz, 1833

CHAPTER 37

Liesel hummed as she scrubbed the wood floor with vinegar and water. Her fingers were wrinkled and her back was sore, but most of the mud was gone now and the rugs were outside drying in the setting sun.

She and two other women had spent the day cleaning out the house and carrying food back down to the kitchen. The others had left a few minutes ago to prepare their families for bed, and she would soon go to sleep in an empty room upstairs.

Throughout the day, she'd glanced out the window to watch Jacob as he cleaned up the streets. She was glad they had been here to help during the flood...and even more glad she was able to see Jacob again after the Elders had told her she wouldn't be allowed to say goodbye.

Her mind wandered again, wondering where Jacob would spend the night.

Sophie was learning to live outside the Colonies; perhaps she could learn as well. She could even learn to shop for food and cook and find a place to worship God. The outside world didn't appeal to her, but she would leave Amana if she must. As long as she could be with Jacob Hirsch.

The front door opened and Niklas Keller stomped inside. "*Guten abend*, Liesel."

She tossed her rag back into the bucket and stood up. "Good evening to you too."

"Is your father awake?"

"He's resting right now."

"I need to speak with him."

She nodded. "Were you able to see Cassie?"

"I was, and my wife is taking good care of her. Cassie said she misses you, though."

"I miss her too."

Niklas studied her for a moment. "You've sacrificed yourself, Liesel, and exhibited Christ's love to this child. We are glad of it."

"It wasn't a sacrifice for me."

Niklas put his hand on the banister and climbed a step before he stopped again. "Did Jacob tell you about his opportunity in Chicago?"

Her insides fluttered. "No."

"His former boss offered Jacob the position of bank president."

"President?"

"It would be a reputable position for him."

She leaned back against the wall. "Is he going back to Chicago?"

Niklas climbed another step. "He told his boss he couldn't accept the job."

She rubbed her hands together, wanting to plead with him for more information, but she calmed her voice. "Why not?"

"He told the man he had to go home."

Home. Jacob Hirsch considered the Amanas his home, just as she did. And this should be his home. He was a hard worker and an honorable man, and he sought after God to give him strength and wisdom.

"Why can't he join the Society?" she asked the man on the steps.

The front door opened and four more men walked into the room. Elders from Main Amana.

"We need to speak with your father," Niklas repeated before he led the men upstairs.

It was approaching ten o'clock, but none of the Amana men stopped working so Jacob continued alongside them. Kerosene lamps illuminated the brown ooze trickling down the street as some of the men bailed out basements and others repaired damaged buildings.

Jacob stayed with Michael and the boat crew to finish clearing the debris out of the muddy street. In the morning, they would clear out the charred brick structure left after the fire.

The door of the Schmidt house opened, and Jacob glanced up at it to see who was coming out so late tonight. Niklas Keller was the first person he saw, followed by several other men in dark hats. The Elders disappeared into the night, but Niklas stayed in front of the house, searching the streets.

Jacob pushed the wheelbarrow a bit farther down the street to begin collecting leaves and twigs that had spread across the gardens, but Niklas called his name, motioning for him.

He'd helped row Niklas and Adam over here, but nothing else had changed. They probably wanted him to move on in the morning, long before he could help Michael clean out the house.

He lowered the wheelbarrow to the ground before he walked toward the kitchen house. In one of Niklas's arms were three worn books, and with his other hand, Niklas pointed Jacob to the bakery next door.

Light from the street lamps seeped into the windows, and Jacob saw a giant hearth surrounded by tables that had been filled with barrels and flour bags. Niklas set the books on an empty corner of the table, and he picked up one of the two wooden stools and handed it to Jacob.

Light danced across the bricks on the hearth, silence pervading as Niklas watched the bricks glow for a few moments before he spoke.

"Do you know the history of the Amana Society?"

"Liesel told me some of your history."

"Our Colonies formed almost two hundred years ago, back in Germany, to protest the dogmatism that was trickling into the Lutheran Church," Niklas said. "Our brothers and sisters believed in the Inspiration of the Bible, but they also yearned to hear God's voice in the present-day as well."

Jacob rested his hands on his lap. He didn't know why Niklas was telling him the Amana history, but he wasn't in a hurry. In fact, he was intrigued to learn more about their roots.

"For many years, God spoke through special men and women called the *Werkzeuge*, who shared these divine testimonies with the rest of the group. This is why we became known as the Community of True Inspiration."

Niklas shifted on his stool, leaning forward. "The Inspirationists grew quickly as a faithful band of brothers and sisters who sought only to follow God's voice, but the German government and church was none too pleased about the Inspirationists' growth or our beliefs. Our ancestors, you see, refused to send their children to public school because church doctrine was being taught in these schools. As a result, many of our predecessors were flogged, persecuted, and imprisoned. They sacrificed their freedom and their possessions to follow Christ."

Jacob nodded. "That is why so many remain faithful today."

Niklas looked over at the light flickering on the bricks again.

"We have followed His voice, and God has been faithful to our community for many, many years."

"Liesel said the Inspirationists came to America fifty years ago."

"I was seven years old," Niklas said, "when the Lord made it very clear to our *Werkzeuge* that we should hold all our possessions in common, so eight hundred members pooled their resources and purchased land to live together in Ebenezer, New York."

The older man continued to watch the lights, lost in the memories of his childhood. "We sailed to America and, under our new constitution, we followed the doctrine set out by the apostles in the book of *Acts*. 'And all that believed were together, and had all things common; and sold their possessions and goods, and parted them to all men, as every man had need.' We believed together in community, and God blessed our fields and our mills and our families."

"And He continues to bless you today," Jacob said.

"*Ja*, that He does. Brother Christian Metz led us to Ebenezer, but when the world encroached on our lives there, he and the Elders began looking for a new place for us to live a simple life, apart from the temptations and anxieties of the world.

"They found this beautiful land of milk and honey in 1854 and named it *Amana* from the Song of Solomon, which means to 'believe faithfully.' From our hands, we have built seven villages and businesses and gardens and herds and a flour mill to feed our people. We have never stopped being faithful to God."

"The work you have done—" Jacob paused. "You have worked together under God and succeeded in building a community isolated from the world."

"Yet the world keeps coming to us..." Niklas's voice trailed off. "Since we moved to Iowa, many have wanted to join our group. The isolation is attractive to some, as is the assurance of food, housing, and medical care, but '*unto whomsoever much is given, of him shall be much required.*' We require our men and women to work faithfully as well as believe."

Jacob weighed his next words. The Elders rarely welcomed new members into the Amana Society, but sometimes people joined the community. More than anything, he wanted to be one of those who joined.

"I believe that God still speaks today, Niklas. He comforted my daughter on the train, in a dream, and he's spoken to my heart many times in the past month. He healed Cassie, and He's comforted and provided for both of us. I haven't always been faithful to God, but even still He has been faithful to me."

Niklas pulled the books from the table into his lap. "Michael tells me you have worked hard on the dredge boat."

"I will always be indebted to you for giving me work."

"Why did you turn down the position at the bank, Jacob?"

"I—I don't belong in Chicago anymore." He brushed his hands over his trousers as he weighed his words. "But I feel like I belong here in the Amanas. If you would only give me the opportunity to stay, I will continue to work hard alongside you and the others. I will serve like you do and believe faithfully."

"We've had men and women ask to join our Society before because they want to marry one of our young people," Niklas said. "Sometimes they stay for a lifetime, but other times they leave in a few years. Of course, sometimes our young people marry another Amana and then leave."

Jacob felt sorry for the man who was trying to save so many from the outside world but had lost his son to it. "I cannot deny my love for Liesel," he said. "But once I give my word to her and to your community, I will stay."

Niklas nodded. "I believe you, Jacob, and so do the Council of Elders. We've been praying that God would show us clearly whether or not you are a diligent and honorable servant."

Jacob flashed back to his moments in the hansom cab, the

money easily within his reach. With God's help, he'd resisted the temptation, but his thoughts had not been honorable. "I am nothing apart from God."

"Neither am I, my friend. Neither am I." Niklas opened the book on his lap. "If you decide to join our community, you must be assigned a job."

His mind raced at the man's words. Was Niklas offering him the opportunity to stay? He flashed back to the sweltering room of the dredge boat. Even if he must feed the boiler to stay in the Colonies, he would do it. "I understand."

"Adam tells me you are good with numbers."

"It was my profession, sir."

"The Elders have shared bookkeeping over the years, but with the woolen mill and our other enterprises, we now have at least a thousand receipts and invoices each month to record and balance. It is an overwhelming task for any of us."

Jacob reached for the journal and glanced down the rows of income and expenses. It was what he knew. What he enjoyed.

"Would you help us keep our books?" Niklas asked.

Jacob smiled. "I would be honored to do that."

"We still need help on the dredge boat, but none of our young people know how to swim."

"Would you like me to remedy that?"

"If you could."

"I'd be glad to," Jacob said.

"I will arrange for a room for you and Cassie in Homestead."

Niklas stood up, but Jacob wasn't finished yet. "If Cassie and I stay…I would like very much to ask Liesel Strauss to be my wife."

Niklas put his hat on his head. "The Elders thought you might want to do that."

"And what did the Elders say?"

"They said you'll have to talk to Liesel."

His heart leaped. "So I have your permission…"

"Ja."

Jacob clapped his hands. "Can you keep this a secret for a few days, please? So I can talk to Cassie first?"

"Of course."

"And Niklas…" He hated to ask for anything else, but there was one more issue that must be resolved. "I missed Liesel terribly during the days I was in Chicago. I can't imagine being separated from her for a year."

"You have a young daughter to care for," Niklas said with a smile. "The Elders will make an exception to that rule."

Love will burst through its restraining dam and, together, love and mercy will pour forth, seeking and flowing into the lowest valleys of the land and heart.

Barbara Heinemann, 1820

CHAPTER 38

Majestic purples and pinks breathed calm into Liesel's bedroom as the sun set over Homestead. It had been three days since the Iowa River washed through Main Amana. Hundreds of men and women came from every village to help with repairs, cleanup, and the reconstruction of her childhood home.

Yesterday she'd left her father in Dr. Eisenberg and Margrit's good care to harvest the wet garden in Homestead, but as glad as she was to see Cassie, she was sad to leave Jacob without letting him know she'd returned home.

She hadn't spent time with Jacob since that glorious morning she'd awakened him in the barn and they'd eaten breakfast together on the rock. Every mealtime she'd caught his eye, he always smiled back at her, but they hadn't been able to steal away together again. As the days passed, she prayed he hadn't changed his mind about her like Emil had.

"Orange is my favorite color," Cassie said over her shoulder, and Liesel reached out and put her arm around the girl as they watched the beauty of the setting sun.

"Why is orange your favorite?"

"Because Papa always calls me his pumpkin."

"Your father loves you very much, Cassie."

"*Ja!*" the girl said, sounding very much like the *Kinder* she played with every day. "And I love him too."

Cassie reached for Liesel's hand, and when she squeezed it, she felt something hard around the girl's finger. She lifted the girl's hand to the fading light and examined the dainty silver ring. "Where did you get this?"

Cassie's smile was as bright as the sunlight. "Papa gave it to me this morning."

"You didn't tell me you saw your papa."

She shrugged. "He told me it was a secret."

"A secret from whom?"

"From you, silly."

Liesel sat back in her chair, the colors in the sky beginning to dull. Why was Jacob trying to keep his visit a secret from her when she wanted so badly to see him?

The Elders had told her to guard her heart, and she hadn't heeded their warning. Instead she'd practically handed her heart over to Jacob, unprotected, and now... she could only pray he wouldn't crush it.

There was a soft knock on her door, and she glanced at the time on the clock. It was almost 9:30. Before she could open the door, Cassie ran to it and pulled it open. Outside stood Greta with her baby in one arm and a goofy grin across her face.

"Are you busy?" her friend asked.

"We're getting ready for bed."

"You can't go to bed just yet."

Liesel put her hands on her hips. "Why in the world not?"

"Because there's a surprise waiting outside that you can't miss."

"A surprise?" Liesel looked back out at her window. "What are you talking about?"

"I can't say another word," Greta said. "I promised I'd keep a secret."

Cassie's smile was almost as big as Greta's.

"It seems like everyone is keeping secrets." Liesel reached for Cassie's hand. "Do you want to go outside with me?"

Greta stepped forward. "Oh, no. She needs to go to sleep."

"But she can't stay here by herself."

"I'll be right across the hall." Greta tousled Cassie's hair. "You'll let *Tante* Greta know if you need anything, right?"

Cassie grinned. "Right."

"Are you certain, Greta?"

Her friend gave her a little shove. "Go."

Liesel leaned down and kissed Cassie on the cheek. "You go right to sleep."

"I will."

"No messing around near the window."

"I'll stay in my bed."

"Promise?"

Cassie nodded her head as Liesel stepped out of the door.

"He's waiting for you at the apple orchard," Greta said.

"Jacob?" she asked, but Greta buttoned her lips closed.

Liesel shook her head at her friend's silliness. As she walked down the stairs, she glanced up one more time to make sure Cassie had left the door propped open in case she needed to call out for Greta—and then she laughed out loud at herself and her worry over Cassie.

When had she started fretting so much about this girl? She may want to be Cassie's mother, but unless Jacob decided to pursue something more, she was only Cassie's caretaker and friend. Not her parent.

Still, she couldn't help but worry.

The street was quiet when she stepped into it, the stars beginning to twinkle overhead. The freight train spouted off its whistle as it cruised through their village, but it didn't stop tonight, traveling off to another city beyond her world.

She could no longer imagine her life without Jacob, but neither could she imagine leaving the Colonies. If Jacob asked for her hand in marriage, she would be happy to be with him yet she would still grieve leaving her home. She would never tell him that, of course, but he would probably guess at her reluctance to move away.

Ahead of her, something glowed in the orchards, glittering like the stars in the sky. Enthralled, she walked faster now, her eyes on the dozens of lights scattered among the trees. Candles sprinkled throughout the orchard. She'd never seen anything so breathtaking, with the flames dancing in the night.

"Jacob?" she whispered.

And then he was there, right beside her.

"Are you hungry?" he asked.

Her voice shook. "I don't know."

He smiled as he took her hand and led her gently through the labyrinth of lights until they came to a blanket stretched out between the trees. On it was a bottle of rhubarb wine along with cheese and crackers and a bowl of strawberries.

"How did you do this?" she asked.

He smiled again. "I had a little help."

"It's marvelous," she said. "But I don't understand...."

He motioned for her to sit on the blanket, and then he poured her a glass of wine.

"I have an important decision to make, and I wanted to see if you could help me with it."

She sipped the sweet wine. "How can I possibly help you?"

He sat across from her, his long legs stretched over the blanket. "When I was in Chicago, I received some reward money...and I'm trying to decide how to spend it."

She tried not to sigh but couldn't hide her disappointment. She didn't want to talk about money tonight.

Jacob didn't seem to notice. "One option is that I travel on to Spokane and set up a home for Cassie and me."

The breeze blew across her face, rustling the leaves around them as she tried to smile. "It would be good for you and Cassie to have a home."

"That's what I was thinking as well," he said, scooting a little closer to her. "Of course, the other option is that we find a place a little closer to the Amanas."

Her heart skipped a beat. "I would like it if you and Cassie were closer."

"How close, Liesel?"

The wine splashed out of her glass, onto the blanket, and she set the glass down. "Are there any other options?"

"There is one more option," he said, another smile washing over his face. "Niklas Keller and the other Elders have asked me if I'd like to join the Amana Society."

"What?"

"They would like me to live here in Homestead and take care of their bookkeeping."

"Jacob—" Her thoughts raced, trying to form words. If Niklas and the others had asked Jacob to stay, he didn't have to leave the Amanas…and neither did she.

"I would have to give my reward money to the Society, of course, so I won't have any left over to purchase a home. Cassie and I would live as part of the community."

She wanted to both squeal and drop onto her knees and thank God for His goodness, but she couldn't seem to do either.

"Are you okay, Liesel?"

"I'm trying to sort it all out in my head."

"What do you think I should do?" he asked, inching closer.

She swallowed hard. "I think you should stay."

He reached forward, taking both of her hands in his. "That's what I was hoping you would say."

Then he took her into his arms, pulling her close to his

chest, and her body warmed with his touch. She'd never known what it was like to be held like this, and she didn't want him to let her go.

Slowly he tilted her face up to his. "I spent a bit of the reward money before I left Chicago."

His lips were inches from her ear. "On what?"

Gently he unfolded her fingers, and she felt the coolness of metal in her palm. Looking down, she could see a silver ring in the candlelight. "It's beautiful, but—."

"I know you can't wear it, but I still wanted you to have it so you don't ever forget my promise."

She tried to say something, to ask about his promise, but she couldn't speak. "The Elders agreed that I could join the Society, and they also agreed to make an exception to one of the rules for me."

"An exception—" she whispered. "Which rule?"

"I told them I couldn't join unless the woman I loved agreed to be my wife."

Her heart seemed to stop.

"I also explained that I couldn't wait for a year to get married to the woman I love."

He pulled her to him again, kissing her softly, and she went limp in his arms. "Liesel Strauss, would you consider becoming my wife?"

She closed her eyes as he stroked the back of his hand down her cheek. There'd never been a sweeter moment than this one. She didn't want it to end.

Opening her eyes again, she looked into his face, candles glowing on every side of them.

"I will go wherever you go, Jacob," she said, recalling the words from the book of Ruth, before he stopped her with a kiss.

"This is home, my love." He sat back and smiled at her. "I will never ask you to leave."

*Behold the work of the old.
Let your heritage not be lost, but bequeath
it as a memory, treasure, and blessing.*

Christian Metz, 1846

EPILOGUE

TWO YEARS LATER

Apple tree branches rustled in the orchard beside them, and along the kitchen house trellis, hundreds of red and green grapes glistened in the sun. Liesel pushed her heels in the grass and the tandem lawn swing rose and then dipped under the tree.

On the bench beside her, Sophie Keller rested her head on the rope, breathing in the aromas of the ripening fruit and summer blooms on the trees. Her friend looked beautiful, dressed in a pale pink dress with puffy sleeves. Sophie's skirt was gathered tight with a fancy buckle decorating her thin waist, and bursting out of her tea hat was a mass of pink and yellow tulle, feathers, and lace.

Sophie smoothed her gloves over her lacy dress and closed her eyes. "I still miss it here."

"I miss you being here." Liesel watched Cassie lift up Sophie's young daughter to reach a handful of grapes. "Aren't they sweet?"

Opening her eyes, Sophie followed her gaze across the gardens. "I wanted our children to grow up together."

"They'll grow up together," Liesel replied. "They just won't see each other as often as we'd like."

Sophie sighed, pushing their swing again. She and Conrad had rented a home in Cedar Rapids, but Conrad now handled all the legal work for the Amana Society. Whenever he traveled to Amana, Sophie and little Meredith visited Liesel and Cassie for a day or two in Homestead. Liesel wished Sophie still lived here, working in the gardens beside her, but she savored every moment of their visits together.

The two girls fell into the grass, giggling together before Meredith dropped a grape into the red-stained mouth of her six-year-old friend.

"They'll be the best of friends, won't they?" Sophie asked wistfully.

Liesel laughed. "I think they're already the best of friends."

"Sometimes I worry..." Sophie leaned back again. "I worry about raising Meredith in the outside world."

Liesel grasped for the right words to console her friend, but she couldn't imagine raising her daughter outside either. "You will guide her, and you will pray."

"*Ja*. I pray every day for her." Sophie took off her gloves and put them on her lap.

"You are a good mother, Sophie."

"And so are you."

Liesel's hands traveled to her belly and the bulge hidden under her loose calico dress. "Thank you."

"You should come visit me in Cedar Rapids."

"I can't."

Sophie looked down at Liesel's hand, still resting on her belly. "Liesel Hirsch, are you—"

"Hush," she whispered. "Jacob doesn't know yet."

"Good heavens, Liesel. Why not?"

"After what happened to Katharine...he'll worry too much."

"He'll be angry if you wait too long."

"Mama!" Cassie shouted.

Her daughter ran up to her with a cluster of grapes in her hand and kissed her cheek as she held out her bounty. Liesel's stomach rolled at the thought of eating the fruit, but her heart was full.

"Thank you, sweetheart."

Cassie hugged her neck. "You're the best mama in the whole world."

Liesel smiled at her daughter, relishing her tender words. She couldn't imagine being any more blessed.

Meredith toddled up beside them and nudged her finger into Cassie's chest. "My sister."

Sophie winked at Liesel and then clapped her hands together. "Yes, she is."

"Come home with me."

"Some day," Sophie said, ruffling the yellow bow in her daughter's hair. "Some day she'll come for a visit."

A faint whistle trilled from the side of the kitchen house, and Liesel sat up a little straighter on the bench. The moment Cassie heard the whistling, she let go of Meredith's hand and sprinted around the brick building. Seconds later, Liesel watched her husband lift Cassie and twirl her around in his arms.

Jacob's hair was wet from his weekly lesson at the river, where he was teaching a dozen or so Amana boys how to swim, and his smile was wide. She didn't imagine it could be possible, but she thought he was even more handsome now than he was two years ago, when she and Cassie visited him on the dredge boat.

They'd married within a month of the great flood, and during his first year in the Amanas, Jacob won the admiration of the Board of Elders with his meticulous bookkeeping. Now he was a respected member of their Society. No one ever talked about him being "worldly" anymore—at least, not in front of them.

In the first months of their marriage, she'd worried that he would grow frustrated with their plain lifestyle, afraid that one day he would leave the Colonies like her mother had, but she rarely fretted anymore. Jacob seemed contented with his new life, as if he had been reborn since arriving in Homestead.

Some days she still wished she could work in the *Kinderschule* instead of in the gardens, but in the meantime, she was content with the *Kind*—her hand rolled over her belly again—the *Kinder* God had given her.

Her eyes locked on her husband's gaze as he moved toward them. She'd braided his ring into her hair and hidden it under her sunbonnet, but in his eyes, she saw love and hope and a quiet promise that he would never leave.

"You are blessed," her friend whispered.

Liesel nodded. God was in heaven, and all was truly right here in her world.

AFTERWORD

I became intrigued by the Amana Colonies many years ago when I lived in Iowa. As I researched this novel and *The Society*, it was a tremendous honor to return to Iowa and spend time with Amana men and women whose parents and grandparents had built these beautiful Colonies.

In the 1700s, the Amana Church was known as the Community of True Inspiration, a name given by people outside the community who heard the *Werkzeuge* (Instruments) speaking testimonies inspired by the Holy Spirit. The Amanas believe these testimonies are God-breathed revelation, and these Words have blessed and guided their community for more than two hundred years. While the testimonies are woven into the core of their faith, the Amanas also believe the Bible is the preeminent source of God's revelation to His children. Each inspired testimony was tested against Scripture in the eighteenth and nineteenth centuries to determine if the words were from God.

While the Amana people lived as a communal society for eighty years, a devastating fire destroyed the Amana flour and woolen mills in 1923, and then later in the decade, the Amana youth began to rebel against the Society's rules. While the members still operated as a commune during this decade, many of the residents sold handiwork and produce to purchase items not available in the Colonies. The financial state of the tight-knit Society began to deteriorate as more and more outside workers were hired to provide for the community.

In February 1932, members of the Amana Society voted to reorganize, and the Amana Church was separated from the profit-sharing corporation known as the "Amana Society." In the Amanas, this period was known as the Great Change.

After the Great Change, every member was guaranteed a job within the new organization, but they no longer lived as a commune. Members had to learn how to cook, pay taxes, and purchase items for their homes—and many of the older members missed the companionship of cooking and gardening with their friends.

The Amana Society still exists today, as does the Amana Church. In 1934, George Foerstner began to sell refrigeration coolers in the Amanas, and this business grew rapidly over the years as it produced washers, dryers, dishwashers, ovens, and air-conditioning units. Amana Appliances, now owned by the Whirlpool Corporation, is located in Middle Amana.

As the Amana Church follows the Spirit's voice today, the inspired testimonies continue to enlighten and instruct its members. And the businesses in the Colonies continue to thrive as visitors from around the world escape to these peaceful villages.

Because of communal Amana's unique and inspirational past, I relied on a number of new friends for information, and I'm grateful to each of the following who helped me understand the Amana Church Society's history and faith. Thank you to:

Emilie Hoppe (*Seasons of Plenty: Amana Communal Cooking*), Barbara Hoehnle, Lanny Haldy, Peter Hoehnle (*The Amana People: The History of a Religious Community*), and Brandi Jones for providing me with an abundance of historical information.

And unpublished author Henrietta Laubly—finding her original essay in the State Historical Society of Iowa was like finding a treasure. Her vivid recollections from her childhood visits to the Amana Colonies were invaluable to me.

I am blessed beyond words to have a husband and two daughters who cheered me along as I wrote about these remarkable colonies. Thank you, Jon, Karly, and Kiki, for all of your love and grace.

And thank you to our Lord Jesus Christ who is the same yesterday, today, and forever. I pray that each of us, like the Amana people, would continue to listen and follow the "holy and mysterious rushing" of the Spirit's roar.

~Melanie

LEGACY OF LOVE SERIES

Legacy of Love by Melanie Dobson is a historical romance series based on the courageous people and significant events that wove together the rich tapestry of America's freedom and faith.

Now Available:
The Masquerade (Gilded Age)
The Runaway (Underground Railroad)
The Imposter (Revolutionary War)
The Christmas Bride (Colonial America, Moravians)
The Journey (Oregon Trail)
The Society (Civil War, Amana Colonies #1)
The Stranger (Amana Colonies)
The Silent Order (Prohibition)

THE SILENT ORDER

PROLOGUE

"Let's go home," Nikki whispered, her lips quivering. Even her toes, squashed into the sharp points of her strapped Mary Janes, wouldn't stop shaking. "Liz…"

"Hush," her sister hissed as she swung open the side door of Mangiamo's. Nikki held up the small battery-powered lantern, and the shiny countertops in the kitchen glowed.

Nikki's knees knocked under her navy blue skirt, and she pressed them together as the door creaked closed behind them. Her father's employees had left the restaurant hours ago, around midnight or so. Everything inside was still except her heart, which had been hammering in her chest since she and Liz snuck out of the house. Somehow Liz had secured the key to the back door of Mangiamo's, but she wouldn't tell Nikki why they needed to get inside.

Their parents and older brother were asleep in their large home, a few blocks up Murray Hill. As she and Liz snuck down to Mayfield Road, the usually bustling streets in Cleveland's Little Italy were draped with an eerie fog. The silence unnerved her—even the alley cats had stopped howling for the night.

As Nikki followed her sister across the kitchen, Liz pulled a second key out of her purse.

She gasped. "Where did you get—"

"I told you to shut up," Liz barked as she pushed the key into the lock of another door—a door that kept the kitchen staff out of their father's private lounge.

Nikki leaned closer. "Papa's going to kill you."

"He'll have to catch me first." Liz laughed, sounding more like she was twelve than twenty-one.

Her sister teetered daily between the frivolities of her youth and the weight of adulthood. The shiny red barrette in her bobbed black hair matched the red bow on her scalloped dress. Even in the dull light, she exuded glamour.

Until this moment, Nikki never thought to ask why Liz was dressed to the nines—she was still trying to wake up after her sister shoved her out of bed in the middle of the night, saying she needed help. She hadn't told Nikki why they needed to come here, but it didn't matter. Nikki always seemed to be on call for her older sister, and Liz knew it. She covered for Liz whenever her sister slipped away to visit one of Cleveland's many nightclubs.

But never before had Liz tried anything as daring as breaking into Mangiamo's back room. Their father's sanctuary.

Their brother was allowed inside this room when invited— and he bragged about it often—but Salvatore never talked to either of his daughters about the place. Didn't really talk to Nikki at all. She knew the extent of his fury, though, and she feared him almost as much as the spineless henchmen who bowed to him like he was God on earth. She'd never bowed, but she usually cowered when he was around, hoping he wouldn't notice her. He rarely did.

Her sister wasn't afraid of anything, including their father. She had the gift of being able to charm almost any man. If their father discovered them trespassing in his den, though, no charm would work. Discipline would be swift. And painful.

The knob turned in her sister's hands, and as she cracked open the door, the stench of cigar smoke mingled with the lingering smells of spicy sausage and cheese from the kitchen behind them.

"Liz—" she repeated.

Liz grabbed the lantern from Nikki's hands. "Tell me if someone comes to the front door."

Light illuminated the gray stone that lined the narrow staircase below them. Her sister stepped down and slowly descended into the dungeon.

Nikki propped the door open with her heel, waiting in the darkness. She had thought there was a small room in the back of the restaurant, not a basement, but she wasn't surprised. Secrets bound their family together like the tangled silk threads layering the web of a black widow.

The girls at Nikki's school envied these seemingly luxurious threads, but she knew that the Cardano money only covered the secrets with a blinding sheen that most people couldn't see past. She and Liz knew the truth. They were trapped in their family's web for the rest of their lives.

Her mother refused to talk about their family's secret life, and her father usually refused to talk to her, period. Silence stopped even the walls of the Cardano mansion from sharing their secrets, but the walls knew. They knew about her father's mistress over on Woodland Avenue. They knew about the bitter tears her mother shed. And they knew about the dirty money that surged through her family like water from a fire hose, money that never seemed to extinguish the smoldering inside her father for more.

Nikki watched the light in her sister's hands turn the corner at the bottom of the steps, and she rested her back against the post, praying Liz would hurry.

Light from the city lamps trickled in through two small windows at the side of the room, illuminating the shiny tops of the kitchen ovens and the draped tables that filled the dining room. Instead of windows by the imposing front door there was a wall filled with paintings of Italy.

The restaurant couldn't possibly support the Cardano family lifestyle, nor could the factory where her uncle's refined sugar, but there was always plenty of money. Some mornings she walked down the stairs and the dining room table was hidden under silvery green mounds of cash. Someone supplied her father with thousands and thousands of dollars at least once a week, but she didn't know who paid him, nor did she want to know. She just wanted to rush out the door each morning before the others woke up to join her friends at Saint Anthony's.

Their mother liked to pretend that her husband's business ventures were perfectly legitimate as she tried to induct her daughters into the high society circles like they were members of Cleveland's elite. Two years ago, Liz began rebelling against the dog-and-pony show and decided to flaunt herself in circles not so pleasing to their mother. The more their mother and father disapproved, the happier Liz seemed to be.

Salvatore ignored Liz's exploits for a long time, but everything changed in July. For the past three months, their father had kept Liz home around the clock, under surveillance. On the rare occasion that Salvatore let Liz go outside the estate, she was escorted by two of his bodyguards.

Tonight, however, the man who was supposed to be standing guard outside Liz's door was sleeping beside it instead. Nikki assumed Liz, with her smooth words and alluring smile, offered him a couple of drinks from the stash she snuck into her room under her longer dresses.

The lantern light blinked below her.

"Liz?" she called in a hushed voice.

When her sister didn't answer, her gaze wandered back toward the six rows of tables that separated the kitchen and the front door. The chairs and table settings appeared to be in their proper place; there was no hint of the loud patrons who had departed four hours ago and no bloodstains left from the man shot inside the parlor back in March.

Nikki shivered. Did the man's ghost stay behind to haunt those who'd murdered him?

She glanced back down the staircase, at the light bobbing on the wall below. She should have asked Liz why they needed to come here in the middle of the night, but it was much safer to play along than ask questions.

A sharp click sounded in the dining room, and her heart leapt. Turning, she squinted in the dull light, but nothing moved. No one was in the restaurant at this hour, she told herself. No one but her and Liz.

She whispered her sister's name one more time, but Liz didn't respond.

Holding her breath, she pressed her hands against the doorframe and pretended to be one of the Sicilian statues in her father's pictures. If the murdered man had come back for vengeance, perhaps he wouldn't see her. Surely he would know she didn't have it within her to hurt a soul.

She peeked around a column as the front door crept open and a man walked inside, built thin as a rail and a good head taller than she was. The evening was warm, yet he wore a dark overcoat and hat, the uniform of a Cleveland Mafioso.

And he looked very much alive.

She stepped down into the stairwell. If anyone except their father caught her and her sister, they might bump them off, and there were no guarantees with their father.

She and Liz had to get out of here.

Nikki locked the door behind her, and as she rushed down the stairs, she struggled to catch her breath. Air didn't come until she reached the bottom, but even then, her breathing was shallow. The room in front of her seemed to spin.

Steadying herself against the wall, she took a deep breath and hiccupped.

The basement was one room, a dank space fortified with cold stone and a solitary brown hat rack that hovered in the corner. An old table stood in the middle of the room, surrounded by folding chairs, where the men probably dealt business ventures along with their cards. At the side of the room, a much shorter set of steps led up to a storm door.

Liz swiveled around by an open closet door, a narrow metal box clutched in her hands. "I told you to stay upstairs."

"But someone's—" Nikki didn't finish her sentence. The door above her swung open, banging into the wall. Apparently her father wasn't the only one with a key to this place.

Liz shoved the lantern into Nikki's hands and tucked the metal box under her arm. Then she stepped toward the second set of stairs. Nikki followed her lead, but at that moment, the storm door began to shake. Someone else was outside.

Liz swore and grabbed Nikki's arm, shoving her into the closet. Liz squeezed into the tight space beside her and yanked the door closed, the lantern shining like a beacon until Liz punched the button on top. The closet turned black.

On the other side of the door, Nikki heard muffled voices as several men greeted each other. At this time of night, surely this meeting wouldn't last long. They'd finish whatever deal they'd come to resolve and disappear back into the night. She and Liz would escape minutes later, going home to the safety of their beds before daylight. No one would be the wiser.

Her ear pressed against the door, Nikki strained to listen to the men's words. Rough talk about the Puglisi family, interfering coppers, and the blessed Volstead Act floated under the thin crack beside her feet, burned her ears. They were making a pact to work together under the nose of the government.

A hiccup swelled in her throat again, and she swallowed hard, holding her breath for a good minute. When she finally released her breath, her hand raced to her mouth to squelch another hiccup, but in her panic, her fingers knocked the lantern in Liz's hands. She groped for the lantern in the darkness, trying to stop its fall.

Liz reached out to catch the lantern, but when she did, the metal box in her arms fell to the floor, and the crash echoed around them.

Nikki froze.

Liz swung open the door to the closet, pushing Nikki in front of her, and Nikki stumbled forward. Chairs slid back, and the men at the table opened their coats. She saw her father's face first. The anger etched in his eyes. And there was another emotion she'd never seen before.

Fear.

Her brother sat there, stunned. And all three of her uncles.

There was another man beside them. A man with bushy blond hair.

Nikki watched in horror as the blond man reached for his gun.

"Stop, Heyward," her brother yelled, but she could see the malice in Heyward's eyes. He wasn't going to stop.

"Blast it, Nikki." Liz shoved her toward the storm door, her eyes still focused on the blond man. "Run."

Heyward shouted, commanding the others to shoot. Nikki snapped out of her stupor when she saw the gleam of his gun. Racing up the stairs, she slammed open the storm door and burst outside.

Cool air flooded over her as a gunshot echoed down the alleyway. Lifting her skirt, Nikki ran into the billows of the fog, but with every step, her sister's face trailed her. The faces of the men haunted her soul.

Another thread for their family's web of secrets. A thread she could never escape no matter where she fled.

ABOUT THE AUTHOR

Writing fiction is Melanie Dobson's excuse to explore abandoned houses, travel to unique places, and spend hours reading old books and journals. She enjoys stitching together historical and time-slip stories, and her novels have won awards for historical romance, romantic suspense, and historical fiction. Melanie has published almost thirty books including *The Silent Order*, *The Curator's Daughter*, *Catching the Wind*, *Chateau of Secrets*, and *Memories of Glass*. Her Legacy of Love novels have been revised from her previously published Love Finds You and American Tapestry books (legacyofloveseries.com).

Melanie loves connecting with readers! The best places to find her online are:

melaniedobson.com
comments@melaniedobson.com

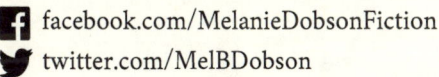

facebook.com/MelanieDobsonFiction
twitter.com/MelBDobson

Copyright © 2020 by Melanie Dobson

Cover design by Roseanna White Designs

Art Direction by Ink Map Press

Cover images used under license from Shutterstock.com

Map of Amana by Kristin Stroup

ISBN: 978-1-7366791-0-4

All rights reserved.

No part of this book may be reproduced in any form or by any electronic or mechanical means, including information storage and retrieval systems, without written permission from the author, except for the use of brief quotations in a book review.

Made in the USA
Columbia, SC
22 January 2024